# ASHES TO ASHES

## A Ludington – van der Berg Mystery

## M.M. LINDVALL

LEVEL
BEST BOOKS

"The job of the detective is to restore the state of grace in which the aesthetic and ethical are one."

—W. H. Auden

# Praise for Ashes to Ashes

"A minister uncovers an old secret in the basement of the manse revealing a nefarious past within the church as well as his own personal struggles. M.M. Lindvall has penned a true mystery mixing the spiritual, the criminal, and modern technology inspired by my own hunt for the Golden State Killer." — Paul Holes, Former Cold Case Detective Contra Costa County and author of *NYT* Best Seller *Unmasked: My Life Solving America's Cold Cases*

"M.M. Lindvall, a father-daughter writing duo, has cracked the code for a great mystery novel. This first in the Ludington-van der Berg series not only offers up fascinating characters and a fast-paced plot, but plumbs profound moral and spiritual issues that stay with you long after you've finished the last page. Can't wait to read the next one."—Katie Couric

"Bones in the pastor's cellar. Secrets and sin. The Reverend Seth Ludington tugs at a set of mysterious threads that entangle his predecessors in the Old Stone Church pulpit and touch on his own shadowed past. In *Ashes to Ashes*, M. M. Lindvall has penned a gripping whodunit that gives fresh perspective on the human need for confession and grace."—Scott Black Johnston, Senior Minister of the Fifth Avenue Presbyterian Church in New York City and author of Elusive Grace.

# Chapter One

"**M**anse" had always struck Seth Ludington as a curious anachronism. It is used nowhere except in the Church of Scotland and among American Presbyterians, more or less that church's spiritual descendants. The term refers to the house where the minister lives, traditionally one owned by the church. Ludington assumed that it would no longer apply to the fifteen-foot wide brownstone that he and his wife had just purchased from the congregation he served as minister. He was rather saddened by the loss of the crusty name used for the last half-century to identify 338 East 84th Street. Being one himself, Ludington was fond of anachronisms.

"Reverend, I gotta tell ya, this place is a wreck."

The building inspector Ludington had hired, a Staten Islander with the accent to prove it, pronounced the word "Revrunt." Ludington was far too polite to ever correct people who used what was properly an adjective as a title, however they pronounced it.

Ludington had chosen him among the slew of private inspectors he found on the internet because his bare-bones website noted that Vincenzo D'Amato had "years of experience working with the New York City Department of Buildings." Ludington knew that he would need a guide—a Virgil—to lead him through that labyrinthine Hades of a bureaucracy when they renovated the house.

1

As the inspector made notes while standing in the kitchen following his two-hour inspection, he summed up the bad news. "I mean, it needs everything. You gotta do all new plumbing. I showed you the leaks. You gotta redo all the electric; whole house has to be rewired, means tearing up plaster, you know, walls and ceilings both. A lot of it's old knob and tube. Can you believe it? This kitchen is, like, 1968. You got some structural issues with the fourth and fifth floors. You got some sag there you better deal with."

He then pulled Ludington out the kitchen door, pointed dramatically at the front façade of the house above them, and leveled what might have been his parting shot. "And look at the brownstone, needs redoing all over the place." Like many New York rowhouses called "brownstones," 338 East 84th Street was actually a brick house covered with brown concrete cladding made to look like the real thing. Even on a gray spring day with no sun gracing the façade of the house—a row house on the south side of a narrow street, Ludington could see what the man was pointing out. Fissures and flaking here and there on the front of the house reminded him of a dry lakebed.

Back in the kitchen, building inspector D'Amato had to look up at Ludington as he regaled him with the tidings of what was shaping up to be an even more outrageously expensive restoration project than he and Fiona had imagined. D'Amato may have been pear-shaped, but he was not that short. Rather, Ludington was that tall, as tall and trim as the inspector was not.

"Revrunt, what ya pay for this place, if I may ask? You bought it from your church, right?"

Ludington would have been embarrassed to name the sale price. At the very least, he'd feel he had to explain it, which he'd sooner not do. He knew it was too high; the church knew it was too high. D'Amato would also know it was too high and would surely whistle his shock, or at least raise an eyebrow.

So, he answered, "Doubtless too much."

Unlike most parish ministers, the Rev. Seth Ludington was wealthy. It was family money, the "Ludington fortune," five generations old. The original source was one James Ludington, a Midwestern lumber baron, and land speculator, a notorious clear-cutter who had reaped millions in the middle of the 19th-century raping the great white pine forests of lower Michigan. James had never had children. To perpetuate his name, he had paid ten thousand dollars to a Michigan village with the evocative name of "Pere Marquette" to rename itself "Ludington." Even though he owned half of the place, James Ludington never once deigned to visit his namesake lumber town on the shores of Lake Michigan.

At James's death, the money not only stayed in the family, but unlike many a 19th-century fortune, it grew with the family's careful husbandry. One hundred and fifty years later, it made Seth Ludington an extraordinarily well-heeled thirty-nine-year-old pastor of a struggling little Presbyterian congregation in the Yorkville neighborhood of Manhattan. Ludington had long borne his wealth uneasily. It wasn't simply the money itself—the "camel through the eye of the needle" business—but where it had come from. Every time he wrote a large check, he saw the sepia-toned photo in a family album that he had contemplated as a teenager. It showed two proud Mason County lumberjacks, one hand on a hip, the other leaning on an axe, standing next to the stump of the towering white pine they had just felled. In the background lay an endless sea of stumps.

The purchase of the manse had been occasioned by another tower about to fall. The steeple of the Old Stone Church on 82nd Street between First and York had been encased in scaffolding for a decade. It was ambitious as Presbyterian steeples go, dwarfing the more modest Gothic-Revival sanctuary it rose above. The latest estimated cost to repair—the third estimate sought in the last ten years—was 5.8 million dollars, a sum unimaginable to the Session, the nine-member board that governed the congregation. The estimate to remove it altogether was half that. The scaffolding alone, mandated by the City, had exhausted the church's reserves. Yorkville, even with the coming of the Second Avenue subway and creeping gentrification, was still a poor cousin to the famously moneyed Upper East Side to the south and west.

Without so much as an appraisal, Fiona and Seth had agreed that 5.8 million dollars was to be the purchase price of the manse, a house they had lived in for just over a year. They realized that number was well over market, but they liked the twin prospects of a renovation project and a rescued steeple. Money was not an issue. In the end, it was a way of making a gift to the church without doing so directly, which would have been awkward in the extreme. The Session, indeed the entire congregation, understood this. No one said anything, of course. The steeple would be saved from a felling, and the erstwhile manse would be renovated to its former glory.

"A buck over three-and-a-half, maybe four mil and you paid too much, Revrunt."

The familiarity of D'Amato's appraisal was perhaps occasioned by Seth's offer of coffee, which to his surprise, the inspector had accepted. D'Amato sat down at one of the two chairs on either side of the small oak table and watched as Ludington set water to boil on the "like, 1968" electric range. Ludington thought to himself, "We'll get gas—'like, stainless steel'—when we remodel." He then ground some of the coffee beans he had picked up at Grace's Market the day before, a Haitian dark roast he and Fiona favored. He ground the beans coarse, as he was going to use the French press. As he spooned the beans into it, he noticed Fiona's birth control pill packet for the month lying all too conspicuously on the counter. He opened the nearest drawer and deftly swept the pills in and out of D'Amato's sight. "Forever forgetting them," he thought to himself as he quietly closed the drawer. When the water began to boil, he poured it over the freshly ground coffee at the bottom of the press and let it steep for exactly four minutes. He liked his coffee robust.

"Milk, Mr. D'Amato?"

"Sure, yah, thanks, milk."

Ludington poured a half cup of whole milk into a saucepan and set it on the stove to heat.

D'Amato watched this coffee preparation operation with silent interest as Ludington slowly pushed down the plunger on the coffee press.

"The wife and me, we got us one of them Keurigs," he said. "Gave it to

4

each other for Christmas. Pop in the capsule, push the button, and badaa bing, you got yourself cup a coffee."

Ludington recalled the awkward conversation he'd had with his mother about capsule coffee makers. His parents owned a fleet of them, stationed in their three homes—one on Lake Michigan between Pentwater and Ludington, the second in Charleston, and one on Lyford Cay in the Bahamas, where they retreated in deep winter. As his mother was making morning coffee during Seth and Fiona's recent post-Christmas visit to the Bahamas using four capsules in a row, Seth had made a careless comment about packaging waste and all the plastic in the ocean. His mother said nothing, but Seth sensed she was hurt by the remark which he immediately wished he had not made. The issue had doubtless never occurred to her. Seth told his mother that the coffee was "really quite good," which was true enough.

He said nothing to D'Amato about capsule coffee makers and packaging waste. The building inspector complimented Ludington on the coffee and had a second cup before he rose to leave. The man had given Ludington both more time and counsel than his fee required. Seth liked him and couldn't help but respect both his technical knowledge and New York forthrightness.

As he gulped down the last of his coffee, D'Amato said, "Tell you what, Revrunt, I'll give a call to some buddies at the DOB and, you know, grease the wheels, get all the inspections for your permits on the fast track."

Ludington thanked him, stood, and showed him out the kitchen door into the small patio just below street level. As he was about to close the door, the man turned to Ludington and gestured vaguely in the direction of the cellar.

"And you better clean out that ash pit in the cellar under the living room fireplace. It's totally full. Don't look like nobody's emptied it in a hundred years."

# Chapter Two

Nearly a week later, Ludington had downed his two cups of coffee and eaten half a bagel with cream cheese and raspberry jam by 8 am. He had scanned both the *Times* and *Journal*. He was an early riser, not from self-discipline, but from a constitution that insisted on waking with the sun, even in a darkened bedroom. Fiona was traveling again with her work, but was to return from Nicaragua that afternoon. To welcome her home, Ludington imagined a fire in the living room fireplace and a bottle of the Chateauneuf du Pape from the case he had ordered when they closed on the purchase of the manse. Best to clean out the ash pit before another fire. Then they'd eat at Elio's. He should really make a reservation when they opened. The place was predictably packed, even on weeknights. Wednesday was normally a work day for him, but he had spent his day off—routinely Monday—visiting an elderly parishioner at New York Hospital on 68th and York. He owed himself, he figured, but would stop in at the church later in the afternoon after he took care of the ash pit.

As in most New York townhouses, the kitchen was on the lower level of the building, just below street level. Three steps led down from the sidewalk to a small patio landing and the kitchen door tucked under the front steps. In the old days, it was a door that would have been used only by the help, but now Seth and Fiona used it routinely. The main entrance was a dozen steps up from the street. That grand door—presently painted an unfortunate robin's egg blue—was layered with a century of repainting. It opened into a foyer, a room often called a "gallery" by old New Yorkers. Double pocket doors, long stuck in their pockets, led from the foyer into a spacious living room with a fireplace to the left, surrounded by a magnificently carved marble mantle. To the rear of the room were two sets of exterior French doors. They opened onto a shallow elevated brick patio with a curved staircase descending to the rear garden, long unkempt, but full of promise and facing south, blessed with sunlight.

On the lowest level and behind the kitchen was the room D'Amato had called a "cellar" in the course of his inspection. It housed the ancient oil-burning furnace, a slightly more recent hot water heater, a terrifying old fuse box, and assorted detritus left behind by former residents. For the last 50 of the house's 100 years, those residents had been a string of ministers who called Old Stone Church's manse their home. At the center of the cellar wall to the left, behind a pile of boxes filled with moldy and dated biblical commentaries from the 50s that had been wisely left behind by some former Old Stone preacher, the building inspector had pointed out a rusty cast iron door some eighteen inches square. Behind that door lay what he had named "the ash pit."

D'Amato had explained to Ludington that a lot of older houses with living room wood-burning fireplaces ("WBFPs" he had said, displaying his fluency in realtor-speak) had a large rectangular opening in the floor of the WBFP's stonework. The opening was under a removable grate. Lifting out the grate, one could then lift up the hinged metal door and sweep ashes directly into a brick-lined pit a floor below. They could then be removed through the clean-out door in the cellar rather than from the fireplace itself.

"Whole arrangement kept the upstairs cleaner, I suppose," the building inspector had opined after coming back into the kitchen from his tour of the lamentable utilities in the cellar. "Servants did that kinda dirty work back then."

Ludington rinsed out his coffee cup and went upstairs to the living room to find the metal ash shovel that leaned up against the fireplace mantle. He went back downstairs and retrieved an empty 50-gallon plastic garbage can from the kitchen storage room and wheeled it through the kitchen and into the cellar. He moved the boxes of old commentaries out of the way and yanked open the cast iron clean-out door to the ash pit.

The door was low, the bottom of its opening some two feet above the cellar floor. Crouching for the work would be uncomfortable, so he slid one of the book boxes in place and sat down on it. He put on the leather work gloves Fiona had bought him last week and took the fireplace shovel in hand. The ashes formed a solid wall in front of the opening. They were not soft and dry as he had expected, but dampish and semi-solid, pale and the texture of fine soil. Rain down the chimney when the damper was left open had doubtless seeped through the opening in the fireplace's floor and slightly moistened the contents over the years. Sealed up as they were, they had never quite dried out. Ludington plunged his little shovel into the wall of ash and began the slow and messy process of loading ages of old fires into the garbage can. He thought of the fire to come that night, the Chateauneuf, and Fiona. Well worth the effort, this was.

With the fifth shovelful, Ludington discovered that ashes were not the only contents in the ash pit. And it was not "totally full," but full only to the top of the clean-out door. As he emptied the fifth shovel into the garbage can, he saw a tiny tin box labeled "Certs Peppermint Breath Mints" fall into the bottom. He retrieved it and examined it. He had never seen one quite like it; it looked old. A few shovels later, he encountered a small glass bottle in a shape he vaguely remembered as that in which Bayer aspirin was sold in the days before that remedy was eclipsed by acetaminophen and NSAIDs. He rubbed it clean. Indeed, its label read "Bayer Aspirin." Clearly, the fireplace had been used over the years as a handy living room trash basket and incinerator.

Ludington began to shovel more carefully. As he did so, his mind went back to the summer he and Fiona had met on an archeological dig in Israel. Cleaning out the ash pit was rather like their work on that dig. It was the summer of 2007. He had graduated from seminary—Princeton—two years earlier. He'd wandered Europe with friends for a while and then volunteered as an archeological grunt with the dig at Herod's Tomb on the slopes of

Mount Herodium south of Jerusalem. One of his Princeton Old Testament professors, a man with contacts at Hebrew University, had landed him the job, not that it paid anything and not that he needed to be paid.

Herod the Great, the Jewish King of Judea at the time of Jesus's birth, was an unapologetic Roman lackey and an ambitious builder of monuments, including the Second Temple in Jerusalem. He was also one of history's more notorious serial killers, though he did his murdering—whether his wife, his children or, most infamously, the innocents of Bethlehem, by proxy. He had always said he wanted to be entombed in the desert. Their dig at Herodium aimed to determine if he had gotten his wish.

Two years after seminary, Ludington was still wandering, not only geographically, but vocationally, struggling mightily to dodge a pull to the ministry that refused to let him free. He was still sometimes trying to slide from under the weight of it a dozen years later, though there was less fight in him now. When they had first met, Fiona had just finished her undergraduate studies at St. Andrews and was planning on taking up law at Aberdeen in the fall. She was a daughter of the manse, her father the minister of the Canongate Kirk on the Royal Mile in Edinburgh. It was he who had arranged for a summer spot on the Herod dig for his only daughter.

Seth and Fiona experienced something close to love at first sight, though initially, it was mere physical attraction for both of them. She was a Viking Scot, curling blond-to-red hair, of medium height but statuesque, hauntingly beautiful, though not quite in the classic way. The freckles took care of that. He was much taller, his usual pallor tanned by the Middle Eastern sun, with sharp, classic features. His hair was jet black, straight, and worn long, his eyes a discordantly light blue. The two of them ascended into a passion that soon relaxed into love. The relationship that took shape was part of neither's plan for their futures.

They had dug side-by-side at Mount Herodium through the summer. Laborious work it was, with shovels the size of spoons, examining each bit of earth for some hint of what once was. Ludington learned what archeologists know: the deeper you dig, the farther you go back in time. This was true at both Herod the Great's tomb and in the ash pit of 338 East 84th Street.

His next find in the ash pit dig was a pipe tobacco tin—"Prince Albert," Victoria's German husband still discernible, standing ramrod straight and decked out in his tails. Digging deeper, below the tobacco tin's layer of ash, he came upon bits of newspapers, probably remnants of less-than-successful kindling efforts. One remnant was the corner of a page from the *New York Times.* He could easily make out the date, "Friday, December 17, 1970."

A bit more ash excavation and Ludington next came upon his largest find so far—the nearly complete front page of a *Life* magazine. It showed a full-page black and white photo—a paparazzi snapshot, not posed—of Rose Kennedy in an evening gown and a slender young Ted in a tuxedo a step behind his mother. The date was clearly legible—"July 17, 1970," when the Kennedy clan was still in their popular ascendency despite Teddy's missteps. As he shook ashes off, the image reminded Ludington of how disconnected the appearance of a perfect and pretty family could be from a complicated reality. He laid it carefully on top of one of the book boxes.

Ludington was now becoming more a curious archeologist than mere ash pit cleaner. He fetched a flashlight from the kitchen to see better into the dark pit. He dug carefully, intrigued with what bits of the manse's history he might unearth. Just under where the *Life* magazine cover had lay, his shovel hit something hard, something that was neither ash nor paper. Shining the flashlight closer, he could see that what his shovel had struck was white, bone white, and thin. Remembering his dig days in Israel, he rushed back into the kitchen and found a teaspoon and a stiff one-inch paintbrush.

He spooned ash away delicately, using the paintbrush to sweep away ashes from what was looking more and more like a set of bones, doubtless those of an immense New York City rat or perhaps an unfortunate squirrel that had somehow fallen first into the fireplace and through the opening in its floor into the ash pit. Ludington had never been squeamish; in fact, he found himself growing intrigued. As he spooned and brushed away ash, the multiple bones reclining in the bed of ash soon shaped themselves into what was clearly a skeleton. A few brush strokes at one end of the stretch of bones disclosed a tiny skull. Ludington jerked back, dropped the paintbrush and the spoon to the floor, and whispered, "Oh, my God." Those words were no trespass of the Third Commandment; they were an earnest prayer. The bones that lay in the ash pit were in the general form of a disconnected and scattered skeleton. They were small and delicate—almost bird-like—but obviously human.

# Chapter Three

*Wednesday, March 27—The Nineteenth Day in Lent*

L udington left the little bones where they lay on the soft bed of ash on which they had long rested. He needed time to think. He left the plastic garbage can, a third full of ashes and debris, his fireplace shovel, the kitchen spoon, and the little paintbrush in the cellar and went to their fourth-floor bedroom to shower and change clothes. He cast a long glance at the living room fireplace on what they thought of as the second floor as he mounted the stairs to the third. The third floor consisted of the library facing 84th Street and a smaller room to the back, which older church members called "the sewing room," though no sewing had been done there in anyone's memory.

The fourth floor was given over to an expansive master bedroom and bath suite larger than most 100-year-old houses. Both had been updated, but less than well and some fifty years ago when the house had passed into the church's hands and first used as a manse. Old Stone Church had deeper pockets in 1969 and had been able to finance a bit of modest manse renovation.

Ludington showered even though he had already done so earlier that morning. He put on his black clergy shirt and clerical "dog collar," gray wool slacks, black penny loafers, and a blue blazer, an ensemble Fiona called the "Presbyterian preacher uniform." He usually wore clerical garb on days he worked. It helped him remember who he was even when he'd sooner forget.

Dumbfounded by what he had come upon in the ash pit, he decided to walk through Carl Schurz Park along the East River south of Gracie Mansion. It was another dark and cool day. Save for a few nannies with their charges and a couple of dog walkers, he had the park to himself. He had neglected to grab an overcoat when he left the house and was suddenly cold. But he sat down on a bench facing the river and stared across the gray water to Astoria on the other side.

He thought to himself, "There is a skeleton of a very small child in the fireplace ash pit of my house, a house that has been occupied by my predecessors in the pulpit for half a century."

His first thought had been to phone the 19th Precinct. You find a body, you call the cops. Ludington was sure that there must be some law requiring as much. He had gone into the kitchen after his discovery and pulled out his cell phone to do so. But he had hesitated. If he reported his discovery, how long would it be before it became common knowledge? His decade in the ministry had taught him that anything known to more than one or two people was not long a secret. And what if the *Post* or the *Daily News* got wind of it? Tabloid headlines composed themselves in his imagination as he stared across the river: *"Baby Body Discovered in Parsonage Basement." "Preacher Finds Infant's Body in Fireplace."*

It had lain there silently for decades. He had decided it could lay silent for a few more hours. He went to church, arriving in his study just before three o'clock. No one was in the building. The church sexton came in five mornings a week, mostly to tidy up after the Sunday morning worship service or the AA meetings the night before. Ludington's very part-time volunteer secretary came in Tuesdays and Thursdays, though she was always happy to stop in Wednesdays and Fridays, in fact, most anytime if Ludington needed her for something. He sat down and checked email on his computer. He sorted through the snail mail on his desk. Nothing important. He couldn't concentrate. Ludington was relieved when his cell rang, and he saw that it was Fiona.

"Afternoon, my love," she said in the chipper Scots accent he adored, barely diminished by a decade of living in the States.

"Two-hour layover in Miami. I'm on the three-thirty-five to La Guardia. I should be home by six. Looking forward to that lovely wine and fire you promised."

"There may be one, but not the other."

"Which one don't I get?"

"No fire in the fireplace, I'm afraid,"

"Another broken thing in our lovely old pile, I suppose."

"You could say that. I'll tell you about it when you're here. And you just used up two of your 'lovelies.'"

"Righto then. They're boarding. Must run."

Eighteen months earlier, Fiona had landed a prestigious job as a lawyer for the United Nations' High Commissioner for Human Rights. Her focus was currently exclusively Central America; it had been largely so since she had started. That she had dual American-U.K. citizenship and spoke fluent Spanish had been her leg up in the competition for the position. That she was smart and passionate had not hurt either. She loved and hated her work. Hated it because of the parade of inhumanities she witnessed, often in horrific detail; loved it because she dared to believe that she and her office were capable of making a difference.

It was her U.N. job that had brought them to New York. They'd lived in Philadelphia for most of their first decade of marriage. Seth had brought his Scottish bride to an iffy neighborhood of that Pennsylvania city New Yorkers call "the Sixth Borough." He managed to get himself ordained and had worked for an inner-city mission project called "New Philadelphia Ministries," first doing advocacy and youth work, then more and more "development work"—taking other people with money out to lunch to ask them for money. Fiona went to Penn Law and took a job in the city D.A.'s office after passing both the Pennsylvania and New York bar. A decade later, when she got the U.N. job, she had sublet an apartment in Stuyvesant Town and moved to New York ahead of Seth. He came a few months later and looked for some kind of job in ministry in the New York metro area.

Old Stone Church had been without a full-time pastor—"vacant," as Presbyterians say—for several years. It was not a plumb position—a small and aging congregation, the minimum allowable salary, a wreck of a manse, and a collapsing steeple. But Ludington accepted their call. The congregation was intrigued as to why such a promising young man—and so attractive—would ever take the job. The church was convenient to Fiona's U.N. office, though she was in it only half the time. But it was not merely location and availability that had called him to Old Stone. Though Ludington's sense of call to the ministry was often vague and vacillating, he had felt an irresistible pull to this church, a dogged little band of stalwarts who managed to love each other most of the time and were not at all ready to yield, whether to rising secularism or falling steeples.

When Fiona's yellow cab pulled up to 338 East 84th Street, Seth was shifting anxiously in one of the two red leather wing chairs in front of the fireplace. He stared into it, empty and cold as it was, barely touching his wine, not the Chateauneuf he had thought to open that morning, but a bottle of less celebratory red. As he heard her unlock the kitchen door, he galloped down the stairs, took her in his arms, and planted a kiss on her forehead, holding her longer than he usually might have after a mere three-day absence.

"Missed you, my dear. I'm really glad you're back."

"More than usual?"

"Yes, more than usual. We have to talk."

He poured her a glass of wine as she moved her roller bag to the corner of the kitchen and sat at the table. He sat down opposite her and told her of the building inspector's visit, his warning about the ash pit, Seth's own decision to clean it, and finally, after taking a deep breath, what he had discovered.

Fiona set down her wine, pushed the glass away, and offered the same three-word swear prayer Seth had whispered eight hours earlier, "Oh, my God."

She asked, "Have you called someone?"

"No, not yet."

They sat in silence for what seemed an eternity. Fiona interrupted the awkwardness of the moment. "I want to see it, Seth." Seth tried to dissuade her, but she insisted.

They went from the kitchen to the cellar. Seth flipped on the lights. They approached the ash pit slowly, almost reverentially. He opened the cast-iron door, and Fiona peered in. She sat down on the book box Seth had used as a chair earlier in the day. She rested her chin on two fisted hands. She stared for an eternal moment and then dropped her head between her hands.

"It's an infant, Seth. A little baby, a very little baby. Somebody's child." She wiped away a tear with the back of her hand and said, " I want out of here, out of this house."

As they left through the kitchen door and walked up the three steps from the lower patio to the sidewalk, a voice—a throaty smoker's voice—called from directly across 84th Street, addressing them in the Hungarian way of speaking to clergy. "*Tiszteletes*, Mrs. *Tiszteletes,* good evening to you."

The last person in the world either of them wanted to talk to was Orsolya Tabor, the older woman who occupied the ground floor of the five-story walk-up at 337 East 84th Street. They smiled faintly and waved barely as they dashed down their side of the street toward the restaurant. Seth and Fiona called the woman "the last Hungarian," though not to her face, of course. Yorkville had once been home to a thriving Hungarian community, now much diminished. Orsolya was one of the remnants. Now a chatty 75-year-old widow, she was faithfully perched on her front stoop every morning at 9:00 o'clock and every evening at 5:00—even in the foulest of weather. She smoked three cigarettes and drank two large cups of coffee in the morning and smoked three cigarettes and drank two glasses of bull's blood in the evening. She retreated to her ground-floor apartment promptly at 11:00 each morning and at 8:00 each evening. She then pretended to watch television, but her eyes were as much on the street outside her window as on the old Magnavox in front of it. Passing her without stopping for conversation always entailed pretending to be in a rush.

In the disorientation of the day, Seth had forgotten to make a dinner reservation at Elio's. It was their favorite restaurant in the neighborhood, if not the City. Italian, of course, and run by real Italians. It was filling up as they arrived, but Giorgio said that he could always find a table for "Father Seth and Mrs. Father." Giorgio knew full well that Ludington was a Protestant and that Protestant clergy married. But he was repeatedly pleased with his little R.C. witticism and offered it up nearly every time they ate at Elio's. As they were shown to a corner table in the back and wove their way through tables of diners, people looked at them curiously. Seth, especially in his clerics, was achingly handsome. Fiona always enjoyed the stares, Seth less so.

Seth ordered a bottle of mineral water from Giorgio. Fiona called after him as he turned away, "And two glasses of the house chianti, Giorgio, please."

She turned to her husband, sighed, and said softly, "I'm not a criminal lawyer, but I'm pretty sure the law requires you to report any discovery of human remains, recent or otherwise. Seth, do you have any idea how long that child's skeleton has been there?" Merely uttering the words "child's skeleton" was not merely uncomfortable; it was sickening.

"Actually, I do." He told her about the nearly intact *Life* Magazine cover and the bits of dated newspaper he had found right above the bones. "Just like archeology, the deeper you go, the farther back you go. Herod's tomb, remember. The skeleton must have been there before the magazine and the newspaper. One's dated July of 1970, the other December. Maybe the child ended up there days before, maybe years before, but only if nobody swept anything into the ash pit for a long while. After the body, I mean."

"So, it's been there nearly fifty years, at least. But Seth, the passage of time—a day or half a century—I don't think it matters to the law. We have to report it."

He took a sip of the San Pellegrino and said, "I suppose you're right, but I'm going to talk to Harry first. You know he's retired NYPD. He's Clerk of Session at church. I have to tell him sooner or later, and I think sooner is better. I've been thinking about it all day. Those bones have been there half a century. I think they can wait one more day. And we don't know what, if any, crime was committed. "

"Oh, Seth, a crime was committed. Even if the child died a natural death, it was surely as much against the law in 1970—or whenever—to dispose of a human body in your ash pit as it is today."

17

"There are so many possibilities, Fiona. I thought about it for a long time in the park. Miscarriage, fetal death, SIDS, an accident, and, well…child abuse, or outright infanticide. Murder. We don't know. The body could have been placed directly in the ash pit, I suppose. But I looked, and the bones are so clean. And I noticed that they're charred in places, as if they were burned. Remember Professor Netzer at the Herodium dig telling us about excavating through old fires? Bones and pottery shards that had survived fires were usually charred."

Their waiter, a no-idle-chatter older man with a thick Italian accent who often served them, came to take their order at this precise and awkward moment.

"I don't know," Fiona responded when asked what the *signora* would like. She hesitated. Seth picked up his menu and stared at it, even though he knew it by heart.

"Maybe your regular?" the waiter suggested, growing impatient.

Unable to think about food, they both nodded their assent. Their regular was saltimbocca for Seth and linguini Bolognese for Fiona. To the waiter's consternation, Seth added, "Make the saltimbocca chicken."

Both picked at their dinners, superb as they were, and said no to dessert.

"Whatever happened," Seth said following the long after-dinner silence that sat between them, "Whatever it was, it's such a cruel world we live in. I mean, such horrors happen. It's all so screwed up. You've got to wonder about bringing children into it at all."

This was a regular lament on Seth's part. At first, Fiona had heard his reluctance about starting a family as merely his desire to wait. She had not been ready herself… until recently. Her work, both in Philadelphia and now with the U.N., had filled her life—her time, energy, and passion. She was six years younger than Seth. But now, at 33, she had begun to feel the clock ticking. She was recently inclined to hear his anxiety about parenthood not as delay but as fear—fear about bringing a child into a world filled with uncertainty and packed with fearsome things. It was also, she suspected, fear about his own ability to be a fit father, yet another incarnation of his self-doubt.

18

"Seth, remember what I do for a living? If anybody knows how cruel this world can be, it's me. But you have to push back, I mean you've got to resist the cruel and well, just risk it."

Seth looked at his water glass, swirled the Pellegrino, gulped it down, and did not respond. He understood that his anxiety about fatherhood had roots that crept deeper into him than Fiona knew.

# Chapter Four

*Thursday, March 28—The Twentieth Day in Lent*

Seth phoned the only cop he knew at 7:30 the next morning. He normally did not phone parishioners before 9:00, but he was desperate to catch the retired detective, who, as Old Stone's Clerk of Session, was the ranking lay leader of the church. He wanted to reach him before he and his wife returned to Vero Beach. Seth knew Harry Mulholland to be a fellow early riser. The couple had been in church the Sunday prior, and Harry had mentioned that they might not be there the next Sunday. They were thinking about going back down to Florida for a few days to shut down the condo. Or perhaps they would call the handyman and have him do it. But whatever they decided to do, Harry assured his pastor that he would be in town for the next Session meeting, and of course, for Holy Week and Easter in three weeks.

Harry Mulholland was faithfulness incarnate. He was the grandson of Ulster immigrants to New York. He had been baptized at Old Stone, attended Sunday School at Old Stone, and was a member of the Old Stone High School Youth Group in the days when such a thing existed. As a Protestant from the North, he did not quite qualify as an Irish cop. He did not fit the stereotype either. Harry was soft-spoken and reserved, on the cusp of dour, given to short sentences, grunts, and close-mouthed nods. Seth had come to admire the older man's consistency and steady affection for his church. Early in their acquaintance, he had detected a patient compassion and deep faith behind the man's matter-of-fact exterior. Seth liked Harry Mulholland very much and was pleased that he and his wife had signed up to be part of the church tour group traveling to Scotland the coming summer.

Weeks after his retirement from the NYPD seven years earlier, Harry had agreed to serve as Old Stone Church's Clerk of Session, the previous Clerk having died after filling the position for 38 years. The Minister at the time, as well as the Session—the congregation's nine-member governing board—were desperate to find somebody to take on the job. It was not especially demanding. It entailed keeping the minutes of the Session's meetings as well as other records—baptisms, marriages, and deaths, but Harriet helped with that. Harriet van der Berg was the church's part-time volunteer secretary. She was also intimidatingly competent. Even though the duties of the Clerk might be manageable, the job did demand being present for all the board's monthly meetings. Harry and Georgia Mulholland had recently bought a two-bedroom condo in Vero and planned to spend winters there. But Harry said yes to the clerkship anyway. He'd fly back from Orlando for winter Session meetings. He was honored to be asked, even though he knew they had asked others before him.

Seth had come to better know and understand Mulholland in the course of their purchase of the manse. As Clerk, Harry had shepherded the transaction through the Session and the subsequent congregational meeting. The man had not raised an eyebrow when his pastor had told him that he and Fiona would be interested in purchasing the house if the church wanted to sell. He had not blinked when Seth named the price they would offer, a number curiously equal to the latest estimate of the cost to repair the steeple. After the closing, Mulholland had taken Ludington's hand, held it long, looked him square in the eye, and said, "Thank you, Seth, thank you." It was the first time he had addressed him by his first name.

When Ludington called, Harry detected the urgency in his pastor's voice. He told Seth he would come to his study at 9:00 sharp. Ludington had risen early after a restless night. He had skipped breakfast, called Harry, and left the house at 7:50, walking the two short blocks and one long block to the church on 82$^{nd}$ Street. Sun was threatening to break through the grim weather of the last several days. He unlocked the door to the Parish House, the four-story building attached to the church itself. The Parish House held classrooms, a parlor, and kitchenette, plus several offices—including the pastor's study—these last on the ground floor. Seth punched in the code to turn off the security system, but instead of turning to the right toward his study as he usually did, he turned left and walked through a set of double oak doors with small leaded glass windows and entered Old Stone Church's sanctuary.

He sat in the last pew of the long, narrow, dark room. He had not turned on the lights, and most of the natural morning light that might have come through the row of six stained-glass windows was blocked by the sidewalk scaffolding erected to protect pedestrians from bits of steeple that regularly fell to the sidewalk along 82$^{nd}$ Street. Like many of New York's churches built in the later 19$^{th}$ and early 20$^{th}$ centuries, Old Stone's building was Gothic Revival, that noble architectural attempt to import the silent mystery of the Medieval to the cacophony of the New World's greatest city. It was beautiful space, if a bit moody—bare Bedford limestone walls to the right, a massive oak hammer-beam ceiling above, the row of lancet stained-glass windows to the left, and before him and three steps up, the elevated divided chancel with its massive communion table that Old Stone members insisted on calling "the altar." He had given up correcting them. An elevated pulpit with a suspended sounding board above was to one side of the chancel, a lectern to the other.

Ludington had never felt he needed to be in sacred space to pray. He did most of his praying on the sidewalk, on the subway, or in taxi cabs. He had long ago come to understand that the poetry he was given to writing was actually something close to prayer. He seldom shared his poems, and when he did, it was only with Fiona and only when she asked. He was repulsed when she had suggested looking for a publisher. Prayer and poetry are both books open wide in the presence of the Transcendent One, laid prostrate, truth naked, every fear and dream exposed to Eternity.

Sitting in a pew in his own church to pray was not something he customarily did. He knew he should not pray for the nameless child whose bones lay in the ash pit of his home. Presbyterians do not pray for the dead. "What's done is done" was their thinking. But he could not help himself. The child had a mother and a father. He was not sure exactly what to pray for. Forgiveness? Mercy? Peace? Justice? He had no idea. He mostly prayed for his church and for himself, that some path through this thorny thicket might break open, that he might be shown what he should do. Ludington waited, but there was mere silence, silence broken only by the cant of yellow cabs and T-plate Ubers and Lyfts on First Avenue tapping their horns at each other as they hunted for fares and jostled for pick-up position. He sat still for a very long time, finally glancing at his wrist and the Shinola Runwell Fiona had given him for Christmas. It was five till nine. He rose from the pew, afraid of what he thought he was going to have to do.

Ludington arrived in his office a moment before Mulholland. He nodded a clipped good morning to Harriet van der Berg as he passed through her small office and entered his. He turned on his computer, only to be jolted—as he always was—when the ancient 70s intercom on the corner of his desk offered up its annoying buzz. He pressed the "listen" button and heard van der Berg say, "Dominie, the Clerk is here to see you. Shall I send him in?"

Ludington pressed the "speak" button and said, "Of course, of course." He pushed the "speak button to turn his microphone off. As it occasionally did, it stuck in place. He jammed it hard with his finger, muttering to himself, "Nothing in this place works right."

When Mulholland entered the room, it occurred to Ludington that though he knew the man was a retired NYPD detective, he had no idea what kind of detective Mulholland had been. He didn't even know what categories of detectives the force had, though he assumed there were those who specialized in homicides, others in burglaries, others who dealt with drugs, and others fighting who-knows-what in the catalogue of malefactions that plagued humanity. Would Mulholland even know the law as it applied to old skeletons in ash pits?

"Mr. Clerk," said Seth as he swiveled his desk chair around and rose to greet Mulholland, "You're not in Florida."

He suspected that Harry liked the little formality of being addressed—at least now and again—as "Mr. Clerk." A compact man in his mid-'60s, trim, balding, and presently wearing a Florida suntan, Harry Mulholland was clad in a heather-colored Harris tweed sport coat, one of his small collection that now resided in New York and never visited Florida. He also boasted a green and blue regimental tie, rather too wide for current fashion. The man still donned a tie six days a week when he was in New York. Saturday was informal. His adoring wife, Georgia, patient with her husband's sartorial traditionalism, had told Ludington that he had trimmed tie-wearing back when in Florida. She had then smiled broadly, "Holly's idea of informal is loosening his tie when he goes fishing."

"Flying down next Monday. At least that's the current plan," said Mulholland. "But I'll be back for the Session meeting." They shook hands, and Seth motioned to the pair of faux Chippendale chairs on either side of the coffee table at the other end of his sizeable book-lined study. Ludington disliked speaking with people over his office desk.

"How's your dear wife, Seth?"

"Well, thank you. Back home yesterday. Off to Scotland tonight. Her father's birthday."

"And the renovation? Have you had the place inspected yet?"

"Well, Harry, that's what I need to talk with you about. I had an inspector go through the house last week. It needs a lot, but we knew that. He said, 'she's a grand old lady, but she's led a hard life.' He also told me that the ash pit under the living room fireplace was full and that I should clean it out. I started to do the job yesterday morning. Wanted to have a fire for Fiona when she got home."

"My brother's place in the Catskills has one of those ash pits in the basement. Nasty job to clean out if you let it go too long."

"Well, the one in the manse has been let go too long, to say the least. Not sure it was ever emptied. Harry. I found something in the ash pit that I need to tell you about. That's why I called. I need to talk to you about it, as both Clerk and cop."

Mulholland cocked his head to signal concern and interest.

24

"Harry, when I was cleaning out that ash pit, I found bones, a skeleton, more or less. It's an infant, a human infant, very small."

Unlike both Seth and Fiona when they first saw the bones, Mulholland said nothing, but he appeared more than jolted at this news. He sat silent, leaned back in his chair, and sighed—a long, knowing sigh offered by a man who had seen a surfeit of human pain in the course of his life, but had managed not to be hardened by it. He looked directly at Seth. Then he shut his eyes and winced.

"The bones have been there a long time, Harry."

Ludington told Mullholland about the *Life* Magazine cover and the bit of the *Times,* as well as his experience with archeological strata and dating. "They've been there since the summer of 1970, maybe before that, but I doubt much before. The bones were right under the cover. No ash or debris to speak of in between that paper and the bones."

"Summer of '70? Are you sure?"

"Well, probably the summer of '70, maybe a bit earlier or later. Depends on how many old fires were swept into the ash pit before and after and how long somebody might have held on to those copies of *Life* and the *Times* before using them as kindling."

The dates seemed to interest Harry. "I'm the first person you've told?"

"I told Fiona last night. Nobody else. I was going to call the precinct, but then I decided to talk to you first. The bones have been there for fifty years. I didn't imagine another day would matter."

Harry said nothing for a moment. Then, in his no-nonsense manner, counting the points he made on his fingers, he responded. "Seth, three things are for sure. One, legally, you're required to report the discovery of human remains. Two, whatever happened to that little one and its bones ending up in the ash pit of the manse, some law was broken, and somebody was hiding something. Three, if and when we report it to NYPD, I have no doubt that it'll get buried. Fifty-year-old cold cases that may or may not be a homicide are just not a priority. Too much fresh and pressing for-sure crime.

"So, what should I do, Harry? I've gotta do something. I can't pretend they're not there, that nothing God-awful happened in the manse 50 years ago. It needs some sort of resolution. I need it. The church needs it. The bones need it."

Mulholland played accordion rhythmically, his fingertips pressing against each other, back and forth for a full minute. He appeared to be staring at nothing but Ludington's penny loafers.

Finally, just as Ludington was about to break the silence with another declaration that they had to do something, Mulholland spoke.

"Like I said, this is a fifty-year-old cold case. And it's not clear what the crime was. Maybe murder, maybe not. If we report it, it probably wouldn't even get funneled to homicide."

"Are you saying we keep it quiet, Harry? There's a toxic history of churches covering up crimes against children. Doing nothing smells like that. Whatever happened to that little one needs to be known, known by someone. We can't just bury them quietly and anonymously and forget about it." He fell silent as those last words tumbled righteously from his lips. He remembered how adept he was at forgetting.

Mulholland finally broke free of his own brooding, "So maybe you should do something, Seth. DNA. A DNA sample from the bones. Then maybe you poke around, and maybe you can figure out what happened. Maybe it was a crib death or a miscarriage. And whoever put the body there might well be dead. DNA samples are easy enough to obtain. I mean samples from people who lived in the manse over the years. That would be your predecessors in the pulpit, I guess. So how about this? You get me DNA samples. We see whose matches the bones, if any, and whose doesn't. Maybe we won't have to report it."

Ludington was pleased that it was Mulholland who first suggested that he be the one to pursue the matter. It was what he had come to both understand and fear while sitting in the sanctuary that morning. But he was loath to appear eager. In fact, he wasn't eager. Rather, he felt cornered to act, cornered by circumstance.

Mulholland said, "I can help with DNA analysis. There's a guy at the NYPD lab who owes me a lifetime of favors; he's good, and he won't ask questions. Get me one little bone, just one, and I'll get it to him. But don't move anything else; leave the bones where they are. I don't dare touch this more than that myself. I can't risk more than opening a backdoor to the forensics lab. I guess, 'do something' means mostly 'you do something.'"

He looked away and then back at Ludington.

"Seth, I was in homicide my last decade in the NYPD. I saw things you never want to see. I saw raw evil, of course, but I also saw dumb kids do dumb things. I saw decent people do stunningly stupid stuff. Out of control anger, sometimes justified, fear, drugs, all tumbling into another sad little tragedy, and a life was gone. Sometimes nobody exactly meant it to happen. I believed in justice then. I still do, but justice isn't always so simple. It can be complicated, damn elusive, especially after the passage of time."

Mulholland continued, "So, if you don't get anywhere, we call it in. Actually you do. They'll do a report, the report will be stuck in a file and probably forgotten. Or maybe somebody sees it, recognizes a juicy story, and tips off the *Post*. If we end up going to the precinct and it gets buried or leaked, we'll just have to live with it, live with it either way."

Ludington was again shaken by the distinct possibility—even probability—that one of his predecessors at Old Stone was somehow complicit in the death and cremation of a child. He said as much to Mulholland. Yet there was an emptiness that had been carved in him by the bones, both the first and second times he had seen them, a void that ached to be filled. And he knew it could only be filled by somehow setting the horror of it right. And setting it right could be done only by knowing, the knowing of whatever the horror had been, and why, and who was responsible, and then going wherever the knowing might lead. And perhaps it would help to set right his own horror, also long buried. Just maybe.

# Chapter Five

*Thursday, March 28—The Twentieth Day in Lent*

L udington walked Harry Mulholland out of his study and through the door that led into the smaller office of his admin, Harriet van der Berg. He was about to open the second door that led out of Harriet's space and into the hallway when Harry said, "My cap. I must have left it on your coffee table."

Ludington recalled Harry having it on when he arrived that morning. It was a tweed driver cap, a failed attempt to coordinate with his jacket. Seth remembered him laying it on the coffee table between them. Harry went back into the study to fetch it. He heard the man call out, "Found it." He heard these words not only through the open door connecting the two offices. He also heard them clearly through the intercom atop Harriet van der Berg's tidy desk. The "speak" button on his unit that was always sticking open. He looked at Harriet. She looked away.

When Mulholland had left, Ludington sat in the spare chair in Harriet's cramped office. It was to the side of her desk, so there was nothing between them. "You heard?"

"I could hardly help hearing your conversation, Dominie. You must have inadvertently left the button on that devil's tool of an intercom device in the 'on' position. I did not want to interrupt you and the Clerk. You know I am unable to turn it off from my machine. What could I do?"

This was not strictly true. She might have turned the volume down or left her office.

Harriet van der Berg was tall and slender, almost scrawny. When standing, she invariably did so with her back arched, ramrod straight. Her posture gave her personality away. She insisted on addressing Ludington in the manner of speaking to clergy that she had been taught growing up in one of the old Dutch Reformed worlds far up in the Hudson Valley. And she named herself a "secretary," eschewing the modern "administrative assistant." When Ludington had suggested a sign on her door identifying her as such, she resisted, saying, "In no time, it'll be 'admin,'" a word she spat out disdainfully.

Harriet van der Berg had been a "secretary" for fifty years, and was not about to change her vocational title for the sake of merest political correctness. She had moved to the City immediately after high school and enrolled in the Katherine Gibbs School on West 40th, that venerable institution devoted to the training of New York secretaries. Competent and tireless, she had risen as high as a woman and secretary of that era might, serving several Wall Street types as "executive secretary." Now in her mid-seventies, she had retired a decade earlier. She had not married, and still mourned the death two years earlier of Margaret, her apartment mate of 50 years. When speaking of Margaret, Harriet referred to her as "my dearest friend." The two women had joined the Old Stone Church together half a century earlier and had come to be much loved by the congregation. No one spoke—at least not openly—about the nature of their relationship.

As was typical of her, van der Berg seized the conversational high ground, "I must commend you, Dominie, on your decision to attempt to save Old Stone from the perils of scandal. You must fear that should you go forthwith to the police, it is only too likely that the tale would be leaked to the press. The tabloid newspapers do love sin-in-the-church stories. It could be most deleterious to our congregation. We are rather at a crossroads just now, and with the steeple to be repaired and under your leadership, I have renewed hope." Decades as an executive secretary to powerful men had taught her exactly how much flattery she could get away with before slipping into fawning.

Ludington was still shaken by the fact that a fourth person now knew about the skeleton in the ash pit, but he was able to answer, "Thank you, Miss van der Berg, but you know how closely guarded this must be."

Van der Berg, insulted by the insinuation that she might be anything but absolutely discreet, answered with a firm, "Of course! You know that you can depend on me."

Which, Ludington had come to know over the last fourteen months, was quite true. He could indeed always depend on Harriet van der Berg, even though he often found the woman guarded and remote. She was deferential in the extreme toward Ludington, which also grated on him. He suspected that she was always secretly evaluating him, measuring him against all the Old Stone clergy she had evaluated over the last half a century. But the woman was more than capable. She was also, he had come to understand, very bright. Unlike most septuagenarians, she was computer savvy, more so than he. And she knew the Old Stone congregation inside and out. Fifty years a member, she knew everybody's back story. Ludington had once said to Fiona, "She knows where all the bodies are buried." "But not this one," he presently thought to himself. Van der Berg was also embarrassingly generous with her time. Ludington had to be careful not to ask too much of her, even though she offered "to be supportive in whatever manner I might" with regularity.

"Dominie, you are going to need assistance with your impending investigatory endeavors. I am more than willing to assist, should you assent. And Holy Week and Easter will soon be upon us, a most intense and demanding period of time for you." When he had first met her, Ludington was incredulous that anyone in the early 21$^{st}$ century would actually speak like Miss van der Berg. Conversing with her was like reading a Victorian novel. He especially disliked her insistence on addressing him as "Dominie." He retaliated by calling her "Miss van der Berg."

He was silent; she continued. "You are aware, surely, of the depth of my knowledge of Old Stone Church—its history, its members, and the various clergymen who have served us over the years." This last was obviously offered in response to what she had overheard about the need to explore the several ministers whom Ludington had named to Mulholland "my predecessors."

Ludington understood several things. First, she was right about the depth of her local knowledge, as deep as his was shallow. And Holy Week and Easter were just over two and three weeks away. But more importantly, he understood that it didn't much matter what he said in response to her offer. Now that she knew the story, one way or another, she would find a way to "assist him in his investigatory endeavors."

He had little choice but to say yes to her, thinking as he did so what a curious Watson she would be. One that was probably more clever than his Holmes. She was clearly pleased with his response, suggesting with what approached intimacy that he should perhaps now address her as "Harriet" rather than "Miss van der Berg."

"Not until you stop calling me 'Dominie.'"

# Chapter Six

*Thursday, March 28—The Twentieth Day in Lent, and Friday,*
*March 29—The Twenty-First Day in Lent*

L udington left the church shortly after 5:00. Fiona had stopped by
his office with a farewell kiss before she climbed into an Uber on
her way to JFK and a direct to Edinburgh. Her father's birthday was
Sunday, the 31st. She was booked on a return flight Friday the 5th. She never
missed his birthday, faithful daughter that she was. She would be there for
this one even though she'd see her parents in Scotland in ten weeks' time.
The past fall, Seth had cajoled her into going along on the church tour he
had been cornered into leading by promising her that the itinerary would
include Orkney. Fiona had long wanted to visit those remote islands to
the north of Scotland proper. Her maternal grandmother had been raised
there and still returned for months every summer. Seth had decided not to
accompany her on this birthday visit as he would see his in-laws in a few
months' time. If anyone would understand his son-in-law's absence on a
Sunday birthday, it was another minister.

As Ludington walked out the parish house door, he said a good evening
to the sexton who was vacuuming the worn burgundy carpet in the church
lobby. He knew the man had been more than pleased when he and Fiona
had bought the manse from the church. It was one less aging building with
an endless list of code violations for him to worry about.

As Ludington turned the corner onto 84th Street, he spied Orsolya stationed at her post on the stoop across the street from his house. As he unlocked the manse door, he turned to see her wave her paper cup of bull's blood in his direction. It occurred to Seth that the woman was a classic "watcher."

When he was a teenager, he recalled his father telling him, only half in jest, after an afternoon of sailing on Lake Michigan that every harbor had a watcher. Seth and his dad were motoring up to the Yacht Club dock Pentwater on a perfect July day. Docking a boat well is a bit of a challenge for even the best sailor. As his father steered their 37-foot Tartan toward the dock in a still southerly breeze, carefully gauging wind speed and direction as well as the vessel's inertia and the manner in which the stern would walk to the side when he slipped the engine into reverse, he told Seth about watchers.

"Every harbor has one. All they do is sit on the shore and watch boats come in, waiting for you to make a mistake. When you make one, you can count on it, the watcher will see it. Your mistakes never go unnoticed."

As Seth waved back at Orsolya, he thought, "And every New York street has a watcher. Just waiting for you to make a mistake."

Ludington steeled himself to go directly to the cellar, a room he had avoided since his discovery. He was somehow uneasy about violating the little skeleton that had so long been at peace. But now discovered, its peace was unavoidably troubled. Retrieving a bit of bone for Harry was as discomforting as it was necessary. He sat on one of the book boxes, hesitated, breathed deeply, and reached for the handle of the ash pit door. As he slowly pulled it open it protested with a loud screech that he did not recall having heard before.

All was as it was, as it had been for some 50 years—the bones of a tiny skeleton, more than a bit disjointed and scattered, but still recognizable as such, sleeping in its soft cradle of gray ash. With some trepidation, he reached into the pit and removed what appeared to be the tiniest bone, that of the fingertip of the little hand lying nearest the opening of the ash pit. It seemed a violation as he did this, like the body snatchers of 19th Century Edinburgh. He knew it was necessary, and he also knew that in time the entire skeleton would have to be removed. By whom, and under exactly what circumstances, he did not know. Where it would then go, he did not know. Ludington placed the minuscule bone in a small brown pouch envelope and walked it over to Harry Mulholland's apartment on 84th Street east of Lexington. As he left his house, the ever-vigilant Orsolya called to him from across the street, "Going again out so soon, *Tiszteletes?*" Though her accent was slight, her word order was often curious.

Harry's place was not in a doorman building, so when Seth buzzed the Mulholland apartment, he said he'd come down, rather than have Seth come up. Georgia Mulholland, Ludington assumed, was not to be apprised of his discovery, the impending investigation, or Harry's involvement. Just as well. The fewer people who knew, the better.

Mulholland and Ludington walked a few steps down the block toward Third and stopped. Mulholland opened the envelope, peered inside, and said, "I'm only going to give my guy part of this bone, so small that it won't be recognizable for what it is, a finger bone I'm guessing. He needs precious little for the DNA analysis. He'll email the profile to me asap and I'll forward it to you. Harry said "ASAP" as if it were a word.

He tucked the envelope in his jacket pocket and went on, "Then maybe—just maybe—you poke around and maybe snag some DNA and we can figure out who this baby was related to. And if you know that, you can maybe—just maybe—figure out what the hell happened."

Seth looked at the cop-turned-clerk, "Well, okay, but that's a lot of just maybes, Harry."

Mulholland took a few steps down 84th Street, stopped, and turned back to Ludington. "You're going to get other DNA samples for me to pass on, Seth. I ask one thing only. Give me a pair of initials with each of them, to keep them straight you know."

"Okay, Harry, I'll do exactly that. Let's call this one 'L.O.—Little One.'"

* * *

Ludington arrived at Old Stone Church at 9:00 the next morning. He was not surprised to discover Harriet van der Berg parked at her desk waiting for him, even though Friday was not one of her regular volunteer secretary days. She clearly had a plan for the first step in their investigation. He could guess what it was. It was doubtless the same first step that had occurred to him, obvious as it was.

His plan for the day also included preparing Sunday's sermon. As every preacher knows too well, Sunday rolls around with cruel regularity. No matter what might consume the days prior—emergency hospital visits, disastrous weddings, sudden deaths, leaky pipes in the church kitchen, broken organs, tedious committee meetings—there would be a congregation, small as his was, sitting more or less expectantly in the pews come 11:00 Sunday morning.

"The Session record books, Dominie," she said without preamble as he walked through the door. That is precisely where we must begin."

"That occurred to me as well," Ludington answered—a bit defensively—as he sat in the chair to the left of her desk. "Where are they? I mean, the old ones, the ones from the late '60s and early '70s? They should tell us who lived in the manse and when."

"Oh, I know precisely who the ministers were back then. There were only two in that time frame—the approximate period of your *Life* magazine cover, that is to say. But it was fifty years ago, and I don't recall precisely when one moved out of the manse, and the other moved in."

"Precisely," Ludington had noticed, was one of van der Berg's favorite words. And she would always call 338 East 84th Street "the manse" no matter who owned it.

She continued, "The older Session record books are kept in the storage room next to the boiler room in the basement under the sanctuary. Those I have here in my office only go back to January of 1980. I have time to investigate just now if you do, Dominie." "Investigate" struck Ludington as a strange word to tumble from the older woman's lips.

The storage room in Old Stone Church's basement was as disorderly as van der Berg's office was orderly. Cardboard boxes stuffed with old Sunday bulletins, church newsletters, and carbon copies of ancient correspondence were stacked in no discernible pattern around the walls of the room. Several pieces of discarded furniture were piled together in the center. Happily, van der Berg knew where the boxes of Session record books were.

"I occasionally receive inquiries from people engaged in genealogical research asking for information about the baptisms, marriages, and deaths of antecedents whom they believe were connected to Old Stone Church. Any records prior to 1980 are located here. This room may be a disgrace, but the Session record books are arranged in chronological order. I have seen to that, at least."

Indeed, lined up against one wall of the room were half a dozen boxes neatly labeled "Session Record Books," with the years that each box contained noted on the sides in neat lettering. If, in the course of human history, Presbyterians are remembered for nothing else, they will be remembered for their near-pathological zeal for record keeping. The exhaustive minutes of every meeting of the Session—who made what motion, who seconded it, and what the vote was—all recorded for eternity. Every baptism, communion service, wedding, funeral, all recorded for eternity. Every set of minutes dated and signed by the clerk of the Session and counter-signed by the moderator of the Session, usually the minister at the time.

Harriet pointed to the box labeled "Session Record Books, 1964—1972" directly under the one labeled "Session Record Books, 1973—1979" and on top of "Session Record Books, 1956—1963." Harriet had been organizing. Ludington removed the box they were seeking and opened it. Inside were four leather-bound books, rather larger than standard letter size, each about two inches thick, stacked atop each other.

"It'll be the second book down, Dominie, labeled '1966 and 1971,' I believe. Most books contain several years of minutes."

Ludington removed the book, handed it to van der Berg, and extracted two old ladder-back chairs from the pile of furniture behind them. As they sat down, van der Berg said, "I clearly recall who our ministers were in the pertinent time frame, that is to say, 1969-1970. There were two, the Reverend Malcolm McCrae and the Reverend Philip Desmond."

Ludington knew Desmond, or more accurately, he knew *of* Desmond. The man was something of a Presbyterian rock star, one of the so-called "liberal lions" of the more tumultuous days of the last century. Desmond was Hollywood handsome, an earthy and engrossing preacher who had held serial leadership positions in the denomination. He was about as famous as a clergyman might be in a secular age.

"The Rev. McCrae was the Interim Minister prior to the Rev. Desmond," Harriet went on. "But I cannot quite recall precisely when the guard was changed, as the English say." She gave Ludington a look that seemed to apologize for her less-than-exact recall of events that had unfolded half a century earlier.

"I do know that Rev. Desmond and his family lived in the manse. Margaret and I frequently attended fellowship events they hosted there. Such a superb young minister, Rev. Desmond. And he remained with us for nearly twenty years, twenty grand years for Old Stone Church. And his wife was the perfect first lady of the church. 'Penelope' was her name, though people called her 'Penny,' even Reverend Desmond. Unfortunate. Margaret and I always called her by her actual name, of course. And those three lovely daughters."

He knew that the man had once been the minister of Old Stone, but he had not known exactly when. The fact that "when" included the year 1970 was profoundly disconcerting. In an indirect way, Philip Desmond was part of the reason Ludington had ended up at Old Stone Church. Ludington knew Desmond both by reputation and through a common friend. Moses "Moze" Washington had been Ludington's boss at New Philadelphia Ministries. Washington and Desmond were an ecclesiastical matched-set—two very successful pastors, fast friends, both focused on social justice. Their relationship had become emblematic of the struggle to bridge the chasm between black and white churches. The well-known fact that they had been seminary roommates only made them more intriguing.

When Fiona got the U.N. job, and Ludington told Washington he would be following her to New York, Moze had mentioned to him that Desmond's former church, Old Stone, was vacant again. "Maybe you're ready for the trenches, Seth, the parish church, that's where it's at, man." Washington had then noted that Desmond had left Old Stone in good shape some three decades earlier, but the rumor was that the place was in a precarious condition these days. Desmond, he added, had gone on to become the Senior Minister of a large and prestigious congregation in suburban New Jersey. Then he had himself "left the trenches" to become the president of a seminary in Philadelphia, a career-capping position from which he was about to retire.

Van der Berg interrupted Ludington's musing, repeating, "The Rev. McCrae came as Interim Minister prior to Rev. Desmond. This was shortly after Margaret and I joined the congregation. We joined in the winter of 1969 –'70. Old Stone had weekly guest preachers when we were first members. Margaret and I used to rate their sermons on a scale of one to ten, like the Olympics." Van der Berg smiled at the memory of youthful mischievousness and went on, "But I cannot recall precisely when Mr. McCrae arrived or when he left. His wife…her name was Dolores. Quiet, she was. In fact, they were both reserved in their manner. They were perhaps in their late '30s, at least he was. They did not have children. I assume they lived in the manse, but they did not host social events there."

"Well," said Ludington interrupting her waxing nostalgia, "the Session records should tell us precisely when the guard changed." He smiled at her with his use of her preferred adverb. She did not smile back. Ludington guessed her reluctance to exchange a smile was born of her dawning realization that the names they were searching out in musty books in a dingy basement were those of clergy, men—and they were all men then—one of whom was somehow connected to the hidden death of an infant. The horror of it seemed to preclude returned smiles.

Their quick examination revealed that the first minutes of a Session meeting that had been signed by Malcolm McCrae were those of June 1969. They noted that McCrae had started work at Old Stone at the beginning of the month and had first led worship on Sunday, June 8, 1969.

"June the 8th. Margaret and I were present. I can recall the day."

The last minutes signed by McCrae were those of May 20, 1970. The first set of minutes signed by Desmond were those of the meeting of September 16, 1970.

"Desmond was an installed minister," Seth noted. "He would have been elected at a meeting of the entire congregation. Those congregational meeting minutes have to be here as well. And they should tell us exactly when he arrived at Old Stone."

He paged back in the Record Book and found the brief minutes of a Congregational Meeting held following worship on Sunday, April 19, 1970. They recorded that the Pastor Nominating Committee had presented the Rev. Philip Davis Desmond as their nominee and that the congregation had elected him as Old Stone Church's Senior Minister by vote of 172 to 8 with 3 abstentions. The minutes further noted that Desmond would begin work on June 1, 1970. The minutes then offered Malcolm McCrae what read like muted thanks for his service to Old Stone Church.

Ludington read them aloud and said, "That gratitude offered to McCrae was decidedly perfunctory, don't you think? But the point is that they moved out of the manse sometime in late May, and the Desmonds must have moved in around his June 1 start date."

"Well," said van der Berg sitting upright in her chair, "Philip Desmond may have lived in the manse in the summer of 1970, but one simply cannot imagine him or his family having anything at all to do with your unfortunate discovery, Dominie."

# Chapter Seven

*Friday, March 29—The Twenty-First Day in Lent*

Ludington knew exactly where he could find the Rev. Dr. Philip Desmond—in the office of the President of Philadelphia Theological Seminary. At least he would find him there for the next few weeks. The last time he had spoken on the phone with his mentor, Moze Washington, the man had mentioned that Desmond had announced his retirement, a long-anticipated event scheduled for that spring. On the other hand, Seth had no idea where Malcolm McCrae might be, even whether the man was still alive. He would be in his late 80s if he were.

The sermon could wait till the afternoon. He looked up the phone number of the Presbyterian Pension Fund on their website. Every Presbyterian Minister is required to participate in the denomination's pension system, and they keep track of their members—whether they be living or otherwise and—if the former where they do their living. Ludington worked his way through the tiresome telephone prompts to find the extension for the Church Consultant assigned to the New York metro area. He had actually spoken to her a year earlier when he'd taken the job at Old Stone. Alyson was her name, Alyson Weed. She might remember him. She picked up on the first ring.

"Alyson Weed," she chirped.

"Alyson, it's Seth Ludington calling. We talked last year when I accepted the call to Old Stone in Manhattan."

"Of course. I hope you're settling in. Great old church. All's well, I hope."

"It is. But it's not me I'm calling about. I'm doing a bit of, well…, historical research into the congregation. Trying to better understand the place, you could say. History matters, you know. So, I'm wanting to speak with some of my predecessors. There's one I can't locate. I'm hoping you can help. 'The Rev. Malcolm McCrae.' He was Interim here in 1969 and 1970. It was a pivotal time for the church, and I'd love to track him down and have a conversation. He'd be in his 80s now. Just an address and a phone number. That's all I need."

"Let me log in here and see if I can find your Rev. McCrae. How's it spelled? The Scots manage to spell a simple name fourteen different ways.

"CC,' Ludington answered, "M-c-c,' and 'r-a-e.'"

"Give me a minute…." Two full minutes of phone silence ensued, and then she said, "Humm, here we go. I'm so sorry, but Malcolm McCrae died in 2002. He was 72, just 72. But let me see here… His widow is still living. She's receiving a survivor's pension. Dolores, Dolores McCrae. Do you want her contact information?"

Ludington couldn't say whether he was disappointed or relieved that McCrae was no longer living. But he said, "Sure. Why not? It could be helpful to talk with her about those years."

"Okay, 'Dolores McCrae, age 85, 7000 Westminster Gardens Drive, Apartment 420, White Plains, New York, 10602.' Only one phone number, landline, I'd guess. '914-606-2831.' That address is the Presbyterian retirement community in Westchester, by the way. We have a number of people up there. Pleasant place, as they go."

He thanked Alyson, hung up, and immediately dialed the number she had given him for Malcolm McCrae's widow. This could be a clumsy conversation, even though he only planned to ask if he might pay a call. It would be an odd request, an unbidden visit from the minister of a church her husband had served for just one year fifty years earlier. But, Ludington reasoned, retirement home residents, especially single ones, ache for visitors, any visitors.

He was about to hang up after the seventh ring when he heard the click of a landline being answered and a voice, strong and surprisingly deep, saying. "Hello, Dolores McCrae speaking." Old style telephone manners, Ludington thought to himself.

"Mrs. McCrae, my name is Seth Ludington, the Rev. Seth Ludington. I'm the minister of the Old Stone Church in Yorkville, in Manhattan. Our records note that your late husband served our congregation some years ago."

Dolores McCrae hesitated before responding. Then she said, "Well, yes. Malcolm was the Interim Minister there. But it was a very long time ago, and we were only there for perhaps a year."

"Mrs. McCrae, I'm trying to understand Old Stone Church better. You can't understand who you are without understanding who you were." Cliché, Ludington thought to himself, but dead true. "I'm doing a bit of research, you might say." All this was the truth, but it was hardly the whole truth. The line separating generalization from prevarication can be thin.

Again, there was hesitation in her voice. She answered with a perfunctory "Yes?" spoken with an inflection that made the little word a question.

"Mrs. McCrae, I was planning to be up your way tomorrow and was hoping I might pay a call. I'd love to hear your memories of Old Stone back in the late 60s." With those words, the Rev. Ludington took his first clear step on this investigative journey into the world of needful dissembling. Yes, he was planning to be "up her way," but only if he could see her, and the memories he was curious about were very specific and potentially very uncomfortable ones.

Once more, the woman hesitated before answering, "Well, I have my exercise class in the morning and my bridge group in the afternoon. People assume that we just sit in our rooms at Westminster Gardens, but life is really very active for many of us."

The answer was, Ludington assumed, a soft "No."

He pressed her gently, "I wouldn't take much of your time. Perhaps I could drop by between your engagements. It would be such a help to me. I'm trying to understand Old Stone, and your husband served the church at a crucial time. So much was going on in the City in the late 60s and early 70s, such turbulent years. Very formative for a congregation."

Quite true, but not at all what he planned to talk with her about. Trespassing the Eighth Commandment could be so nebulous.

She relented, but reluctantly. "Perhaps just after lunch, shall we say one o'clock? I'm not sure I can be of much assistance. It was a very long time ago, and as I said, Malcolm and I were at Old Stone for only a year."

Ludington thanked her profusely, hung up, and ambled into van der Berg's office to tell her that he had managed to arrange an interview with Dolores McCrae.

"I shall accompany you, Dominie. I shall play your amanuensis, the silent taker of notes for your historical queries. And Dolores McCrae, you must consider, is much in my age cohort, and a woman. She might well be more candid with me present."

Ludington judged van der Berg correct, sensing—and not for the first time—that the woman was enjoying the chase.

"I'll fetch my car from the garage and stop for you at noon...better make it 11:45. Don't want to be late, or she'll be off to her bridge game."

The fact that Dolores McCrae played bridge at the age of 85 was, Ludington thought, a hopeful indicator of the keenness of the woman's memory.

\* \* \*

He hung up and decided that lunch would be his regular sermon day indulgence—a slice of pepperoni pizza from La Mia. Both he and Fiona tried to eat healthily, but one of the things he most loved about New York was its pizza. He allowed himself to collapse before its lure once a week. He ate the pepperoni slice on the bench outside La Mia, wiped the pizza grease off his fingers with the napkin stuffed in the paper bag, and headed back to his office for the Friday inevitable. Even after more than twelve months at it, Ludington was finding the relentlessness of weekly sermons a trial. Some Fridays, he found himself staring at the screen of his Mac, resorting to prayers that words might come, words faithful enough to carry a 2,000-year-old passage of Scripture across the chasm of time and make it somehow relevant to the eighty-some twenty-first-century souls gathered at 11:00 in Old Stone's gloomy sanctuary. Distracted as he was by the bones in the ash pit and the strange visit scheduled for the next day, he sat down before the empty screen of his computer and sighed.

Ludington was a lectionary preacher, meaning that he generally preached sermons based on one of the Bible passages assigned for the day by the Revised Common Lectionary, that pattern of readings used by most of the world's churches. Without the discipline of the lectionary, Ludington knew he would fall back to preaching on the Bible passages he liked, dodging the many that made him uncomfortable.

The Gospel text assigned for March 31, the Fourth Sunday in Lent, was the Parable of the Prodigal Son. Familiar as it was, Ludington was unsure whether it was one of those passages he liked or one of those that made him uncomfortable. Perhaps both. It certainly discomforted him every time he read it, even while he knew he needed to hear it.

Like most of the parables in the Gospels, this one fell on different ears in different ways. If you had screwed up your life and finally determined to fly straight, you identified with the Prodigal, the self-serving wanderer who went home and received forgiveness and got a party before he had even managed to ask for either. If you were a parent of a wayward child who had finally returned home, you identified with the father who ran out to greet his child, lost but now found, throwing your arms around the rogue before he had managed to blurt out his carefully rehearsed apology. Or if you—like Seth Ludington—were an older child with a prodigal sibling, you might identify with the big brother, the kid who kept his nose clean and worked his tail off on dad's farm, only to watch his useless little brother enjoying dad's indulgent love, the big party, the fine wine, and the veal chops. Seth Ludington's younger sister by three years had left the Midwest for Marin County after dropping out of college and was still deciding at age 36 whether to be a potter or a yoga instructor. Neither paid well, and living in the Bay Area in the style to which she was long accustomed was outrageously costly, both of which necessitated annual appeals to her parents for yet another advance on one of her trust funds, actually one of *their* trust funds.

Ludington resented it and felt guilty for resenting it. He grew uneasy every time he read the parable and came to the line about the older brother standing outside the party tent with his arms crossed, complaining to his father about how faithful and hardworking he has been but never got the big party, yet *"when this son of yours came back, who devoured your property with prostitutes, you killed the fatted calf...."* In fact, nobody had ever said anything about prostitutes. Big brother just imagined them. And the parable says nothing about the older brother crossing his arms, but Ludington had always envisioned him with his arms crossed.

He had preached this Parable once before at Old Stone. On that occasion, he had then gently reminded the congregation of the temptation to self-righteousness, which more-or-less decent people inevitably face. Yet, he sensed that it was the parable's straight-up forgiveness that most people wanted to hear, a pulpit proclamation of pure grace, cheap grace, or at least low-cost grace—"no matter how many times and how royally you mess up, just say 'sorry,' and God will forgive you."

True enough, though with some caveats, Ludington admitted. But as he stared at the screen of his Mac, his mind settled on the memory of a print of a painting he had recently seen. The original, he learned, hangs in the Dallas Museum of Art, a haunting depression-era masterpiece by the Midwestern Regionalist, Thomas Hart Benton. It pictures a gray-bearded old man, hat in hand, suitcase held together by ropes and set at his feet, staring at a fallen-down abandoned farmhouse. The skeleton of a full-grown cow lies at his feet, front left—the remains of the fatted calf. "The Prodigal Son," Benton had entitled it, the Prodigal Son come home...but way too late.

The painting begged questions about the passage of time and whether forgiveness becomes easier or harder as the offense ages. The bones in his ash pit asked these very questions, Ludington thought. No matter how hideous or stupid or careless was the death of that child, is the crime—whatever it was—somehow more forgivable after half a century? Is it easier to forgive a wrong, especially a grievous one, after the passage of time? After half a century, has it become too late to expect anybody to "come home" and own the death of the child, a child that would now be a fifty-year-old adult? When—if ever—does enough time ever pass that it's best to let old bones lie in peace? Maybe never. Decades had passed, but a child was dead, dead in secret.

Ludington was careful about permitting his penchant for poetry to find its way very far into the pulpit. Poetry's rhetoric was so compact, so intense that it had to be allowed only rare sermon cameos. He was averse to ever using his own, so he would only quote other poets, but even then sparingly.

He decided to quote a bit of George Herbert's "Love III," familiar, but perhaps not so to many in the congregation:

*"Love bade me welcome. Yet my soul drew back*
*Guilty of dust and sin.*
*But quick-eyed Love, observing me grow slack*
*From my first entrance in,*
*Drew nearer to me, sweetly questioning,*
*If I lacked anything."*

Ludington would not preach about forgiveness and the passage of time this Sunday. He was presently unsure about just how deep forgiveness could reach. Rather he would preach the urgency of coming home to your mistakes and failings, owning them to others, to God, and to yourself. And doing it now, before they might devour you. The phone rang as he prepared to punch save. It was the church landline, not his cell.

"Call for you, Dominie, a young woman, I should think. She did not identify herself."

He heard the click that let him know van der Berg had transferred the call.

"Hello," he said, "Seth Ludington."

"Reverend Ludington?" the voice answered, a question in its rising tone, as well as an emphasis on the "reverend" that hinted at skepticism, or perhaps irony.

"Yes. That's me."

"You probably don't remember me. My name is Cara Lundberg, but you'll remember my sister."

He could find no words. Bile rose in his throat. He felt drops of sweat forming on his forehead.

"I'm here in New York City," she said. "I'd like to meet with you. There are some things I'd like to talk over with you. I think you probably want to hear what I have to say, reverend." Again, that title—one which Ludington had always borne uneasily—was weighted with satire as she spoke it.

Ludington gulped, audibly he guessed, and said, "Well, okay. It would be good to see you." The lie tumbled from his lips before he had a chance to catch it.

Cara Lundberg took charge. "How about later this afternoon? Not in your church. though. Maybe a bar somewhere."

He had no choice but to meet the woman. The Michigan accent vouched for her identity. He could only guess what she might know about her sister, young as she had been at the time.

He said, "There is a place in East Harlem, The Lexington Social, on 104th Street, actually." He had never been there, but had recently walked by on his way to Mount Sinai Hospital. He chose it because it was well out of the neighborhood.

Still in charge, Cara Lundberg said, "I'll find it. Six o'clock."

Maybe the woman just wanted to talk, perhaps unload anger on him, no more than that. Or it could well be that she wanted no more than to unburden herself.

As he named the sermon "Before It's Too Late" and punched "save as," he recalled that one of his preaching professors in seminary had said that most ministers tend to preach to themselves. "Rather too much," he had added. Ludington whispered to himself, "I guess that's exactly what we do."

# Chapter Eight

*Friday, March 29—The Twenty-First Day in Lent*

The Lexington Social mirrored the gentrification creeping north up the spine of Manhattan and into East Harlem. Once called Spanish Harlem, the neighborhood was morphing into reluctant hipsterism, a marginally more affordable Brooklyn peopled with young professionals priced out of the world south of 96th Street. The bar was brighter than he had recalled when he had passed it some weeks earlier. He saw that it named itself not just a bar, but a tapas bar.

Ludington had arrived twenty minutes early so he could secure a table toward the back, away from the windows facing 104th Street. He told the sole waiter on duty early on a Friday that there would be two of them. "I'm not sure about food, but I'd like an alcohol-free beer, whatever you've got." The thought of drinking in the presence of Sara's baby sister was revolting. He stared at the frosty amber glass when the waiter set the Caliper down atop a Lexington Social coaster. He watched the foam head slowly settle to nothing as he waited for her.

He had not yet touched it when a woman who could only be Sara Lundberg's sister entered the bar. He had met her but once before, twenty years ago, when he had driven Sara home after she'd finished her shift at the Landing, but not exactly right after the restaurant had closed, a good hour later. Cara had been waiting on the front steps of their family's home in the rolling country east of Pentwater, almost in Crystal Valley. He had never seen her house before and was jolted by the peeling white paint on the clapboard and the two pick-ups perched on cinder blocks in the dirt drive. He also remembered thinking how odd it seemed for a fourteen-year-old to be up at midnight. The girl had waved enthusiastically as he pulled up to the small frame house in his father's BMW 7 Series. Cara had waved—not at him or the car, but at her big sister. Sara did not introduce him to the girl. He recalled her simply saying, "Dumb kid always has to wait up for me." At least that's what he remembered.

This adoring little sister rhymingly named Cara would be in her mid-thirties now. As she walked toward him, weaving through the tables of Lexington Social, she seemed quite confident that she was approaching the right table. Ludington could see the family resemblance. She was heavier than she's been as a teenager, certainly chubbier than her sister ever was, but nearly as tall. She was dressed in jeans, fashionably ripped at the knees, and a green Michigan State sweatshirt. She pulled out the other chair at the table and sat without a word.

Ludington felt compelled to speak into his discomfort, even if it was to say the obvious. "Last time we met, you must have been in middle school."

"I remember. You used to drive her home after work."

Ludington actually recalled only doing so once, but perhaps it had been more.

"Are you still living in Michigan?" He was loath to ask what had brought her to New York.

"Yep, got a house not far from mom and dad. Mom helps with the kids."

"You have a family, then?"

Couple of kids, eleven and thirteen, boy and a girl. She almost cracked a smile at her mention of her children. Divorced. Last winter.

I'm sorry to hear that.

Ya, right, so sorry. Actually, that's what I'm here about. This is how it is—two kids, no husband, and I got laid off at the plant. It's seasonal, you know. Actually, you'd probably have no idea. Asparagus, then cherries and peaches, then no work till next season. It's hard to make ends meet—mortgage, car payments. I'm hoping you could help me out.

She stared at the wine spritzer she had ordered, unwilling to look Ludington in the eye as she continued. "I mean, you're a Ludington after all, an actual frickin' Ludington, for God's sake." She paused and then said what he had feared she might have come to New York to say. She looked up at him as she spoke. "Mom told me what she and Dad know, the whole truth about Sara...and you."

Seth Ludington did the only thing he could imagine doing. He laid a twenty and a ten on the table to cover the bill and left without a word.

Cara Lundberg's chair screeched on the red quarry tile floor as she turned it around to face his back as he strode out of the Lexington Social. "Oh, I'll be in touch. You can be sure of that, Reverend Ludington." Both the title and the name were spoken in disdain.

# Chapter Nine

*Sunday, June 8, 1969*

Harriet and her friend Margaret took the stairs with staccato steps, flying down to a subway platform at Grand Central to catch the northbound IRT. They had heard it screech to a stop as Margaret searched the depths of her purse for two tokens. They made it in plenty of time. The third car from the front of the Lexington Avenue Local was waiting for them, patiently perhaps, but also ominously—doors gaping open, graffiti-smeared on the outside, sauna-hot on the inside. Blessedly, it was nearly empty on a Sunday morning.

Harriet van der Berg and Margaret Whitaker, both in their mid-twenties, were carefully coiffed and conservatively dressed, Harriet more so than Margaret. Harriet, firmly formal in demeanor, was a secretary in a shiny-shoe Wall Street law firm and always cautiously clad, whether she was heading uptown to church on a Sunday morning or downtown to work weekdays.

Margaret worked as a designer for a rising women's fashion company on Seventh Avenue. Harriet sometimes accused her roommate of having quite a lot of flair, no compliment in her lexicon. Margaret regularly ribbed Harriet about her sartorial conventionality, telling her with a sly and affectionate smile that she was starting to look like a tall Mamie Eisenhower.

Miniskirts, said Harriet, as she glanced at a woman she deemed too old for the one she was wearing slither through the subway cars closing doors. The same aesthetic cretans who thought it a good idea to tear down Pennsylvania Station probably invented miniskirts as well.

Margaret, fashion-forward as she might be, was no miniskirt fan, a minority position at her place of work. But she was quite inured to Harriet's fashion-backward views, so she easily slanted their conversation toward the architectural vector of Harriet's comment.

Well, she replied, At least they're not going to take the wrecking ball to our Grand Central Station.

'Terminal, Margaret, Grand Central Terminal.'

This banter, intelligent, sometimes sharp, but always fond, had been part of their way with each other since they had met a year earlier. Their friendship had bloomed slowly after a chance encounter at a tenant meeting. The residents of their building on 39th were contemplating a rent strike. It never happened; the landlord said he would freeze rents for two years and promised to clean up the lobby. Margaret and Harriet caught one anothers eyes as the meeting was breaking up. They exchanged smiles; both said how relieved they were at the outcome, Margaret suggesting a celebratory glass of wine at a spot she knew on Second Avenue. They moved in together a few months later, sharing Harriet's apartment to save money, or so they told their parents.

The landlord reneged on his promised rent freeze and never touched the lobby, so Harriet and Margaret went apartment-hunting uptown. Rents were falling in a city beset with garbage strikes and street crime. Manhattan, it seemed, was beginning to decamp to North Jersey, Westchester, and Connecticut. They found classic six in a prewar building on Second Avenue, more apartment than either had dared to dream of. They planned to move in later in the summer when the lease on Harriet's apartment was up.

Church shopping came right after apartment shopping. Margaret sprang from a family of eight generations of North Carolina Presbyterians, nine if you count the one who got off the boat from Scotland. Harriet had grown up in the fading Dutch Reformed world of the Hudson Valley. She could remember her grandfather speaking Dutch to her grandmother. Both women had the faith planted deep in them, rooted there by family and tradition. They could have rejected it as they had other conventions, but did not.

They had chosen to attend and would soon formally join the Old Stone Presbyterian Church, but not until their move uptown. The church was only two blocks from their new apartment and was, to their pleasure, liturgically traditional, about as high as Presbyterians rise. No guitars...ever. The members were friendly, but not too much so.

Nothing worse than being pounced upon when you visit a new church, Harriet had said the first Sunday they had attended.

Margaret was, after all, a legacy Presbyterian, and the Dutch Reformed, Harriet had informed her with an uncharacteristic wink, were the Presbyterians' continental kissing cousins. The clincher was the fact that the ushers, all four of them men, wore black morning coats, grey striped trousers, and matching gray neckties. How refreshing, Harriet had observed.

A postcard had arrived early that week informing them that Old Stone's new Interim Minister would lead worship and preach on the Sunday coming. *Please plan to attend worship this Sunday, June 8, and extend a warm Old Stone welcome to the Rev. and Mrs. Malcolm McCrae. A Coffee and Tea Reception in the Social Hall will immediately follow the service.* Harriet and Margaret would have been in church anyway, new minister to welcome or no. They rarely absented themselves, sitting dependably in the ninth pew back on the lectern side, the accustomed space to which they found their way on that Sunday as the organ prelude began.

The Rev. Malcolm McCrae was a small man, thin of hair and body. He had a pleasant enough voice, tenor probably, but had a habit of blinking his eyes with disconcerting frequency. He did wear a black Geneva preaching gown, which won him points, but about his neck was a blue tie rather than a clerical collar and tabs. He lost points with both Harriet and Margaret for that infraction. At least the long liturgical stole over his shoulders was the proper color for the season, green for Ordinary Time. And it was not hand-woven in Costa Rica or tie-died by Mrs. McCrae. More points for that. The sermon was longish. Margaret timed it at 24 minutes. It ended with a surfeit of we shoulds. As the Rev. McCrae descended the stairs from the pulpit, holding up the hem of his robe so as not to trip over it, Margaret mouthed, *sotto voce,* six-point-five.

The Coffee and Tea Reception in the Social Hall under the Sanctuary was well-attended, nearly all the congregation having found time to greet the Rev. and Mrs. McCrae. A long table was set at one end of the Hall, the center bedecked with plates of assorted cookies, all homemade. Stationed at one end of the table was a member of the Women's Association pouring coffee; a second dispensed tea at the other. Harriet noted that the church's fine old Wallace silver service and collection of bone china had been rescued from storage oblivion for the occasion.

The Rev. McCrae and his wife stood together at the other end of the Social Hall. A line of church members of various ages, including a handful of youngsters more interested in cookies than interim ministers, snaked from them to the center of the room. Harriet noted that Mrs. McCrae was taller than her husband by an inch or two, and looked rather more comfortable than he with this needful ordeal. Both appeared to be in their mid to late thirties, he perhaps a few years older. Harriet and Margaret chatted with several church members, set down their cups and saucers, and wandered to the greeting line.

Dolores, please call me Dolores, said Mrs. McCrae as she shook Harriet's hand after the latter had offered, Welcome to Old Stone, Mrs. McCrae. The woman's grasp was firm, and her smile broad and genuine.

I'm Harriet van der Berg. This is my friend, Margaret Whitaker. We are neither of us members at present, but plan to join the congregation when we move uptown later in the summer.

Are you actual native New Yorkers? They seem to be thin on the ground, even in this old neighborhood.

Margaret joined the conversation, taking Dolores's offered hand, I'm from Charlotte — Charlotte, North Carolina. I moved to New York four years ago, so I may be on the way to native. I came to the City to work in fashion.

Fashion. How intriguing. Only in New York. Are you in the fashion industry as well, Miss van der Berg?

Hardly. I'm a fashion Neanderthal. A merest law firm secretary, I fear. I came to New York to attend the Katherine Gibbs School. Right after college, that is. I'm from upstate, attended college there as well. Skidmore. Harriet was generally not a name-dropper, but was wont to mention Skidmore whenever she had to confess to being a secretary.

Dolores deftly passed the two women on to her husband, who did not say Please call me Malcolm when Harriet said, Welcome to Old Stone, Rev. McCrae. His manner was dry and stiff, and his handshake wet and limp.

As I said to your wife, neither Margaret nor I are members of the congregation yet, but we do plan to join when we move into our new apartment here in the neighborhood later this summer.

Wonderful, was his voiced answer, but his look—or perhaps Harriet only imagined it—was questioning rather than wonderful, an eyebrow raised at Harriet's we in when we move.

Living arrangements being the topic, he said, "I must tell you how happy Dolores and I are to be living in the church's new manse. The movers arrive tomorrow."

"And I'm pleased for you." Harriet had heard coffee hour talk about the five-story brownstone on 84th that had recently been bequeathed to the church.

After offering up their welcome and dipping an inch into real estate, that favorite focus of so much New York conversation, Harriet and Margaret moved along for those in line behind them. As they walked away, Harriet glanced back to look at the McCraes. The two Anderson children, a little boy of perhaps four and his younger sister, were darting around the Social Hall as they did most Sundays after church, presenting something of a hazard to coffee and tea drinkers. Dolores McCrae was watching them intently. There was no recrimination in her look. Harriet thought it seemed more like longing. No children danced about Malcolm's legs or pulled with boredom at Dolores's arm.

# Chapter Ten

*Monday, April 1—The Twenty-Third Day in Lent*

"What a venerable automobile you drive, Dominie."

Harriet said this right after her doorman opened the door of Ludington's ancient Volvo for her. He had pulled up to her building on 81st and Second at the contracted time of 11:45. He was quite prepared to get out and open the car's door for her when the doorman dashed out of the lobby to do so. He appeared to understand as well as Ludington that Harriet van der Berg expected doors to be opened for her. "Thank you, Sergio," she said, working her lanky frame into the passenger seat. Sergio closed the door, and Ludington helped her with the seatbelt.

"What make is it? I know nothing of autos. I don't even have a driving license, but I don't believe I have ever seen this model before. It's quite unusual. And the color. Would you call it 'teal' or 'aqua?'"

Ludington suspected that, as with many New Yorkers, the only "autos" Harriet van der Berg rode in were cabs. He also guessed that she was thrilled with the adventure that lay before them—a drive out of the City to White Plains for an interview with a person whom she had named to Ludington as "a suspect." Her excitement was inducing an uncharacteristic loquaciousness.

"It's a Volvo PV544, 1965."

"Older than you, Dominie. Some fourteen years older, I believe."

Ludington was intrigued that she knew his exact age. "It was a gift from my father when I graduated from college. He'd bought it as a second—well, actually third—car for my mom. She'd decided she needed air-conditioning and really didn't like shifting gears. It sat in their garage for decades, then he had it restored and passed it on to me. It's ancient but dependable and serves us well, not that we drive it much in the City."

"Well, I approve, Dominie." This unsolicited judgment was passed with a firm nod of her head and a gentle pat of her hand on the dashboard in front of her.

"And if I might say so, I also appreciated yesterday's sermon. It is indeed so important for us to be honest about our failings. I certainly must have some myself. We all do, of course. And owning them to one's self and, as you noted, owning them to God, leads one to integrity."

This synopsis was vaguely what Ludington had said from the pulpit. Van der Berg's next exegesis of the sermon went well beyond anything he'd said, however.

"Truth must out, Dominie. You know the old saying, 'Truth is the daughter of time.' I read a detective novel years ago that was entitled *The Daughter of Time.* Written by Miss Josephine Tey. Margaret read it first. She was quite the detective fiction aficionada. She passed it on to me, insisted that I read it. Miss Tey's detective—I cannot recall his name—sets out to solve a very old mystery, the murders of those two little princes in the Tower of London. That tragic event, as you surely know, occurred five hundred years earlier, not the mere forty-plus as in our case. Well, in his play, Shakespeare had blamed their uncle, Richard III. Miss Tey's detective concludes, quite convincingly as I recall, that Richard was innocent. As you said yesterday, there can be no peace until the truth is known."

Though that was not quite what Ludington had said in the sermon, van der Berg was unknowingly articulating what he was coming to understand to be at the core of his own motivations for what they were doing. People often hear things in sermons the preacher did not say. How curious that she might hear what he had not said, but was thinking. Ludington had never before experienced van der Berg in such a voluble mode.

Her words about the truth coming out cut painfully close to the bone, recalling as they did the awkward encounter he'd had with Cara Lundberg the previous Friday. That meeting had never been far from his thoughts over the last two days. The woman had threatened to be in touch, but had not yet contacted him again. Perhaps she'd drop it, or so he hoped. Nevertheless, he could not but fear that what she knew might become another daughter of time.

"Quite true," he answered stiffly, shifting down into second gear as he turned left off Madison and headed west toward the 86th Street Traverse across Central Park. "It seems impossible to imagine any kind of resolution—forgiveness, reconciliation, peace if you will—if the truth about things is hidden. Even when it's been long buried, truth wants to rise to the surface, even if the rising is painful. I think truth may actually force itself up into the light." As he spoke—in a rather too preacherly voice—he could not but think that Cara Lundberg might be planning to force truth up and into the light. But he only said, "I like your 'daughter of time' metaphor, though I think it often takes a long time for the daughter to be born, Miss van der Berg." In the matter of what Cara Lundberg said she knew, he hoped for a great deal more time.

"Well, Dominie, I guess that's precisely what all this is about—today's little foray up to White Plains and the bone sample for DNA analysis you were to give to Harry. You did pass the sample on to him, I assume. So, as I said, today I shall simply take notes as you interview Dolores McCrae."

"Yes, I gave it to Harry. But calling our visit to Dolores McCrae an interview makes me sound like the cop. I'm thinking about an easy conversation with Mrs. McCrae, a chat about old times. Go back to 1969-'70, go gently, and then move sideways toward the manse and maybe just mention the fireplace, but only if it seems natural. Remember, it's the history of Old Stone I'm supposed to be after. I told her I wanted to know about the church back then so I can better understand the congregation today."

As Ludington said this, he realized yet again that this investigatory adventure was pushing him into the moral fog of deliberate dissembling, into a thickening mist of little prevarications, needful—perhaps justifiable—as they might be.

"Personally, I'd be more direct."

I bet you would, thought Ludington.

"Dominie, you might candidly inquire as to whether any small children or infants—you might even say infants—ever resided in the manse during their tenure. That's a simple enough question. Or you might tell her about your impending renovation project and mention your cleaning of the ash pit. Nothing of what you found, I suppose. That might overstep. After you say this, we both closely observe her reaction."

Ludington crossed Central Park West and headed down the architectural canyon of West 86th Street toward the Henry Hudson Parkway. He was less than comfortable with the directness of van der Berg's suggested approach, so he changed the subject.

"Tell me what you recall about the McCraes. What were they like as a couple? What kind of a person—what kind of pastor and preacher—was Malcolm?"

Even though he was asking for memories almost fifty years old, Ludington had come to appreciate how keen van der Berg's mind was.

"I'd guess they were in their mid or late thirties when they came to Old Stone. They seemed a happily married couple, I suppose. Frankly, Dolores was the more engaging of the two. He—Malcolm—well, how to put this…, he often looked as though he were ill. I don't know that he was, but Margaret always said that 'unwell' was Malcolm McCrae's adopted demeanor. 'Unwell.' That's what Margaret said, and she was precisely correct. We both found him to be a middling kind of preacher. He ended every sermon by telling us what we ought to do. Tiresome week after week. He seemed a faithful enough pastor, though. He sent Margaret and me notes inviting us to join the congregation when we moved into our apartment that summer. I distinctly remember that he sent two separate notes, one to Margaret and one to me. Dolores was outgoing, smart. She seemed such a focused and energetic person. We did not socialize, so these are memories from some distance, but my guess is that Dolores made the decisions in such a way that Malcolm never knew he didn't make them. They didn't have children when they were with us. If they had them after they left Old Stone,

I'd be surprised, given their ages. Of course, they might have adopted."

The always startling expanse of the Hudson River reclined to their left as they drove north up the Henry Hudson Parkway. The Palisades, that long run of basalt cliffs on the west bank of the river, rose Rhine-like in the distance. Harriet ceased offering her remembrances and leaned forward in her seat to take in the breadth of the river of her upstate childhood, the river that had so shaped the city she now called home.

In the first silence of the drive, Ludington dared to trespass a topic he had never trod before. "You must miss Margaret very much."

At first, van der Berg did not respond—and he had not really asked a question. Then she took her eyes off the Palisades and looked at her pastor intently. A heavy silence sat between them for an awkward, though intimate, moment. "Of course." Then her gaze returned to New Jersey in the distance.

In the longer silence that followed those two words, Seth Ludington wrestled with their looming challenge—how in the world to shape what would doubtless be a very clumsy conversation with another old woman, an 85-year-old widow whom Harriet van der Berg had labeled "a suspect"—a suspect in the death of a child.

# Chapter Eleven

*Monday, April 1—The Twenty-Third Day in Lent*

Westminster Gardens of White Plains was hidden in a forest, rather than perched on a plain, white or otherwise. It was a campus of large four-story red-brick boxes looking to have been erected in the 1970s, at what was perhaps the nadir of American architecture. The blandness of the structures was somewhat redeemed by the countless towering maples and the well-groomed eponymous gardens woven gracefully among the buildings of the retirement community.

The website Ludington had perused earlier that morning advertised the place as a "continuing care community," an accidental alliteration that meant its residents might progress from "independent living" to "assisted living" to "skilled nursing," to "hospice care," and finally, he assumed, to "non-resident" status.

Under the words on a newer in-ground sign that read "7000 Westminster Gardens Drive," the address Dolores McCrae had confirmed when he called the day before, was a carved subscript—"Independent Living for Active Seniors." "Independent" and "active" were adjectives that meshed with the impression Ludington had gained of Dolores in their brief phone conversation.

He parked the Volvo near the entrance to 7000 Westminster Gardens Drive, quickly got out of the car and dashed around to open the door for van der Berg, not because he thought she expected such gallantry from a man even when exiting a car, but because the PV544's passenger door had recently been recalcitrant and demanded a firm tug. He yanked it open and offered her a hand, which she regally accepted with a "Well, thank you, Dominie."

They walked side-by-side through the small parking lot and then past early spring gardens promising blooms in a few short weeks. As they neared the entrance to Dolores McCrae's building, Ludington stopped and turned to his unlikely sidekick, "Remember, Miss van der Berg, we go slowly. I do most of the talking. You take notes."

Pulling a spiral-bound notebook from her purse and waving it in front of his face, she assured him, "I understand completely. You can depend on me."

The lobby was presided over by an imposing counter labeled "Welcome Desk." The Welcome Desk was presided over by an equally imposing woman who greeted Ludington and van der Berg with, "Good morning. How can I help you," offered up in a Caribbean lilt. She was not dressed in nurse's white. Ludington guessed that her job was more security than medical services.

"We've come to visit Dolores McCrae in 420. She's expecting us." He glanced at the wall clock behind the desk. One o'clock sharp.

The woman raised one hand to signal "stop" and reached for the phone on her desk with the other. "Please wait as I call Mrs. McCrae."

Ludington could hear several faint rings, an answering click, and then, "I'll send them right along, Mrs. McCrae."

The woman pointed to the lobby elevator to her right and said, "Please take the elevator to the fourth floor and then turn to your right. You'll find Mrs. McCrae's unit at the far end of the hallway to the left. She's expecting your visit." This last comment was punctuated with a broad smile.

Ludington rang the doorbell of unit 420, thinking that "unit" was an unhappy word for a place to live. The door was opened slowly. Dolores McCrae was a tall and angular woman, almost as tall as van der Berg. She looked and moved a decade younger than her 85 years, neatly dressed in black slacks, a trim white blouse, and grey cardigan. She was unsmiling and did not offer a welcome, merely a "Good afternoon, you must be the Rev.

Mr. Ludington." She then cast an inquiring look at van der Berg, a look that silently shouted, "And who would you be?"

"This is my administrative assistant, Harriet van der Berg. You'll perhaps remember her from your Old Stone days. She's helping me better understand the history of the congregation and agreed to come along today. And she was eager to see you again."

Van der Berg smirked at her pastor's sudden ease with truth-stretching and offered a nod to Dolores McCrae that was barely short of a bow. "How do you do, Mrs. McCrae? It's grand to see you again after all these years."

No smile was offered in return. Ludington guessed that McCrae had no memory of van der Berg.

"Well, you might as well come in. And do have a seat."

McCrae turned and motioned to the tidy sitting room behind her. The room was brightened by a large picture window overlooking the gardens below. The compact space was thoughtfully set with a small couch in a bright yellow floral print and two identical wing chairs covered in a light green velvet, all on three sides of a glass-topped coffee table. Then, hesitating as if she might not offer but doing so because the situation demanded it, McCrae asked, "Would you perhaps like coffee or tea?" Ludington and van der Berg answered in a duet, "Coffee, please."

As they moved from the entrance toward the sitting room, several items in the small apartment caught Ludington's eye. A MacBook Air sat on an open roll-top desk placed against the wall between the entrance and sitting room. It was an exceptional device for an octogenarian to own, he thought. To the left of the sitting room was a small and spotless kitchen. Through the kitchen to the left of the sitting room, Ludington could see into the bedroom beyond. Beside the single bed sat a nightstand bedecked with two framed photos, not twelve feet from him. McCrae, close behind them, had moved into the kitchen to fix coffee, but not until she had quietly closed the bedroom door. Ludington had seen the photos, however. One was of a marginally younger Dolores with an unsmiling man who looked older than she, doubtless the late Rev. Malcolm McCrae. The other was of a woman with bright magenta hair who looked to be in her late 60s, with a winsome young child—a boy of perhaps six—perched and smiling on her knee. Both photos had the same blue fake-sky backdrop that betrayed them as church directory photographs.

McCrae entered the silence of her two sitting-room guests, balancing a silver tray holding three delicate bone china coffee cups, a small silver pitcher of milk, and a matching sugar bowl. "How lovely," said van der Berg as McCrae returned to the kitchen for the silver coffee pot.

Their hostess sat herself carefully but easily in one of the wing chairs and looked at her guests without making any comment. Ludington began the interview. It was unfolding as clumsily as he had feared, "I'm fairly new at the Old Stone Church, just over a year. I'm trying to understand the congregation better, and knowing its history is essential to understanding it now. You and your husband were there at such a pivotal time for the church—late 60s and early 70s. New York and Old Stone were undergoing such changes. It was a tough time for both the City and the church. What was it like then, I mean—well—the mood? What challenges did you and your husband face?"

McCrae answered with the first hint of a smile, "The City was a mess, of course. It was dirty, so dirty. And not safe, even Yorkville was unsafe. Mayor Lindsey was doing his best, I suppose, but what with the garbage strike and then the blizzard and the Stonewall riots.... All that was before we got to Old Stone. The police strike was later, but my point is that the City was in chaos, a very different place than it is today. Norman Mailer actually ran for mayor. Incredible. People romanticize those days, but there was nothing romantic about them to my mind. I was working part-time in the Emergency Room at New York Hospital. I'm an RN. What I saw—the muggings, the shootings, the drug overdoses. People were starting to leave in droves, leaving for the suburbs, I mean."

None of this was news to Ludington, nor was it to van der Berg, though she pretended to take notes about events she remembered as well as McCrae.

"And the church? How did the church deal with it all?" Ludington asked.

"Heads in the sand. Like ostriches with their heads stuck in the sand. Members were leaving for Summit and up here to Westchester, Connecticut even. Budget problems. But nobody did anything to deal with it. It was that kind of a place, a bit insulated, a 'silk-stocking church,' you might say. A bit snooty, to be candid. And it's not like it was quite on the Upper East Side, not the real Upper East Side. But they behaved like it was. Malcolm attempted valiantly to communicate to them what they needed to do. That was his calling as Interim Pastor, to wake them up. In every sermon, he tried to nudge them into action. But it was always 'carry on as usual.'"

Ludington could see that van der Berg had stopped pretending to take notes. She was also biting her lower lip, something she invariably did when she was irritated. She might occasionally criticize Old Stone, but she brooked no critique of her beloved church from anyone else. Ludington saw her raise her pencil as if about to speak. He caught her eye and gave his head a quick shake in warning. She bit her lip again and returned her pencil to note-taking position.

But Dolores McCrae was not finished. "They treated Malcolm shabbily, to be frank. No raise, ever. Faint thanks when we left, and that new youngster came. It's all they could talk about, the handsome new minister and his beautiful wife. And we were out the door."

"Well, you were privileged to live in the manse," blurted van der Berg, unable to contain her growing chagrin.

"Big old barn of a place," responded McCrae. "Heating worked off and on. The kitchen was in the basement. I don't mean to sound ungrateful. It was quite a magnificent house, but rather in need of some attention. It's not like they bought it for us. The church had received it as a bequest from a member. I don't recall the details, but it had all unfolded only weeks before we arrived. That would have been in the early summer of 1969."

"Sunday, June eighth, to be precise," said van der Berg, glancing defiantly at Ludington. "I was actually in attendance that day."

She had been unable to maintain her promised secretarial silence. Ludington could see that she was growing evermore perturbed by McCrae's attitude, inching toward a burning indignation he had witnessed but rarely in the year he had worked with her.

Ludington reclaimed the conversation. "That summer you moved in, was it just you and the Rev. McCrae living in the manse? It's only my wife and I now. So much space for two people."

"Of course. We had no children. Just Malcolm and I."

Van der Berg pressed on, driven by inquisitorial inertia, "You would not know that Dominie has purchased the manse from the church and is presently undertaking its renovation."

"Dominie?" asked a perplexed McCrae.

"The Rev. Mr. Ludington, that is to say."

Ludington glared at van der Berg and gave his head a shake to either side, but van der Berg was not to be silenced. She was nearing the heart of the matter and was not about to be deflected by his pastoral discretion.

"Why, he's even doing some of the work himself. The other day he cleaned out the old ash pit under the living room fireplace."

Ludington was stunned to silence, but Dolores McCrae was not.

McCrae said, "That was doubtless wise. I do recall the fireplace in the manse. I wish I had one here, but they're not permitted, not even those electric ones." She glanced toward the clock on the wall over the television set and turned to her guests with a small smile. "Would you care for a second cup of coffee? I guess I could make more."

Understanding that their visit was being curtailed, and suddenly animated by the heedless candor that often comes with age, van der Berg smiled back at her pastor and said to both of them, "Why, Dominie actually found some bones in the ash pit when he cleaned it out."

To Ludington's horror, she pressed on, "They seem to be human bones, those of a small child, believe it or not. We do need to know whose bones they are of course, so we are having their DNA analyzed." Van der Berg offered this up as though it were merely an interesting piece of news.

McCrae was unshaken and glacier-cold in her response. She remained silent for an uncomfortable minute. "How dreadful for you, Rev. Ludington. Perhaps that's what this visit is really about. April Fools' Day on me. You might have simply asked. You would dare to suspect that Malcolm and I had something to do with such an atrocity? Well, I know nothing of it. And I am happy to confirm it." Nodding at the MacBook Air on the roll-top desk, she continued icily, "I have been working on my family genealogy with Ancestry.com. I've learned about DNA. Do you know about DNA? I'll be happy to give you my DNA profile, my DNA fingerprint' as they call it. Now I have a bridge game to attend." She rose, picked up the serving tray, and retreated to the kitchen.

Van der Berg jotted down her church email address and gave it to McCrae. Then she and Ludington left the apartment with no farewell and nary a word between the two of them. Ludington was so furious with van der Berg that he did not open the Volvo's door for her. She yanked at it mightily and almost toppled into a soon-to-bud azalea when it finally sprang open. All he said to her was, "Fasten your seat belt, Miss van der Berg."

They drove back into the City in silence. On the way up to White Plains, Ludington had noticed that the southbound Henry Hudson was down to one lane and backed up for miles, so he decided to take an alternative route home. They crossed into Manhattan on the old Willis Avenue Bridge. As they did so, Harriet glanced down to the Harlem River below, guessing that it was perhaps about to change its direction of flow, tidal estuary that it was. She softly laid a liver-spotted hand on Ludington's knee and said to the river, "I have lived a life of secrets, Dominie. You probably know that. They corrode the soul. I'm getting too old for corrosion." Even though his window was rolled down and the car was far from warm, beads of perspiration formed on Ludington's brow at the mention of secrets and soul corrosion.

# Chapter Twelve

*Tuesday, April 2—The Twenty-Fourth Day in Lent*

L udington had spent the early night sleepless and wrestling with his pillow and top sheet. He finally surrendered and got up, thinking to brew himself some herbal tea and read something. He stumbled down to the kitchen and brewed tea—the cherry-infused he liked and Fiona despised. He added some honey and sat at the little table to worry. There were any number of clouds on the horizon of the next three weeks, but the one that was keeping him awake this night was the dark cloud of prevarication. He had misled Dolores McCrae and would almost certainly be finding words that were markedly less than the whole truth tripping from his lips in the next days. Sleuthing when you were presenting yourself as a pastor and not a sleuth—as well as surreptitious DNA collecting—necessitated dissembling. Even the mundane routines of daily life, Ludington knew, inevitably demanded that you utter words that were hardly perfect truth and that you often refrain from speaking the truth when it was painful and needless. Wasn't there a movie about a guy who has some kind of curse that forced him to constantly speak the whole truth? It didn't end well. Was it Emily Dickinson who had said, "Truth is such a rare thing it is delightful to tell it." At least, he thought it was Dickinson.

His guilt was somewhat assuaged by the fact that something that might lead them to the truth had surfaced, if painfully, before they had left an obviously angry Dolores McCrae in White Plains. That memory led him to think again how curious it had been for her to volunteer her profile so willingly. Moreover, how many 85-year-olds even know they have a DNA profile? He took an Advil PM at 2:30 and slept for six hours. He didn't get to church until 9:45.

Van der Berg was already there of course, perched perfectly erect in her wheeled office chair staring at her computer screen, her French twist facing him as he entered, her hair as tidily in place as it had been since 1955. "Why change hairstyles when you find the one that suits you?" she had once asked him, incredulous that most women regularly do exactly that. Though it might be the same venerable French twist, Ludington had thought, it had changed color with the years, finally settling into a flattering steel gray. It suited her straight and longish nose and equally straight back and longish Dutch legs.

"Good morning, Miss van der Berg."

"Oh, Dominie, I didn't hear you come in." She said this as she swiveled her chair around to face him. "Dolores McCrae has sent along her DNA profile already. She must have emailed it right after we left. No note with it."

Ludington sat down facing her—their knees almost touching—in the only other chair in her cramped office. His anger with her had cooled to lukewarm. He had to admit that the woman's bluntness, inappropriate as it was, had gotten them somewhere.

"Dolores must be totally confident that there's no relationship," he said. "She's a savvy woman. Send it on to me, and I'll forward it to Harry for his lab guy."

"I shall do so immediately. Dominie, I must wonder if the child had a name. Did its parents, or at least its mother, give it a name? I dislike using the pronoun 'it.' Was the child a boy or a girl? I'm not aware of exactly when one names a child, having never had one myself. Children we've baptized at Old Stone always come to us with a name, most always two names, occasionally more. Parents always have the names chosen when they phone to schedule a baptism."

"A name would seem to make our bones a person," Ludington responded. "And dates—date of birth and date of death, the bookends of biography."

He looked at the floor, his straight black hair, which was rather too long for a Presbyterian minister, falling over his right eye as he did so. He raised his eyes to van der Berg flipping his hair back as was his habit.

"Fiona and I are finding it painful—not just painful, agonizing—knowing those bones are in our ash pit. It seems so unresolved, even unholy, to leave them there, but Harry says not to touch anything until we know the story or until we call in the authorities, God forbid. Not reporting is problem enough, but if we have to, we can deal with the delay. We can sort of fudge the date that I found them. You know, let them assume that I only just discovered them if and when we call the precinct. But messing with some sort of a crime scene—if that's what my ash pit is—Harry says that's pretty major. So, for now, our nameless little bones rest in their bed of ashes."

"But," van der Berg protested, "that won't be forever. They'll have to go somewhere eventually. Perhaps into our columbarium."

At that thought a smile broke Ludington's face; he hadn't smiled in several days. "'Columbarium.' Latin for a dovecote," he said.

He forced a second smile, this time at van der Berg, and retreated to his study, sat at his computer and emailed Dolores McCrae's DNA profile to Mulholland. He turned away from the screen to see that the message light was flashing on the land line phone on the corner of his desk. He picked up the handset and hit the code to retrieve messages. There was just one. Left at 7:10 that morning. "Reverend Ludington, it's me. Got a deadline for you. About our talk the other day. Easter Day. I have a place to stay till then. Call me and we can talk about what's the right amount. Oh, and I've got the police report. You know which one I mean. Mom kept copies." She left a call-back number, a 231 area code, West Michigan. Cara Lundberg was not dropping the matter.

He sat silently at his desk, his blossoming apprehension interrupted by the ring of his own cell phone. He pulled it from his jacket pocket and was relieved when he saw that it was Harry Mullholland. "Seth, it's me, Let's be careful with email. Leaves a trail that's too easy to track. Better we talk on the phone, or even better, in person. I got the DNA profile. I'll get it to my guy ASAP. Remember that this is going to take a few days, a week maybe. I can't press him too hard. I'm just a retired cop buddy asking a favor. But Seth, I have to tell you that I'm intrigued that Dolores McCrae was so willing to give you her DNA profile. I'm even more intrigued that she even had it and that she actually knew how to get it to you. Some old lady. Interesting. But the detective in me thinks you better start looking at the other people who lived in the manse in your '69-'70 time frame. I hate to say it, but I guess that means, you know...the Desmonds and maybe whoever lived there before the McCraes. Get your samples, Seth, and we'll get them tested. All I need is initials for each one, okay?"

After the call, Ludington turned back to his Mac and Googled "Philadelphia Theological Seminary." Up popped its home page, a color photo of the façade of one of the several Richardsonian Neo-Romanesque piles of sandstone that comprised its inner-city campus. He had been on the campus any number of times in his Philadelphia days, usually for some seminar or another. The faux-ancient architectural conceit of the campus had always struck him as jarringly inconsistent with the school's flagrantly progressive ethos. Of course, Neo-Romanesque had once been avant.

He hit the homepage's tab for "leadership," and several rows of color photographs of the institution's staff members appeared—professors, administrative types, custodians and the president himself. All the photos were of equal size and arranged alphabetically by last name. Philadelphia Theological was nothing if not aggressively egalitarian.

He found Desmond's photo in the middle row. "The Rev. Dr. Philip Davis Desmond, President." The photo looked to be more than a few years old. It showed a square-jawed and classically handsome man in late middle age offering the camera the merest hint of a smile. The photo was meant to betray raw gravitas. He brought the cursor to the name and clicked on his mouse to bring up Desmond's brief bio, an email address, and a phone number.

A call and visit to Desmond could well be as uncomfortable as those to Dolores McCrae. He had met Desmond on several occasions and liked the man. In fact, he more than liked him, he respected him and his work. And Philip Desmond was part of the reason Ludington had landed at Old Stone.

The thought of considering him a suspect in the matter of the bones in the ash pit turned Seth's stomach.

Philip Desmond was one of the princes of the denomination. He had preached civil rights and declared himself anti-Viet Nam War well before either stance was fashionable. Rumor had it that he had even burned his draft card. More recently he had facilitated "ecology and theology" forums at the seminary, hosting some of the more radical climate change prophets. The seminary had even divested its modest endowment of stocks from companies deemed to be facilitating Israel's "occupation" of the West Bank. If anything, Desmond was to the left of Ludington, who—admire the man as he did—sometimes thought him too unreflective in his instant advocacy of every liberal cause *du jour*.

Whether Desmond be on the side of the angels or no, the bald fact was that he had moved into the manse in June of 1970 and that the charred remains of a magazine dated July of 1970 and those of a newspaper from December that same year lay just above the Little One. It seemed likely that the bones went into the ash pit sometime prior to the end of 1970. It might have been even later, of course. One might hang onto an old copy of *Life* before using it as kindling, but old newspapers were less likely to hang around for months or years. Both dated bits of print journalism were right atop the bones, so it seemed virtually unassailable that the child died sometime in the late '60s or early '70s. Those years encompassed the tenure of the Rev. Dr. Phillip Desmond. Unhappy as this was for Ludington, it meant that another awkward phone call and an even more awkward visit lay before him.

Ludington steeled himself and dialed the number on the seminary's home page. His call was answered by a chipper electric voice that thanked him for calling and then offered a list of extensions. "For the office of the President, press zero one."

"Zero one," thought Ludington, "of course."

The extension was answered by a business-like male voice that intoned, "President Desmond's office." No "how may I help you?"

"This is Seth Ludington, the Rev. Seth Ludington. I'm the newish pastor of the Old Stone Presbyterian Church in Manhattan. It's the congregation President Desmond served for nearly twenty years. I'm going to be in Philadelphia tomorrow and was hoping he might spare me a few minutes. I'm trying to learn more of the church's history, to understand it better. I think President Desmond could be of help."

"Let me check. I'll put you on hold, if I may."

"Hold" at Philadelphia Theological offered not recorded hymns, but smooth jazz.

"Rev. Ludington. I am sorry, but the president is totally booked, booked all day tomorrow. Maybe next time you're in Philadelphia?"

"That might not be for a good while. I really only need a few minutes. Remind him that I'm a friend of Moze Washington."

More hold and more smooth jazz.

"Rev. Ludington, could you do 5:30? But it will have to be brief. He has a dinner engagement at 6:30."

Ludington hung up and mused that being busy—whether you were or not—was code for being important. Well, Phil Desmond was important, and he probably was truly busy as well.

Ludington next called Moses Washington. "Hey Moze, I'm going to be in the Sixth Borough tomorrow. Buy you a late lunch?" The answer was, "Seth, baby! Of course." Washington suggested a restaurant and a time.

The aroma of fresh coffee was drifting into his study from van der Berg's office. She invariably brewed a pot at 10:10 sharp. He wandered through the connecting door to retrieve a cup, sat down, and told her that he was going to Philadelphia in the morning and would see Phil Desmond late in the day.

"I won't have you along for the direct approach, but I do think I'll navigate the conversation to mention the manse and our renovation, the fireplace, and cleaning out the ash pit. I'll see how he reacts."

"I believe it's a waste of your time, Dominie. What a fine man and what a singular family they were. But if you must."

And I'll see if I can purloin some DNA off the fine man. Even seminary presidents must drink coffee and blow their noses."

73

# Chapter Thirteen

*Wednesday, April 3—The Twenty-Fifth Day in Lent*

L udington's cell rang at 9:00 as he was finishing up his morning coffee, solo at the kitchen table. He was about to take a quick dip into the *Times* before heading to the church.

He fished the phone from his jacket pocket, relieved to see that it was a 212 number he did not recognize. "Mr. Seth Ludington?" As soon as he answered, a woman's voice inquired, "This is the New York City Department of Buildings. I'm phoning to let you know that construction permit inspections for your building located at 338 East 84th Street are scheduled for Monday, April 22nd."

Ludington's calendar brain quickly computed that to be the day after Easter. Vinny (as he had told Seth to call him) D'Amato had clearly made the phone call he had promised and "greased the wheels" at the DOB.

At the time D'Amato had made the offer, Ludington had welcomed the prospect of prompt official inspections of his home, inspections he suspected would doubtless be even more thorough than D'Amato's. But now, with the bones laying exposed in his ash pit, he wanted delay. He either needed time, or he needed to move the bones.

"Can I reschedule for a later date?" "A later date" was a request that left the New York Department of Buildings incredulous. "Sorry, sir, it's already set up in the system. I suppose you could cancel and reapply. Maybe in the fall."

"No, it's okay, the 22nd. I'll be here. Any idea what time?"

"Set for 9:00. Plan on them being in your building most of the day, sir. Somehow you've got plumbing and electric and structural guys all coming at once."

"All thanks to a well-connected Vincenzo D'Amato," Ludington thought to himself. The deeper truth, which he was nearly ready to own, was that Ludington welcomed this imposed deadline, ill-timed as it was. This hunt could not haunt him and van der Berg forever. He knew it needed a terminus. This Lent was, it seemed, haunted by Easter deadlines.

He hung up and phoned Harry Mulholland. "Harry, any chance you can talk, I mean in person?" If he could not postpone, maybe he could somehow hide the bones from the prying eyes of New York Department of Building inspectors. If D'Amato had thought to look in the ash pit, so might they.

"Of course, be there ASAP."

Ludington emptied the coffee grounds from the French press, rinsed it and his coffee cup, and set off for Old Stone Church.

Harry stepped into Ludington's study at a quarter to ten, clad in one of his Harris tweed jackets and regimental ties. Ludington left his desk and sat across from his Clerk of Session, the two of them on either side of the coffee table at the far end of the study.

Mulholland began, "So, my guy at the lab has the bone fragment. He says he's backed up, and it'll take him a few days to do the DNA analysis. You understand it'll reveal gender, but not the child's age. That's complicated and imprecise, he says. He said he'd need a whole bone for that, not that we don't know we're dealing with an infant. He'll check it against the profile Dolores sent you. Her name is on it, so we can assume it really is hers. It's almost surely legit, and she was happy to give it to you, all of which probably means you're just getting started with your DNA collecting, Seth."

"Harry, what are the issues around DNA samples, samples that are, well... involuntarily obtained? I mean, that's what I'll have to do. It has to be done if we're going to ever get to the bottom of this, but I gotta tell you, it makes me uncomfortable."

"It's a legal and moral swamp right now, Seth. It's all moving so fast, nobody knows. Yes, there are privacy questions, but it happens all the time. Pregnant women and moms eager to know—or to prove—who the child's father is. Custody battles. Guys who want to prove they're not the baby's daddy. Adult children unsure of who their biological father is, or is not. It's not only paternity issues, but brothers, sisters, aunts, uncles, cousins, even grandparents. There are dozens of labs online. Send in the swab and a few hundred bucks, no 'how-did-you-get-the-sample' questions. But Seth, you don't need to do any of that. My lab guy will do it with no questions. Just get them to me with initials, to keep them straight, you know."

"Harry, here's why I called you. It looks like we're under pressure, I mean time pressure."

He told Mullholland about the impending descent upon the manse of a crew of DOB inspectors. "Harry, they're scheduled for Monday the 22nd, the day after Easter. They won't move it back. If I cancel, I have to reapply. And it could be months. Lots of months." He was not quite ready to admit to Mulholland that he found the deadline, not an altogether unhappy development.

"Like I told you, don't even think about moving the bones." Mulholland knew his pastor well and seemed to have anticipated his thoughts. "Delaying is risky enough. Tampering with what may be a crime scene is serious stuff. I mean, if it ends up we have to report this, we can always fudge the time you found them. But there's no easy way to cover it up if you move them. We just can't risk it."

Ludington considered the implication of the impending inspections of his home and Mulholland's insistence that the bones stay where they lay. He now had a deadline, and that deadline was Easter Day. He looked down at the Presbyterian Planning Calendar on his desk. Today was the Third of April. Easter was the Twenty-First. Today was the Twenty-Fifth Day of Lent, those 40 days prior to Easter, not counting Sundays. So—not counting Sundays—he had fifteen days. A parish minister has more than a few other things to attend to in the fifteen days leading up to Easter.

But he had to confess that part of him was thankful for the sudden imposition of a deadline, even one as consummately ill-timed as this one.

He ached to know, and he was loath to imagine this curious and edgy investigation dragging on, the bones waiting in the cellar of his house.

"One last thing, Seth. Be careful, really careful. Sure, there are some edgy issues with the DNA, but what I really worry about is this. You start poking around dead bodies, bodies dead under questionable circumstances, even ones 49 years dead, and you may cross somebody out there—somebody who's afraid the truth might surface after all these years."

After Harry left, Ludington called the public parking garage where he kept his car and asked for the Volvo to be brought up. The Spanglish-speaking attendant said, "one hora, amigo, busy, busy," which gave him more than enough time for the walk up to East 94th Street and stop by the manse on the way to fetch a book he wanted to give Moze, but had forgotten to bring along when he left the house earlier.

As he locked the manse door, Orsolya called out to him from across the street. It was just after ten. The Last Hungarian was still at her morning watch, a mug of black coffee in her hand, the lit cigarette in her mouth, wiggling up and down as she spoke to Ludington. "You go and come back and go again, *Tiszteletes*, and Mrs. *Tiszteletes* not home."

"The woman misses nothing," Ludington mumbled to himself as he crossed the street to say hello. "I forgot something, a book for a friend."

"You have time to drink coffee with an old lady, *Tiszteletes*? Coffee gets you gassed up for the day."

He did have time, and a cup of coffee with Orsolya Tabor was marginally more attractive than the prospect of sitting in the seedy waiting area at the garage.

"I'd love a cup. Milk, please."

"I'll get it. Plenty in the pot." She retreated up the steps to her apartment.

The coffee was halfway to espresso, but the hot milk she had added civilized it. "Good coffee, Orsolya."

They sat next to each other on the stoop, hands circling hot mugs on the crisp spring morning.

"*Tiszteletes*, you know I don't go to your church because I always go to the Hungarian church, the one down on 69th Street. Farther walk, but still in

Hungarian on Sunday. But most people, they don't live in Yorkville. They come from all over."

As a minister, Ludington had come to anticipate such apologies from people who don't go to his church or any church. It usually grated on him, though Orsolya's excuse was more credible than most he had heard.

"They took us in when we came from Hungary in '56. Helped us with money and finding a house, this house." Tossing her head back to the five-story walk-up behind them, she recited more personal history. "My parents, they bought it cheap then. We lived and worked on the first floor, rented out the top four floors to pay for it. My father was a tailor, excellent tailor. Worked and worked, mother too. I've lived here since 1956, most of my life. When I got married, we lived on the second floor. Low rent from Papa. Alphonse wasn't Hungarian—German—but that was okay with my parents because at least he wasn't Russian. That's what Daddy always said. 'At least he's not Russian.'" The woman smiled, but barely, at the memory of her father.

She looked like anything but the cliched round and rosy-cheeked Eastern European grandmother, thought Ludington as he took another sip of her deadly coffee. No widow's black for Orsolya Tabor. She was rail thin, done up in a pastel polyester pantsuit and a fake fur jacket, topped off with a head of rebellious bottle-blond curls.

"I was only eleven when we came to America. I barely remember Budapest, mostly the tanks." She spat artfully into the garbage bin to the right of the stoop. "This is my home now, 84th Street, Yorkville, New York. I've seen so much come and go over the years, right on this street."

Ludington glanced at his watch. Ten-thirty. The car would be ready, and the garage grew impatient if you did not pick up your vehicle promptly. He gulped down the last of the coffee, winced, thanked Orsolya, and headed north up Second Avenue.

On the road, he stopped to fill up the Volvo with gas at the Vince Lombardi Rest Area at the northern end of the New Jersey Turnpike. As he stood at the pump filling the tank, he phoned his wife, who was in Edinburgh. He mentioned his chat with Orsolya and the meeting with Harry, omitting mention of the man's final cautionary words. Her work led her through a landscape littered with the fearsome. He was reluctant to add yet another worry to Fiona's world, at least not yet.

# Chapter Fourteen

*Wednesday, April 3—The Twenty-Fifth Day in Lent*

**M**oze had suggested lunch at the Sabrina's on 34<sup>th</sup> Street just south of Powelton, an iteration of the local chain, this one lodged in a stone Victorian near the Drexel campus. It lay on the edge of the part of the city that New Philadelphia Ministries had long served, a rugged neighborhood locals called "Mantua."

Seth Ludington and Moses Washington had worked together for a decade, and it was not until the end of those years, during a long and well-lubricated brunch after church one Sunday, that Ludington had dared to remark on his colleague's name.

"How in the world did you come to be named after not one, but two national liberators?"

"My daddy had big plans for me from day one, Seth."

Ludington had gone home that day wondering whether his own father had ever had big plans for him. Seth had long accepted the tender truth that both he and his sister, the only two children of Brooks and Phoebe Ludington, were something akin to lifestyle accoutrements to their father. Brooks Ludington, financially secure in the extreme, lived his manicured life as a succession of experiences to be had and things to acquire, children among them. He loved his son and daughter in his way, but his way was skewed toward himself. Children, he admitted, could be enjoyable embellishments to a person, especially children as attractive as his. He was not at all miffed by the fact that his daughter in California had never exactly worked, though he griped when she called for another advance on her trust. After all, he had never exactly worked himself, save to keep an eye on the financial managers who invested what the family had always simply called "The Money."

Seth knew that his decision to enter the ministry had mystified his father. He had actually said as much when Seth told his father he had been accepted at Princeton Seminary. "Princeton," his father had said with a smile, "but seminary?" His son's decision to work for New Philadelphia Ministries was even more unfathomable. There was a corner of Seth Ludington that wondered and feared that his call to ministry, indeed his faith itself, was no more than a quest to find a father who had big plans for him.

That Moze Washington had lived into his own father's big plans was incontrovertible. He had only just retired from New Philadelphia Ministries after a lifetime of pushing and cajoling, challenging and organizing, preaching, scolding, and when needful, denouncing—an uphill slog to make Mantua and the working-class, mostly Black folks who called it home, a better place to live. His daddy would have been proud.

Washington rose from his table at Sabrina's to greet Ludington, not with a handshake but a bear hug, a clumsy gesture as the top of his head rose only to Seth's chest. Retired though he was, he was still decked out in his trademark cream linen suit and bowtie. Seth should have guessed, and felt underdressed in an open-collared shirt and blue blazer.

"Seth baby, you're a sight for this old man's sore eyes. So good to see you, man. How you doing up there in New York City? How are things going in your nice little white church? How's the lovely Fiona? You still fucked-up about your money?"

Most meetings with Moze began with a flood of "what-about-you?" questions, all designed to focus the conversation away from himself. A meeting with Moze always made you feel like the victim of a pop quiz.

Ludington answered his list of queries in serial order, mentioning the purchase of the manse as part of his answer to the "fucked-up about money" question. He told Washington about the scaffolding around Old Stone's steeple and how it dimmed the already gloomy sanctuary. As he spoke, it struck him that the scaffolding propping up the steeple and darkening the worship space was a metaphor for the state of the congregation. He told him about the pending renovation of their house, all as a preface to the ash pit story that he would soon broach.

But first, he attempted to turn the conversation to Washington with the predictable "How are you finding retirement?" question. He could have guessed Washington's answer. "Still doin' what I always did, just not gettin' paid for it."

They both ordered the pulled pork "sammy," as the menu named it, with mango-berry BBQ sauce, and cold sweet tea. Coffee and conversation would be dessert.

Ludington had already decided he would tell Washington about what he had found in the ash pit and his compulsion to discover the identity of the bones, how they came to be there, and who was responsible. But he decided to wiggle cautiously and sideways toward the edge of that cliff.

"I'm meeting with Phil Desmond this afternoon. He and his family are fondly remembered at Old Stone. People recall his years as a sort of Old Stone golden age. The '70s and '80s were not easy times for churches, but Old Stone somehow held its own through his tenure. There were actually a few more members when he left than there were when he came. I mean, folks were leaving the City in those years. And the boomers who should have been filling the pews were home in bed on Sundays studying the *Times* or the *Journal*. How do you think he did it, Moze?"

"Same old formula. Good preaching, good music, good programs for the kids, dodge fights over what color to paint the church kitchen, and at all cost, avoid scandal. Phil's a fine preacher; he's a genius at sugarcoating his liberal pills for a congregation eight feet to the right of him. He hired good musicians who were not major prima donnas. He found energetic young guys to run the youth group and moms with time on their hands to run the Sunday School. In his twenty years there, there were precious few donnybrooks. And I don't think there was ever a whiff of scandal. I know, boring—no praise bands or projection screens—but it was right for that church, and Phil did it well."

82

"You two were roommates in seminary, right Moze? You obviously kept up when he was in New York, and I know you've worked with Phil and his seminary here. What was he like back when...I mean, when you were a couple of young Turks at Princeton in the '60s?"

"We were out to save the world, both of us. He was probably more—well—out there than I was, more so than he is now."

Ludington braced himself with a slurp of caffeine as he crept to the edge of the cliff. "Moze, there's something I have to tell you. Almost nobody knows this, but you I trust."

Washington set his cup on the table, tilted his head down, and looked at Ludington over the top of his horn-rimmed glasses.

Ludington took a deep breath. "Moze, I found a body in the manse, the body of an infant, very small. It's the bones of a child that died about 49 years ago. Phil could have lived in the manse then. I'll spare you details, but my clerk of Session is a retired cop. I told him, and he's going to help me try to get to the bottom of it before we report it. He thinks the NYPD would bury it. And it could get leaked, and if that happened, it could be devastating. I don't know if we're dealing with a child who was stillborn or died early of something, or was, well, maybe killed. Anyway, I'm trying to see if I can figure it out, and seeing Phil Desmond today is part of trying to find out what happened. I've got to know, not just for me, but for the church, for the bones."

As Seth laid out the details of the discovery and his rogue investigation, Washington remained uncharacteristically quiet, not offering so much as a nod of his head. Then he threw his head back and exhaled through closed lips.

"Seth, I know you. I know your pathological curiosity. You always gotta know about everything, and then you always gotta fix it up. You can never let some old wrong just lay there. For some reason, you always ache to make up for it. There's something inside you, something eatin' away in you, that insists on it. But I like that about you, always have. Seems those two parts of you meet up, I mean the curiosity and the fix-it parts, meet up in this. But this is some shit you're wading into, Seth, smelly and dark. And probably damn dangerous. You gonna waltz into his office and confront Phil with the bones in your fireplace?"

"No, not yet. DNA first. To see if his might match the child's. I'll do this without telling him. Then if it matches, I guess I'll have to tell him. If no match, I spare him ever knowing anything."

"Lord Almighty, Seth. This is deep water, deep, deep water you wadin' into."

Washington's cell rang, perfectly timed to rescue him from wading deeper himself.

He took the call, nodding as if the caller could see him, and said, "Be there in ten."

"My old secretary at the Ministries telling me I'm late for a meeting with my successor. She's still covering my ass. I gotta go."

They parted without the bear hug, only a handshake.

Ludington had a couple hours to kill before his 5:30 appointment with Desmond. He walked toward the Drexel campus and found a coffee shop filled with students staring at their laptops. He was coffeed up, so he ordered a horchata and found an empty chair and a copy of the *Inquirer*.

He was finishing an overly thorough reading of the paper when his cell rang its "Old Phone" ringtone. Nobody in the coffee shop even looked up. The call was from Washington.

"Seth, I've been thinking, thinking till it hurts, about what you told me, and there's something I should tell you. I just hinted at it over lunch. Phil was one radical dude when he was in seminary. He was one of the hot-heads. Anti-war, anti-draft, anti-everything. Never missed a demonstration. I mean throwing blood on cops and burning draft cards. There was no SDS membership book, but he was on board. 'Students for a Democratic Society,' stormtroopers of the left back then. Got himself arrested a couple of times, God bless him. Went to Chicago for the Democratic Convention in the summer of '68, the one that blew up. Mayor Daley's cops totally out of control. He was there in the thick of it and proud of it. I was honored he was my friend, but I gotta tell you, he was one radical seminarian, a total wild ass. You weren't even born, so you have no idea. It was different in those days, different rules. Today you'd never get away with some of the stuff that went on back then."

"So, I've been told. Thanks for this, Moze. Anything else?"

"Oh, well, I don't know, but I gotta tell you this. Nowadays, Phil Desmond is good people."

# Chapter Fifteen

*Wednesday, April 3—The Twenty-Fifth Day in Lent*

Ludington still had an hour to kill; he was reluctant to surrender the parking spot he had snagged, so he decided to walk the fifteen blocks to the seminary, just north of the Drexel campus. As he entered the gated seminary campus, he passed through a set of sandstone pillars topped with a black wrought-iron arch bearing the seminary's name. Not exactly pearly gates. It struck him again that the institution's physical space was joltingly out of synch with its ethos. Romanesque, even when faux and a century old, reached back into the past, a dark one at that.

He found the seminary's administration offices on the first floor of a classroom building that he recalled from a seminar he had once attended. The door bearing a brass plaque reading "Office of the President" was open. He entered the office of the administrative assistant, a buffer space that insulated the president from immediate contact with the rest of the world. He was greeted by the young man he assumed he had cajoled into this appointment the day before. Doubtless a struggling seminarian working to pay the tuition that, in turn, helped pay his boss's salary.

"Afternoon, " the younger man said, somehow making the word sound grave. "The Rev. Ludington?"

"The same." Ludington was a quarter of an hour early and assumed he would have to wait.

"Please have a seat. The President is on a conference call just now. I'm sure he'll be free in a few minutes."

He offered coffee, but Ludington declined. "Maybe later." "Later" being when Desmond might join him, or so hoped, even though it would be late in the day for coffee.

A few minutes turned into twenty-five. Ludington was glancing at his watch when Philip Desmond came charging through the door from his office, looking harried and hurried. Ludington surmised that appearing to be in a rush might communicate several things—"I'm important," "This interview is going to be brief," and "You're lucky to have gotten it."

He strode over to Ludington, who rose to receive an enthusiastic handshake and then a pat on the back. "Seth Ludington. It's grand to see you here on campus. It was even grander to hear that you're up at Old Stone. How's it going?"

With this display of unrestrained *bonhomie* and a broad smile, and a hand still on Ludington's back, Desmond herded him into his office and shut the connecting door behind them.

"Have a seat, Seth. First names okay?"

Without waiting for an answer, Desmond rounded his immense mahogany desk and sat in a brown leather swivel chair, turning to face Ludington, who had perched himself in the straight ladder-back chair on the other side of the desk, a chair with a thinly-padded seat devised to keep meetings brief.

"Can I offer you coffee, or maybe a glass of wine? Richard will be glad to fetch either."

"Only if you're joining me."

"Too late for coffee. I'd be up all night. I've got a dinner with a couple of trustees at 6:30. They like their bourbon, and I'll have to keep up with them, so I'm going to pass."

Ludington was disappointed at this turn. No DNA on a wine glass or coffee cup for him to nick. He scanned Desmond's desk and the bookshelves behind him. Fastidiously tidy. Nary an old coffee mug in sight. When he had entered the office, he'd noticed a second door to his left. He hoped it led to the president's private bathroom. He could check it later.

"How can I help you, Seth?" This question was accompanied by a glance at his wristwatch, a glance that was almost surreptitious enough to be missed, then a curious facial twitch.

"Part of the reason I took the call to Old Stone was the fact that you had served it so long and well." Ludington guessed that a hint of flattery would lubricate conversation. "Must be a strong church if Phil Desmond was there for twenty years."

Desmond accepted the compliment with another smile. He was a youngish 75, his well-carved features having aged quite well. And he had kept the weight off, no small accomplishment for a man who surely suffered endless business lunches and dinners in the course of his work. His hair was still blond, tinged with some gray at the temples. Ludington could not but suspect that he had it touched up. The president was dressed in a perfectly tailored navy-blue flannel suit and a burgundy bow tie.

"It was a long time ago, Seth. I left Old Stone almost thirty years ago. I mean, I was a kid when I was there. Penny and I were both kids. But the memories are mostly fond. They indulged my inexperience with consummate grace."

"Well, I was here in Philly to catch up with Moze and thought to stop by and pick your brain. I'm trying to get a better handle on the place. History matters, as you know. So, how would you characterize your memories of the church?" He could not quite bring himself to address the man as "Phil," and "President Desmond" was too fawning, so he dodged both.

Desmond launched into a chain of Old Stone remembrances, warm but not self-congratulatory, memories of programs the church initiated in his tenure, staff who had come and gone, the gritty mess that was the City in those years, the daunting exodus of members to the suburbs, the three times he was mugged on his way home from meetings. Then he looked at his watch again, this time demonstrably.

The word "home" offered Ludington his chance to skew the conversation to the manse.

"My wife and I just bought the manse from the church. It's in pretty rugged condition. We're about to embark on a major renovation of the place."

"What a house that was," Desmond said. "Imagine a couple of twenty-five-year-olds living in that place. It was straight from dorm rooms to mansion."

Moze Washington had surely told Desmond that Ludington had "deep pockets," as they say in development offices. He had contributed generously to New Philadelphia Ministries, something he guessed Desmond would know. But purchasing a townhouse in Manhattan suggested that Ludington's pockets were even deeper. Seth suspected that this realization had shifted Desmond's interest in him. Every academic president knows how to smell money. Desmond leaned back in his chair, suddenly in less of a hurry.

"We had an inspector go through the house last week. It was worse than we thought," Ludington said with a laugh. The guy's parting words were about the fireplace, actually not the fireplace itself, but the ash pit under it. In the cellar. Told me to clean it out. Said he didn't think it had been emptied in ages."

Desmond appeared unfazed. "Ash pit?" he said with another twitch. "In the cellar? We used the living room fireplace some. Loved having a fire on a cold evening. Penny must have cleaned it out, I suppose. Later, when the girls came along, we got a cleaning lady, a string of cleaning ladies. Never heard about an ash pit in the cellar. Truth is, I'm not very handy."

With another staged laugh, Ludington said, "Well, I emptied it of 100 years of old fires. What a job. Full of ash, ashes, and some other stuff, interesting stuff."

"100 years of ashes? That's about the age of the house. Are you sure it hadn't been cleaned out more recently than that? I would have thought somebody would have looked after it in the thirty years since we moved out. How in the world do you know it was that long?"

"Well, I found some bits of a magazine and newspapers that hadn't burned. Dated from the early '70s."

"Interesting." Desmond was silent for a moment, then rapped out a staccato with his fingertips on the glass top of his desk, looked away, and then back at Ludington.

"So, you saw Moze. How's that craggy old disturber-of-the-peace doing?

Haven't seen him for months."

Ludington could only follow Desmond's change of subject. "He's indefatigable. Undiminished by mere retirement. We got onto old times, seminary times, late '60s, all that was coming down in those years, the war, civil rights, student unrest."

Desmond smiled. "Seems like a lifetime ago, no, actually another life altogether.

Seth, I know you went to Princeton, but Philadelphia Theological might be even more after your heart. You know that our commitment to urban ministry is deep. Some giving opportunities are coming up in connection with my retirement. Maybe I can give you a call? In fact, they're throwing a little retirement event next week, a dinner here on campus. Love to have you attend. "

A soft knock on the office door prevented Ludington from answering.

"Yes?" Desmond called out.

Richard poked his head through the door and said, some urgency in his voice, "It's 6:10, Mr. President. Your dinner engagement is at 6:30, and it's downtown. I thought perhaps you and the Rev. Ludington had lost track of the time."

Desmond stood and rounded the desk to shake Ludington's hand, promising a phone call to "talk about this remarkable institution and its future."

"I'll look forward to it. And maybe I can tell you more about our house renovation project. Thanks for your time today. Oh, and may I use your bathroom before I get in the car and head back?"

"Of course, of course. Right there." He pointed to the second door and left Ludington alone in his office.

Ludington waited to make certain Desmond was out of the building before making his way to the president's bathroom. As he did so, he passed a bookshelf under a dark oil portrait of a 19th-century gent in side whiskers, doubtless an early president of Philadelphia Theological Seminary. Seth thought to himself, "I wonder where he came down on slavery?" The only more recent image in the office was the photo on the corner of his desk that

Desmond had proudly shown him—a shot of himself and the woman who was doubtless his wife Penny, both smiling broadly while seated in a vintage sports car, a dark green MGA.

Lined up underneath the portrait and neatly arranged in order of publication were the books that Philip Desmond had authored in his long career. A few tilted toward the academic, but most were written to a popular church audience.

Ludington entered the bathroom, noting that it was equipped with a shower. "Seminary president must be a sweaty job." He said this to himself as he looked for a waste basket that might contain a tissue or two. Nothing in sight. He opened the door of the vanity underneath the sink and lifted out the small metal wastebasket, and peered inside. Empty. He turned it upside-down to make sure. Still nothing. As he went to put it back under the vanity, it slid from his hand and fell to the tile floor with an alarming racket.

He heard Desmond's admin call out, "Everything alright, Rev. Ludington?" He flushed the toilet to lend authenticity to his bathroom visit and called back, "Fine, just fine."

But it wasn't. He smiled at Richard as he left, a feigned smile, aware as he was that his second foray into sleuthing was a failure.

He walked the mile back to his car at a clip, thinking hard as he went. He turned his conversations with Washington and Desmond over in his mind. He knew one man well, the other barely. As he recalled that afternoon's phone call from Washington, he became increasingly convinced that Moze had more to tell than he had betrayed. Yes, Desmond had been radical, but he sensed Moze had more.

He unlocked the Volvo, started the car, and turned on the heater. The evening was growing chilly. He dialed Moze's cell. The man was a widower and addicted to PBS News Hour. He imagined his mentor and old friend parked in front of his television with scrambled eggs and the single piece of bacon he allowed himself every other day.

Washington picked up on the first ring. "Seth, you on your way home? How did it go with Phil?"

Ludington could hear Judy Woodruff's measured newscaster voice in the background.

"Nothing from Phil. But I have to press you, Moze. I mean, I know you well, I know you ten years side-by-side well, and I have a hunch that there's more you wanted to tell me when you called this afternoon, more than how far out there Phil was fifty years ago."

The silence that followed allowed him to hear every word Judy Woodruff was saying. She was cut off mid-sentence. Moze must have silenced the TV.

"Seth, I didn't want to say anything because I was worried it would give you the wrong idea, lead you where you really don't need to go. I was going to call you tomorrow with it. I've been thinking more about it, I mean, since you told me what you found in that ash pit of yours. It's been eating at me, and, well, I guess you need to know. Probably nothing, but there's this—when Phil came back to Princeton after the 1968 Democratic Convention, that would have been early September, he came back on the bus with a girl he'd met there. I was on campus that summer, doing summer Greek, living in our dorm rooms. The two of them came back late one night, high on anger and indignation, maybe high on more than that. They had obviously gotten close in Chicago. She spent the night. Went back to New Brunswick the next day. She was a student at Douglas. I know they saw each other some over the next year. She took the train down to Princeton once and again, at least. That was a little strange. I mean, Phil and Penny got engaged that year, our senior year at seminary. Penny was a senior at Cornell. They'd been an item all through undergraduate school."

"You recall the girl's name, Moze?"

"I actually do. Rachel Ruvenstein. With a 'v.'" Odd spelling, so it stuck in my mind. I got to know her a bit that year. She came down to Princeton for anti-war stuff a couple of times. I liked her. Nice kid. From the Upper West Side. My first Jewish friend. I was probably her first Black friend. I'm not sure if there was any electricity between her and Phil beyond hating the war. But maybe."

# Chapter Sixteen

*Saturday, August 31, 1968*

M oze Washington was a sound sleeper, but he heard the giggles and whispers. When the hall door to Desmond's adjoining dorm room in Alexander Hall slammed shut, he bolted up in his bed.

"What the hell? Who's there?"

"It's me, Moze. Phil."

More giggles and whispers.

"I can't believe I'm actually in a dorm room at a seminary, with a seminarian. My mom would have a kitten."

Moze sat up in his bed and reached for the blue jeans he had folded and laid on the floor before drifting to sleep while plowing through the last chapter of a laborious textbook about the development of the early Greek New Testament. The turgid volume was required reading for his summer semester language class. He pulled on the jeans, stretched, and went into the next room.

"Moses Washington, my man. A sight for these sore eyes." Phil threw an arm around Washington, turned toward the young woman with him, and said, "This is Rachel, Rachel Ruvenstein. We were in Chicago together."

"Good to meet you, Moze." The young woman extended a hand to Washington. "Phil told me all about you."

She was petite and more than pretty; she was beautiful, the kind of beautiful you steal stares at. Younger than he and Desmond, still in college, Washington guessed. She had a mass of auburn hair, wildly curly, and pulled back in a vain attempt at a ponytail. Phil Desmond towered over her. His hair had grown even longer than it was when Washington had last seen his roommate back in June. Dishwater blond, it now fell over his shoulders, held out of his eyes by a beaded headband. He was in a black leather motorcycle jacket and tight bell-bottomed blue jeans littered with patches.

"Moze, we are, like, totally bushed. Been on a bus, actually two buses, for the last twenty-four hours. Hope it's OK if Rachel crashes here? No way to get back to New Brunswick at this hour."

"Sure, 'course."

Desmond and Ruvenstein set their duffle bags in a corner and sat on the double bed in Desmond's room. Washington lowered himself into the coffee-stained easy chair opposite the bed.

"So, what was Chicago like? I gotta hear it all. Can't believe what's been on the news."

Both Desmond and Ruvenstein started to answer. They looked at each other and laughed. Desmond threw his head back, gestured to the girl, and said, "Go ahead. You tell him, Rachel."

"It was a pig riot, man. The cops were, like, totally out of control. We were there, right in Grant Park, on Thursday night. It was a war zone. Then we were in the crowd at the Conrad Hilton when the cops were bashing heads in front of the TV cameras. We were all chanting, "The whole world is watching." The news said there were 10,000 demonstrators. It was something." The girl's zeal lit her young face. Her rage made her even more beautiful.

Desmond picked up the story. "The Yippies nominated a pig for president. Named him 'Pegasus.' Dailey's cops arrested Jerry Rubin and Phil Ochs, and Pegasus, too."

Desmond chortled at the notion of a pig under arrest and said, "Would have been better than Humphrey. The guy's nothing but Johnson's lackey, his assistant war-monger. The people wanted McCarthy, but the war machine, they would never let that happen."

Washington looked at the two of them, side-by-side, exhausted but animated, and said, "The news has been all over it. I've been glued to the TV when I wasn't glued to Greek verbs. They said the cops even roughed up Dan Rather. Cronkite called the cops 'a bunch of thugs.' I mean Walter Cronkite, Mr. Careful Journalist."

They talked for another hour, unpacking the fresh memories of Chicago, the SDS and the Yippies, the songs they sang and friends they met, a cake of tales frosted with rich and righteous indignation. Rachel told Moze that she was from the Upper West Side of Manhattan and was about to start her senior year at Rutgers.

"My parents wanted me to go to Brandeis. I got in, but I wanted someplace more, you know, diverse."

Exhaustion finally trumped outrage. Moze said, "Well, you guys, I've got church in the morning, my fieldwork church in Trenton. I gotta hit the hay."

He retreated to his room, asking no questions about sleeping arrangements in the other. As he turned to shut the door, he saw Ruvenstein lay her hand on Desmond's tight denim butt and give it a squeeze.

# Chapter Seventeen

*Thursday, April 4—The Twenty-Sixth Day in Lent*

Ludington had phoned van der Berg when he got back to New York late Wednesday evening. He knew that unlike most people her age, she was something of a night owl and would still be up at ten, probably watching whatever happened to be on PBS. He asked her to meet him for breakfast at Gracie's Corner Diner, an invitation she accepted with alacrity. She was doubtless eager to hear what he had accomplished on his trip to Philadelphia. She even asked before she ended the call, but he told her it could wait till the morning. He felt he had little to report, save stealing a peak into Desmond's youthful adventures. But that was all before he came to Old Stone.

The next morning as he walked out his door and went down the street to the restaurant at the corner of Second, Ludington saw the lace curtains in Orsolya's front window twitch. The woman had not yet assumed her front stoop post as it was only 8:30, but that didn't mean she wasn't keeping an eye on 84th Street.

Van der Berg had arrived at the restaurant before him and gotten them a window table. She had already ordered tea for herself and a cappuccino for him.

"You know me, Miss van der Berg. Perhaps too well."

"Miss Gibbs instructed us to be mindful of the needs and habits of those whom we serve."

"Well, thank you. So, do you know what I want for breakfast?"

"I'll let you choose, Dominie. I shall have oatmeal with berries and honey. They make their own oatmeal here, none of that hateful stuff in a pouch."

Ludington briefly scanned the encyclopedic menu typical of New York diners, though he already knew what he wanted. He had not eaten since his lunch with Moze and was famished.

To the harried waitress, he said, "I'd like the corned beef hash, please, extra-crispy, with an egg over medium. White toast."

Though Ludington could see she was bursting with curiosity, van der Berg let them get through their breakfasts before carefully setting down her spoon and saying, "Well? I know it's a blind alley, but I do want to hear about your visit with the Rev. Dr. Desmond. You passed on my greetings, I hope."

He had entirely forgotten to do so, so he smiled and said, "No DNA. I mean, he's doubtless got DNA, but I didn't get any. No coffee cups, no wine glasses, and either he never blows his nose, or the waste basket gets emptied daily. No Desmond DNA, but some interesting Desmond history."

He first told her about the young Desmond's political radicalism, re-capping much of his first phone conversation with Moze Washington. As he recounted Chicago and Viet Nam, he assumed that van der Berg remembered the brooding anger and eruptive zeal of the '60s and '70s. She would have been a young woman in her '20s, though he could hardly imagine her screaming political vitriol at a Greenwich Village protest.

"It was a tumultuous time, Dominie. My generation was often undisci-plined in their advocacy, but we were generally in the right, about the war and racism, to be sure. Phil Desmond was a man who was—I mean is—most passionate in his convictions, God bless him. But this has nothing to do with our investigatory work, surely."

Then he recounted his second phone conversation with Moze Washington, the one about Rachel Ruvenstein.

"Well," van der Berg sniffed, "he may have stepped out with other young ladies before marrying Penelope."

Ludington smiled at that antique circumlocution. "Stepping out" was a deliciously ironic term for getting tear-gassed together in Grant Park.

Van der Berg continued, "He and Penelope were not married at Old Stone, you know. Their wedding took place on Martha's Vineyard. Her parents had a summer place on the island. I understand the wedding was quite the social event—outdoors on their property overlooking the sea. How gracious it must have been. Penny, I mean Penelope, showed Margaret and me the wedding photos once. Eight bridesmaids. Can you imagine? It looked to have been a perfect late summer's day, the Saturday of Labor Day weekend, I believe it was."

Ludington set down his coffee cup. "But Phil started work at Old Stone in June. And Penny must have graduated college that spring. One would have thought they'd have had a June wedding."

"Not so," van der Berg said, "Penelope told us her father had promised her a grand tour when she graduated college. She showed us the slides." For Ludington's benefit, she explained, "Those little transparencies projected on a screen. Such a trip it must have been—London, Paris, Vienna, and Rome, of course. The wedding was planned for a few weeks after she and her traveling companions returned. Nowadays, an engaged couple might see Europe together before the wedding, but not then, not in Penelope Worthington's family."

Ludington downed the last foamy remnant of his cappuccino and said, "Very interesting. So, Phil was alone here in the City all summer. Would you do this, Miss van der Berg? As confident as you and I may be of Phil Desmond's probity, I would like to see if we might find Rachel Ruvenstein-with-a-'v' and perhaps even arrange a visit. The 'v' should make her a bit easier to find. She was a New Yorker back then and may still be here."

"For what it may be worth, I shall search her out, Dominie."

"Thank you, Miss van der Berg."

"Another thought. I think we need to expand the time parameters we're assuming for the child's death. Here's what I mean. Think this through with me... the bones went into the ash pit sometime before that July 1970 *Life* magazine and that December 1970 *New York Times* did. We know that. But it could have been long before if we assume nobody had swept any ashes into the pit for a while. And if somebody held on to the magazine and the newspaper for a long time, the bones could have gone into the ash pit months, even years, later, which would have been when the Desmonds were living there. They were in the house for almost twenty years. Remember, there was a lot of ash and bits of stuff on top of those two dated periodicals, so it does seem somebody used the fireplace and the ash pit with some regularity in the years following. That other stuff, I mean the aspirin bottle and the tobacco tin, I did some checking online, and they're pretty old, earlier than 1989 when the Desmonds moved out.

"I have to remind you yet again of my confidence in the consummate decency of Philip and Penelope Desmond. I trust you are suggesting that we move to focus on those who may have had access to the fireplace prior to the McCraes. I must say that their culpability appears unlikely, given Dolores's readiness to share her DNA profile with us. Thus, I am also inclined to look earlier."

"Quite right, Miss van der Berg, precisely." That last word he said with a wink. "So, remind me again who it was who gifted the house to the church before the McCraes took residence in June of 1969? Harry told me it was given to the church by a member. And when was that exactly, Miss van der Berg? How long before? It could have been months, maybe even years, before the magazine and the newspaper if fires were few or the ash pit unused. So, who lived there before the McCraes?"

"I only know the house was given to the church about the time Margaret and I began attending. We were not as of yet formal members and thus could not vote at a congregational meeting. We would not have attended, of course. I don't recall—perhaps I never knew—who the benefactor was or precisely when the church acquired the house to utilize as a manse."

"Well, Miss van der Berg, that we can easily ferret out. As you perhaps know, any transfer of real property to or from a Presbyterian church must be approved by vote of the full congregation. There will be minutes of the meeting. It's back to the Old Stone dungeon and those musty Session records books that you have so efficiently tidied up and organized."

Van der Berg took a sip of her now cold tea and said, "Precisely."

Ludington paid the bill, and they left Gracie's, walking on the south side of 84th. They passed Orsolya Tabor on her stoop on the north side, avoiding an encounter as she was blessedly engaged in an animated conversation with a dog walker she had captured.

When they got to Old Stone, they went straight to the basement room with its repository of old church junk and record books. Ludington found the box with the books they had scanned before and located the same book that had led them to the McCraes, the one labeled "1966-1971." They decided to bring it up to van der Berg's office, where the light was better.

Sitting next to each other at the desk in her small office, they paged through the minutes of meetings of both the Session and the congregation, arranged chronologically. They began with minutes from meetings held in 1967, the year before Harriet and Margaret had begun attending the church. Ludington said they could skip Session meeting minutes as it would require a meeting of the entire congregation itself to approve the receiving of a gift that included real estate. They easily located the minutes of the several Annual Meetings of the Congregation, as they were invariably held in the month of February. Those of 1967, 1968, and 1969 made no mention of a vote to receive property.

Ludington said, "The vote must have been taken at a specially called meeting, not a regular Annual Meeting. That would make sense. When you're offered the gift of a valuable piece of property, you'd surely want to act promptly to accept it."

Working laboriously past page after page of the minutes of Session meetings, they, at last, came upon a single page of minutes headed, "Called Meeting of the Congregation of the Old Stone Presbyterian Church, Sunday, May 18, 1969."

"Here we are, Miss van der Berg." He pointed to the typewritten minutes. The Clerk had noted that prayer was offered by a Moderator appointed by the Presbytery, that a quorum was present, and that there was but one action item—"to approve the receipt of a gift of real property located at 338 East 84th Street, New York City."

They worked down the single page of minutes to the paragraph that offered the information they sought:

> *"The house at said address so bequeathed shall be held in trust as a manse or parsonage for the minister of the Old Stone Presbyterian Church in the City of New York as long as said congregation shall be incorporated under New York Religious Corporations Law and continue to employ the services of a minister.  In the event of less favorable financial circumstances and if the church is no longer able to employ a minister, the Session, functioning as Trustees, with the approval of the congregation and the Presbytery, may sell the property; the proceeds of such sale, after expenses, shall be held by the Session, functioning as Trustees, in an endowment to be named 'The Cunningham Fund,' the income of which may be disbursed in accordance with law for the support of the Old Stone Church. In the event that the Old Stone Church ceases to exist under New York Religious Corporations Law, the Cunningham Fund shall be transferred in its entirety to the Presbytery of New York City, and the income be used, in accordance with law, to support the mission of said judicatory."*

The next sentence in the minutes recorded the unanimous vote of approval and the profuse appreciation of the congregation for the generous gift from the late Oscar Cunningham, Sr.

Ludington had read all this aloud. Van der Berg, after hearing that the Cunningham named was one *Oscar* Cunningham, leaned back in her chair and whispered, "Oh my God. I knew Oscar Cunningham. I mean, I knew of him from Wall Street. So, it was he who gave your manse to the church. I never would have guessed. His secretary and I were friendly. Believe it or not, I actually attended his funeral with her, right here at Old Stone. I accompanied Sally, his secretary, that is. She was anxious about going to the service alone. And Dominie, his wife—whatever her name is—is still a member of the church. Never attends, but she's on the membership roll."

"I never thought I'd hear you take the Lord's name in vain, Miss van der Berg."

# Chapter Eighteen

*Monday, December 9, 1968*

H arriet van der Berg and Sally Wilcox ate lunch together once a week, usually on Mondays. The two women had met when Sally had worked as a receptionist for the Wall Street law firm that employed Harriet as secretary to one of its senior partners. A few years later, when Sally landed a secretarial position at the competing firm of Jansen, Smith, and Cunningham, they had agreed—without so much as discussing it—to maintain their office friendship. They enjoyed each other's company, but they especially enjoyed gossiping about the goings on in their respective firms.

They most always ate at the Horn and Hardart on 14th Street. The prices were right for secretaries, the coffee was excellent, and they found eating at one of the City's handful of remaining automats to be a retro pleasure. Harriet stuffed nickels in a slot, the little glass door opened, and she fished out her regular chicken salad sandwich. She watched as Sally did the same for her generous bowl of the chain's famous mac and cheese. They sat at their accustomed back table; coffee would come later, as would the latest episodes of tales from their respective law firms.

"I really don't think the Arthur Anderson case is going well at all." Harriet had just finished the last of her sandwich and was thinking about coffee. "Lots of late meetings, too many phone calls, and Mr. Crenshaw is unusually cranky. He tends to get short when the case gets long. He's normally such a pleasant man to work for."

"Well, Oscar Cunningham is a bear to be around these days. He's short all the time, short with everyone. I mean, he's short—short-as-in-rude though he's also short-as-in-stature." She offered this comment about Oscar Cunningham with a smirk to congratulate herself on her wordplay. "I told you how handsy he always was, the office flirt, especially with me." Sally had shared this tale with Harriet before.

"Sally, you must let the man know precisely how you feel about those touchy hands and sexual innuendos of his. A girl has to let them know what you will and won't stand for."

"Well, I thought of talking to old Mr. Jansen, the senior-senior partner. But you have to worry about repercussions. Girls get let go when they talk. I need the job, Harriet." Sally was looking a bit green as she pushed her bowl of beloved mac and cheese away. She had barely touched it. "Anyway, it may be moot now, though. Little Mr. Oscar has pivoted to the new receptionist at the front desk."

Harriet had always guessed that Sally's reports of her boss's overtures were perhaps both hopeful and exaggerated. She was not an especially attractive young woman, pug-nosed, moon-faced, and already rounding to pear-shaped, though her head of flame-red hair was fetching, even in Harriet's staid judgment. But you never know with philanderers, Harriet thought. And you never know with young women vulnerable to the attentions and manipulations of powerful men.

"Oh, I keep a very close eye on old Oscar and little Miss Receptionist. All of the sudden, he couldn't keep either eyes or hands off her. She started last month, and he was all over her in a week, I mean *all* over her."

There was an edge to Sally's voice, a brittle rise in pitch that suggested not only moral indignation, but a deeper and more personal anger.

"Sweet young pretty, eighteen if a day, none too bright and way too skinny. I think she's dumb enough to imagine that his attentions might further her career. And him a married man well into his thirties, closing in on forty maybe, and such a big church-goer."

"How do you know he's a church-goer, Sally?"

"I cut the monthly checks to the Old Stone Church uptown. Not very large checks, mind you."

"Old Stone? Why, Margaret and I have been attending there for a while now, and I must say that I've never seen him nor heard of him."

"Well, that doesn't surprise me. But here's the thing. His little receptionist just dropped off the face of the earth last week. Never came back to work after the weekend. Not a word from her, not that I heard about anyway. And Mr. "Old-Stone-Church" Cunningham hasn't said a thing himself. But he's been behaving oddly, not at all his old flirtatious, hands-all-over-the-place self. Like I said, dour and sour." Sally pronounced the two words as if they rhymed.

# Chapter Nineteen

*Friday, April 5—The Twenty-Seventh Day in Lent*

The sermon was done by four o'clock. It was not based on the Bible text assigned by the lectionary for the Sunday coming. The lectionary Gospel passage officially assigned for the next Sunday, the Fifth in Lent, was the raising of Lazarus, a story which always seemed to Ludington like Easter come too early, and a rather unsatisfactory Easter at that. After all, Lazarus would live to die again. The story was surely a foreshadowing of the great day, but on that Friday, it felt to him that preaching it two weeks before Easter would be opening the present too soon and finding it a bit disappointing.

So, he wrote a sermon about wolves in sheep's clothing based on Jesus's warning at the end of the Sermon on the Mount concerning *"false prophets, who come to you in sheep's clothing but inwardly are ravenous wolves. You will know them by their fruits."* He knew that some listeners would imagine it to be aimed at the nation's current leaders, perhaps the President, though he named no names. But as Ludington wrote the sermon, it was actually a generous former member and two past ministers of the Old Stone Church who rose to the surface of his preacher's imagination.

Harriet van der Berg knocked on the door separating his study from her office at four o'clock. When she came in on Fridays, Ludington had asked her to do her best to guard him from all but the most desperate phone calls and distressed visitors until late afternoon when his sermon would hopefully be completed. Van der Berg had decided that "late afternoon" commenced precisely at four.

Standing in the door, she said, "Dominie, I have several relevant pieces of intelligence and one intriguing development regarding our investigatory endeavors. The first concerns Oscar Cunningham. I have also obtained contact information for one Rachel Ruvenstein, as you requested. The only such person I could find, and she lives here in the City. And thirdly, I received a most interesting parcel in the mail today."

She entered his study and perched herself unbidden in the chair opposite his desk. "First, regarding the Cunninghams. His widow is indeed listed as a member of Old Stone. Her name is Mildred, aged 87. Her son, and I presume Oscar's as well, is also still on the roll. He's now 63. That means he would have been a boy of fourteen or so when his father died. I have not laid eyes on either of them in my half-century at Old Stone, not even on Christmas and Easter. I mean, not since Oscar's funeral. It's amazing that they're still maintained as church members. Every member we keep on the roll costs us that noxious per capita tax we have to pay to the denomination. Here are their respective addresses and the contact information we have."

She handed Ludington a piece of Old Stone stationary on which she had printed out the two names and their respective phone numbers, email addresses, and in the case of Mildred, a Second Avenue street address.

She said, "I know that building, the one in which Mildred lives. It's an unfortunate mid-rise comprised of one and two-bedroom rentals, mostly rent-controlled, I would guess. Nothing like the home she lived in before Oscar died, the present manse, I mean."

"The second discovery I have made concerns the date of Oscar's funeral. You and I discovered yesterday that the church received the gift of the manse at a congregational meeting in May of 1969. I reviewed our records of funeral and memorial services and discovered that Oscar Cunningham's funeral was conducted here at Old Stone on February 14th, 1969. And it was a funeral, not a memorial service. Meaning Oscar Cunningham's body was present. Mere memorial services sans corpse had not yet become fashionable. I was there, as you know; it was a closed casket. This means, of course, that Oscar Cunningham surely died in early February. You can't wait too long, you know. But then I recalled that the funeral had to be postponed. Lindsay's Blizzard had cancelled everything. I checked the dates online. The storm—a Nor'easter—occurred over three days, February 8 to 10. The City was paralyzed for ages. Everyone blamed Mayor Lindsay. What was he to do? Shovel snow himself? One recalls such weather phenomena."

Van der Berg was clearly pleased with herself, both her research and her memory. She was leaning forward as she spoke, tapping the glass top on Ludington's desk as if marking each factoid with a bullet point.

"A funeral on Valentine's Day," Ludington said. "I suppose it could have been romantic, or maybe ironic, or maybe accidental." He raised his eyebrows at the thought of all three possibilities.

"The service was conducted by a visiting minister from the Brick Church up on Park Avenue. I don't recall his name. But I know we were without a minister in that period. Sunday services were conducted by a parade of visiting clergy. 'Pulpit supply,' they were called. Odd job title, to be sure. Malcolm McCrae did not arrive till that June, of course."

"How old would Oscar have been when he died? He must have been pretty young."

"I checked his entry in the church roll. He was born in January of 1930, so he would have been thirty-nine."

"Very young indeed. But Miss van der Berg, here is what's oddest about all this. He left the house where his wife and young child lived to a church he rarely, if ever, attended. And they had to move out of a big old brownstone on a nice cross street into a cramped rent-controlled apartment on Second Avenue. A generous gift to his church, but one given at the expense of his wife and son. Our records would not list the cause of his death, of course, but maybe we could find out. Something is off about the whole tale."

"Well, he was a prominent Wall Street lawyer, even at thirty-nine. The *Times* surely published an obituary. And *Times* obituaries usually note the cause of death in the case of younger people. But Dominie, I have one more discovery, one quickened by a personal memory."

Van der Berg leaned even further forward, getting her face as close to Ludington's across the desk as she could, and began to whisper conspiratorially.

"When we came across his name in the minutes of that congregational meeting we found yesterday, I said that I knew of Oscar Cunningham, but not from church. I knew of him because a friend once worked as his secretary at his law firm downtown. Her name is Sally Wilcox. We used to work together, but she left our firm when she went to work for Mr. Cunningham. We kept up with each other, ate lunch together for years. I confess that we freely discussed our employers. When I went home last evening, I seemed to recall some gossip—I mean personal observations—that Sally shared with me years and years ago. It must have been over one of our lunches sometime before Oscar Cunningham died."

"You should not be embarrassed by a bit of gossip, Miss van der Berg. You perhaps know that gossip—I mean the sharing of insightful observations about others and their actions—can function as a social control mechanism to restrain aberrant behavior."

Van der Berg lowered her head and looked at him over her glasses. "You sound like one of those sociologists, Dominie. At any rate, Sally and I still exchange Christmas cards. And we phone each other once and again. I telephoned her last evening. She lives in an unfortunate building, a walk-up in the alphabet neighborhood. I asked her what she recalled about Cunningham, especially just before his death. She reminded me that she lost her job some weeks before he died and had to find a new position. She confirmed what I recalled when I heard you read the name yesterday. Oscar Cunningham, she said, was quite the ladies' man, "a rampant philanderer" were her precise words. She told me about a silly young receptionist that he was chasing around the office. And Dominie, that young girl attended the funeral, or at least the reception following. I recall her having words with Mildred Cunningham. There is doubtless a line of inquiry here. Van der Berg tapped the top of Ludington's desk again, this time even more emphatically.

"Did your friend recall the girl's name?"

"No, she did not. It's so very long ago. And the firm closed, you know, so I can't imagine there are any employment records available."

"Not to worry, Miss van der Berg. If the child were Oscar's, we can probably ferret it out. Oscar may be dead and buried, but his son is still with us, as is his DNA. I have a couple of phone calls to make before the day is out."

Not at all ready to retreat, van der Berg said, "As I mentioned, I also received a package of interest in the mail."

As if hiding a surprise gift, the best for last, she took from her lap a manila envelope that had already been opened, reached inside, and withdrew a baggie containing a black plastic comb. "This was sent to us by Dolores McCrae, along with a terse note. She handed both the baggie and the note to Ludington.

He read the latter aloud. *"Since you have come to suspect me and my late husband of some involvement in the tragedy you came upon in the Old Stone manse, I send you this. It is a comb that belonged to my late husband. It surely contains samples of his DNA, the analysis of which will exculpate him, just as you will find that my profile will me. I continue to resent the implications of your visit, and wish to put this matter in the past where it belongs. Dolores McCrae."*

Ludington returned both the note and the bagged comb to the envelope, placed it on his desk, and said, "Well, that's that, I guess. I mean with the McCraes."

Van der Berg harrumphed, rose to leave, and said, "Oh, and here's a phone number for that Rachel Ruvenstein person. It was not difficult to find. She works as a realtor here in Manhattan." Van der Berg reluctantly placed a note with the name and phone number of her real estate office on the corner of Ludington's desk.

Before he picked up the phone, he turned to his computer. A quick Google search for "Oscar Cunningham obituary" brought up his quarry—two identical and longish obits, both without a photograph, in the February 9, 1969 issues of both the *New York Times* and the *Wall Street Journal*. It began, "Oscar H. Cunningham, Sr., New York attorney and partner in the firm of Jansen, Smith, and Cunningham, beloved husband of Mildred and father of Oscar Cunningham, Jr." A few lines down, the obituary noted that he was "survived by his parents" and then added the short list of schools he had attended and a prior law firm he had worked for as well as his legal specialty—"corporate mergers." Then, as van der Berg had predicted, the obituary disclosed the cause of his death. *"Cunningham died from injuries sustained in a one car automobile accident in Nassau County, New York on February 7th."*

"One car," Ludington muttered to himself. "Interesting detail in an obituary."

He picked up the phone and dialed Harry Mulholland's home number. If he knew his clerk, Harry would be about to settle down with his Diet Coke and the ABC local news. He picked up on the second ring.

"Harry, it's Seth. Two things. First, I've got some more DNA for you. Dolores McCrae sent a comb that belonged to her husband. I'll give it to you in church on Sunday. Second is this. Harriet and I did some digging and discovered that the manse was given to the church—as a bequest—by a member named Oscar Cunningham. You maybe remember all this. A little more digging and we found out that Cunningham died in a one-car accident. It was out in Nassau. So, can you give the Nassau County cops a call and see if you can get a copy of the police report? The accident was on February 7th."

"Don't recall who gave the house. But the accident. That was the week of Lindsay's Blizzard, right? Every old New Yorker remembers that one. Long Island got hit hard. Could have been a slip and slide, but one car accident begs the suicide question."

Ludington said, "The blizzard didn't hit till the next day. We checked. The roads were still fine."

"I'm impressed. It's pre-computer, and they may not have anything, but I'll make the call and get back to you ASAP." Again, Mulholland pronounced the abbreviation as if it were a word. "Oh, and we're not going down to Vero this week. Too much going on up here. Be in town through Easter."

Ludington thanked him and added, "See you Sunday, Harry. Don't forget to remind me to give you Malcolm McCrae's comb."

Ludington hung up and picked up the note van der Berg had given him with the contact information for the Cunninghams, mother and son.

He called her number from his office phone. The call was picked up on the second ring. Silence for a second, then a raspy cough and a gravelly smoker's voice, a woman's baritone, barked loudly, "Who *is* this."

Ludington began in his most pastoral tone, too easily rattling off another of his white lies, telling her that he was the new minister of her church and that he was working to introduce himself to all his parishioners. "Mrs. Cunningham, I was hoping I might stop by, just a quick call, just to say hello."

"I don't go to church anymore. Gave it up years ago." She offered up another phlegmy cough so loud that Ludington pulled the receiver from his ear.

"That's quite alright, Mrs. Cunningham, no pressure. A quick visit."

"Well, suit yourself. What did you say your name was?"

Ludington named himself again and then pressed his case. They agreed to 10:30 the next morning. Mildred Cunningham sounded like a miserable woman, but Ludington guessed she was probably a lonely one as well.

He next used his cell to call the number for the Rachel Ruvenstein van der Berg had found, the only one in New York. Obviously, the getting-to-know-my-congregation ploy would not work this time. She picked up on the first ring and offered her name rather than that of her firm. Direct line, Ludington thought.

He introduced himself as Seth Ludington, no "Reverend" in front.

"Ms. Ruvenstein, my wife and I are considering selling our home. It's a brownstone on East 84th. I'd love to have you take a look at it, give us a sense of what it might sell for. If the number is right, we'd hope to list it with you. Your name was suggested by a co-worker of mine." At least half of what he had said was true.

She was as enthusiastic as any realtor might be at such a prospect, but qualified her interest by noting that she was semi-retired and that she and her husband were flying to St. Bart's the next morning for ten days.

"We get back on the 14th. I could stop by the house on the 15th, that's a Monday. I apologize for the delay. I could send somebody else from the office to do the appraisal if you'd prefer."

"It's no problem. The 15^th works fine. Morning okay with you, say 10 o'clock?"

"Ten it is. I look forward to meeting you, Mr. Ludington."

He gave her his cell phone number and the address of the house, then winced at his new ease with prevarication. The delay in meeting her was lamentable. The 15^th was the Monday of Holy Week, a week before the arrival of a pack of building inspectors and the de facto deadline for his investigations. And DNA analysis took a few days.

When he passed through van der Berg's little office on his way out, he saw that she was still there, squinting at her computer monitor. "It's nearly five, Miss van der Berg. You are part-time, you know. And very poorly paid."

"As you know, Dominie, I am entirely unpaid and happy with it. That way I don't have to answer to your every fancy." She offered him one of her occasional smiles, not a grimace, but a smile that lit her barely lined and usually austere countenance.

Ludington tilted his head in her direction. "And a good evening to you, too."

# Chapter Twenty

*Friday, April 5—The Twenty-Seventh Day in Lent*

Fiona had returned from Edinburgh on the red eye that morning. She'd landed at JFK and made it to her office before noon. She had called Seth from the cab, and they made a seven-o'clock date for a glass of wine at home and then dinner at the Lex Restaurant a half block north of 90th, a bit of a walk, but another of their favorite spots in the neighborhood. Assuming there was not a big program at the 92nd Street YMHA up the block that evening, the place would be quiet. Even if there was a pre-program Y crowd, they'd be gone by eight. Seth called the restaurant and asked Nero for their back table. He recognized Ludington's voice and answered in his Albanian-accented English, "No problem, no problem. See you and the Mrs. at eight o'clock."

Ludington was waiting for his wife in the kitchen, glancing out the window every few minutes to see if her cab might be pulling up. He missed her immensely when she travelled. He was especially missing her just now. He had told her about the bones in the ash pit, but she did not know about his "investigatory endeavors," as van der Berg named their attempts to discover what had happened to a nameless child half a century ago. There was a cowardly part of him that had been relieved his wife had been out of the country for the last week. He was uneasy about telling her what he, his church secretary, and clerk of Session were up to. They kept little from each other. And she was, after all, a lawyer.

He saw a cab pull up. Fiona stepped out almost immediately. The cabbie must have let her pay at the last stoplight. He opened the door and took her in his arms, kissing the top of her head first, then a long kiss from which she finally pulled away. "Seth, let me put my suitcase down."

She did; they kissed again, and she turned to the kitchen table where he had set out blue cheese and water crackers, a bowl of smoked almonds—her favorite—two Riedel stem glasses, and the bottle of wine he had uncorked, not one from the case of the Chateau Neuf, but a fine enough California cabernet.

"How lovely, Seth."

"That's one," he said. Like many a Brit, Fiona overused the word "lovely." She used it to describe anything that was vaguely pleasant, though sometimes it was uttered ironically. He kept count of her "lovelies." She was allowed five per day.

She smiled at this and said, "The wine looks... very fine, but I think I'll have a Scotch. 'My heart is in the Highlands.' She sang this line in a passable imitation of the Jo Stafford classic.

"You always get homesick when you go back. How are your mom and dad? How was the birthday?"

"Since it was a Sunday this year, Daddy preached at the Canongate in the morning and out for dinner at Monteith's that evening. The congregation knew it was his birthday, and they sang him a "Happy Birthday" at tea after services. It was lovely, and he was so pleased. That's two, I know, I know."

Seth fetched a bottle of Highland Park, her new favorite, and poured her two fingers, no ice, and himself a glass of wine.

"Let's sit in the living room, my dear. We're not due at Lex till eight." They went up the stairs, balancing appetizers and drinks, and sat in the wing chairs on either side of the cold fireplace.

Fiona asked, "Well, the bones...are they still with us? What's the plan, Reverend Ludington?"

"Still there. You know I talked to Harry. He said to leave them alone for the time being. So, well...we've been doing some investigating this last week while you were away."

"We? You and Harry?"

"Not exactly. Harry's helping with DNA, but the 'we' is me and Harriet van der Berg."

"Harriet? DNA? Good Lord, Seth."

"Harriet was accidental, maybe providential. She overheard our conversation when I told Harry about the bones, and he suggested I do some sleuthing. That damn intercom was on. She offered to help. Even if I'd said no, she would have wiggled her way into it. You know Harriet. But the truth is, she really knows the place, knows the church, knows the history. She's smart as a whip, and she keeps her counsel."

"And the DNA, Seth? DNA?"

The case hangs on two things, my dear—timing, that is to say, who lived in the manse when, and gathering DNA.

"The case, Seth—*case*? Who do you think you are, Sidney Chambers on BBC?"

"No, of course not. Old Stone is hardly St. Andrew and St. Mary, and Yorkville is no Grantchester. "

Ludington reminded his wife of the dating suggested by the *Life* magazine and a bit of the *Times* in the ash pit just above the bones. Then he told her about his and van der Berg's visit to a minister's widow up in Westchester named Dolores McCrae, his trip to Philadelphia and failure to obtain a DNA sample from Philip Desmond, and lastly, the discovery that the erstwhile manse, now their home, has been owned and lived in by a lawyer named Oscar Cunningham."

"I need another finger of Scotch, Seth, maybe two."

He went downstairs and poured her a dram of the Highland Park, then back up to the living room to find her staring into the fireplace.

He sat down, took the barest sip of his cabernet, and said, "It's like this, Fiona." He leaned forward in his wing chair, glancing like her into the dark fireplace. "As I was saying, the question hinges on who lived in the house during a specific period of time—the months, maybe a year or more, from the tail end of the 1960s into the early 1970s. Three families lived here in that time frame—Oscar and Mildred Cunningham and their son, the interim minister and his wife (that's Malcolm and Dolores McCrae), and Phil and Penny Desmond. The Cunninghams had lived here for some years, lived in the house until the late spring of 1969. More precisely, it would have been just Mildred and the boy from February to sometime in May. Oscar had died in February. The McCraes moved in June of that year and moved out the following May, May of '70. He was a one-year interim. The Desmonds moved in early that summer of '70, probably in June. Actually, only Phil moved in. He and Penny didn't get married till September. Dolores's DNA is being checked for a match. Not a likely match, as she volunteered it. And she sent us an old comb that belonged to her husband. It seems as if two of these guys—Oscar Cunningham and perhaps Phil Desmond—may have been, well, playing the field. A very awkward pregnancy is possible, possible for both Cunningham and Desmond. Harriet and I are following up these leads. I'm visiting Mildred tomorrow morning."

"Crivvens, Seth. Leads? You're not a detective, officially or otherwise, and Harriet van der Berg is certainly not one."

"Fiona, I have little choice. There's just no one else. Whatever happened might turn out to be horrific. Or maybe just pathetic and tragic. But whatever it was, it needs knowing. Somehow it needs to be put right. And now we're under time pressure. The Department of Buildings is sending their inspectors the day after Easter."

Mention of that day reminded him of the other looming Easter deadline in his life. He was not ready to speak of it, so he said, "Harry's anxious about moving the bones. Says don't do it. But we'll have to before the inspectors start poking around. And they haunt me, down there, here in our house. I'm guessing they're haunting you, too. All this was partly Harry's idea. Depending on what we find or don't find, we may not have to go official. He's thinking that maybe the whole world won't have to know. Maybe, just maybe."

As he spoke those sequential maybe's, Seth Ludington could only hope that maybe, just maybe, the whole world did not need to know every last secret. But all he said to his wife was, "If there was a crime, then we'll have to think about going to the police. They may bury it; they could leak it."

"I know you've come to love this sorry little church, Seth. I have as well. But you can't hide a crime to save it. I know you understand that, and I know you wouldn't do it. But I'm also only too well acquainted with your damnable, insatiable zeal to set the whole damn world right, even if it sinks your lovely little church."

"That's three. Let's go to dinner."

# Chapter Twenty-One

*Saturday, April 6—The Twenty-Eighth Day in Lent*

Ludington walked down 84th Street to Second Avenue, moving as though he were in a hurry so that Orsolya would not imagine she might waylay him with her fatal coffee. He saluted as he passed on the other side of the street; she waved her cigarette hand back.

He was not really in a rush. Mildred Cunningham's building was only a few blocks north on Second. He had left himself plenty of time. If Fiona were not travelling, she seldom worked on Saturdays. Seth generally used Saturday mornings for counselling meetings, often with couples planning weddings and others who could not take time away from jobs to meet during the workweek. He also took a Saturday morning hour to tune Sunday's sermon. They did their best to keep Saturday afternoons for themselves.

To kill a few minutes and avoid arriving at her building early, Ludington detoured down 86th Street. If Yorkville had a main drag, it was probably 86th east of Lexington. On this April Saturday, it was crowded with shoppers ducking in and out of stores and people dashing to the subway stations at Second Avenue and Lexington. The newly opened Q subway line running north and south down Second was reshaping the neighborhoods in its path, making them increasingly desirable. Commutes on the Q to jobs in Midtown, Downtown, even Brooklyn, were less sardine-like and markedly faster than on the old Lexington Line. Maybe the flying Q would remake Yorkville and save Old Stone Church as well. So Ludington dared to hope.

Mildred Cunningham's building was as sorry as van der Berg had warned. No doorman, of course. He found the button labeled "3D Cunningham" among the four rows of buzzers on the wall of the airlock between the building's inner and outer front doors. He pushed it and waited a very long time before he heard the same "Who is it?" voice that had answered his phone call the day before. "It's Seth Ludington. Pastor Ludington."

He did not especially like the title "pastor." Shepherds are shepherds only if they have sheep. He did not mind being a shepherd, but he guessed most of his flock would be less pleased about being the sheep. He used the title with Mildred Cunningham anyway. "Reverend Ludington" might have sounded pompous.

"Oh, you. Give me a minute. I have to push the button to open the damn door."

Ludington heard the buzz that told him the inner door to the small lobby was being unlocked. He moved quickly to open it and looked back as he heard Mildred yell through the intercom, "Third floor, then to the right." Another wet cough exploded through the speaker.

The elevator was small and wobbly. The inside walls of the car were not paneled with wood like Park Avenue elevators, but covered in some slick Formica-like stuff—not slick enough to avoid a few Magic Marker graffiti tags and a mild obscenity scrawled above the button panel, however.

The elevator car jerked to a halt at three, the door screeched open, Ludington turned right, found 3D, and knocked on the door. It opened immediately upon his knock, but slowly. Mildred had clearly been waiting for him on the other side. Nevertheless, she opened it only a crack, peering at him for a moment to make certain it was a visiting minister and not some kid up to no good. Ludington had thought to wear his dog collar as clergy ID.

She opened the door and retreated into the apartment without a word. Ludington assumed he was meant to follow. She led him through a tunnel of old magazines stacked five feet high on either side of the small entry gallery that led into the living room. He knew about hoarders, but had never met one. He imagined they did not often entertain.

119

The living room was lined with not only old magazines, but piles of oddments balanced atop each other. He spied an old bread maker in an open box, a silver tea set perched on a kitchen stool, piles of haphazardly folded towels and blankets, and more magazines, mostly women's fashion magazines—old copies of *Vogue*, *Town and Country*, and *Elle* in precarious stacks. The room was dominated by a television set, large, wall-mounted, and looking fairly new. Eight feet back from the TV sat a Naugahyde recliner, also new-looking, and a small side table set with the television remote, a pack of Winstons, and a lighter. The only other piece of furniture in the room was a single mahogany dining room chair set at a right angle to the recliner. Clearly, the visitor's seat. Seldom used, Ludington guessed.

Mildred Cunningham, hoarder of fashion magazines, was a large woman, close to obese. Underneath it all lurked the faintest hint of the fine bones that had doubtless once made her a beauty. He guessed that like many a New Yorker, she lived on take-out food. Her hair was an unnatural jet black, cut short, and not looking to have been recently washed. She was dressed in a tent-like floral house dress that fell just below her knees and red satin slippers with low heels. One little stab at fashion, Ludington thought. She lowered her bulk into the recliner, pointed at the dining room chair to her right, and said, "You might as well sit down."

He did, and after thanking her for her time, fell into his now familiar speech about getting to know his congregation.

Mildred coughed in response, cleared her throat, and said, "Well, you're not going to get me there. Why would I? Haven't been in the place since his funeral."

This declaration was followed by a rosary of complaints, first about the building's super, about her neighbors on the third floor, then about the impossibly complicated television remote control. She skipped a beat and circled back to the church. "Why would I go to some church that stole my house from me, stole it from me and my son?"

Ludington said that he had been told that her late husband had bequeathed it to the church when he died. "Exceptionally generous," he said, deciding it was not the time to tell her that he lived in the house, a house he had recently bought for over five million dollars.

"Generous," she barked, "More like guilt. Both start with a 'g,' but not the same thing. He hardly went to that church. Joined it for the Wall Street contacts, and then he up and croaks at the age of thirty-nine, gives our house away, and his wife and son are on the street. We'd lived there for eighteen years. His parents bought it for us when we got married, bought it for us, not only him. He just gave it away, like it might atone for his sins. Randy bastard, he was. Fat chance. You can't buy forgiveness, you know."

When he had planned this visit, Ludington had thought to find some confirmation of Oscar's extra-marital affairs. He clearly had. He had not thought of Mildred as a potential mother of the bones. What motivation might she have had to cover up a pregnancy or birth? She was married to the man, no reason for scandal. But it now occurred to him that this cauldron of bitterness sitting before him might be—and might have been fifty years ago—capable of anything. He eyed the lace handkerchief Mildred had coughed into yet again and changed the subject.

"I understand you have a son, Oscar Jr. He's also a member of Old Stone."

"I have a never-married son, and he's sixty-something years old. Lives a subway ride away and never seems to find much time to visit his mother."

Her liturgy of unhappiness droned on until she fell at last into silence and started fondling the TV remote, which seemed to indicate that they were finished. Ludington stood, spoke the polite necessities, and let the small prayer book he had brought but not opened slip out of his hand to the floor next to the lacy handkerchief that he had seen slide off the side table. He bent down, picked up both, and stuffed them into his jacket pocket. Mildred Cunningham did not get out of the recliner as Ludington saw his way out through the tunnel of fashion magazines—"the gates of *Elle*," he sighed.

Just as he stepped onto the Second Avenue sidewalk and headed south to the church, his cell phone vibrated in his jacket pocket. He fished it out and saw that it was Harry Mulholland.

"Seth, it's me, Harry. Nassau County just emailed me a photocopy of the accident report. It's dated February 7, 1969, just like you said. Impressive that they could put their hands on it after 50 years. They must have a warehouse full of old paper reports somewhere out there. I'll read you the germane sentence. *'Vehicle, 1968 model Cadillac Sedan DeVille, struck the abutment of the Cantiague Road bridge, Hicksville, on the Northern State Parkway, travelling eastbound at high rate of speed at approximately 1:00 AM. Impact was directly head-on. No evidence of skid marks. Victim later identified as Oscar Louis Cunningham, Sr., 338 East 84th Street, New York City. Deceased was not wearing a seat belt. Road conditions were dry.'*

"That's one of those old bridges on the Northern State, beautiful things, something Robert Moses did right. Seth, looks to me like the guy just may have offed himself. They say that upwards of a third of single car accidents are suicides."

Ludington thanked him and added, "See you tomorrow, Harry. Don't forget to remind me to give you Malcolm McCrae's comb... for what it's worth."

Back in his study and before taking an editorial pass at the sermon, Ludington phoned Oscar Cunningham, Jr. Church records did not have an address for him, but van der Berg had found a phone number, doubtless a cell, and an email address. He picked up on the third ring with one of those chipper, questioning "hello's," his tone rising on the second syllable and making it into two. Ludington introduced himself and recited his "getting to know my congregation" speech. He was taken aback when Cunningham said, "I'm glad you called, Reverend Ludington. I've been meaning to reach out to you for some time. Listen, I'd like to get together if you have the time. Can I buy you lunch sometime? I'm downtown these days. Would Midtown work?"

This was not at all the response Ludington had anticipated. He said yes; Cunningham suggested Le Grenouille. "It's on 52nd just east of 5th."

They agreed on 12:30 on the coming Monday, Ludington's regular day off.

# Chapter Twenty-Two

*Saturday, April 6—The Twenty-Eighth Day in Lent*

Huw and Gina Griffiths were among the precious few younger couples at Old Stone. Like Seth and Fiona, they were in their thirties and had quickly become their closest church friends. They, too, had been childless, but unlike the Ludingtons, had ached in tandem to have a child, a longing that was too often the default subject of conversation when the four of them got together for dinner. This was much to the discomfort of both Seth and Fiona, especially Seth, who remained at loggerheads with his wife on the matter of children.

Seth had seen the couple weep after each of the outrageously expensive and unsuccessful procedures they had undergone at the hands of their superb Manhattan fertility specialist. Finally, over a dinner at Elio's a few days after Thanksgiving, Gina had told them that they had decided to adopt. Huw had taken Gina's hand and smiled his agreement. They asked Seth to write a reference letter to the adoption agency. He said yes—they would be ideal parents—but dreaded composing the letter. Huw had grown up at Old Stone, was confirmed there at thirteen, had disappeared for high school and college, but now attended faithfully with his wife. Gina had been raised Roman Catholic, but planned to join her husband at Old Stone.

The child slept through the entire pre-baptism meeting, an afternoon meeting as happy as the morning's with Mildred Cunningham had been unhappy. Close friends as the Griffith's were, Ludington found it awkward to instruct them on the theology of baptism and the gravity of the commitment they would make in affirming the questions he would set to them the next morning at the baptism. The conversation in his study soon drifted away from theology toward the adoption process they had just experienced. It had been surprisingly easy. A beautiful child had landed in their arms more suddenly than they had dared hope.

"We would have preferred an open adoption," Huw had said, "But the birth mother was insistent that it be closed."

Gina then rehearsed much of the conversation that had unfolded over a celebratory dinner with Seth and Fiona a few days after the call from the agency had come in late February. Gina said, "Someday, she may well want to know who her birth mother was. Maybe her biological father as well. We honestly think it's her right to know. She may want to know for medical reasons. And some adopted children want to know when they are older. I can understand that. Others are just not interested."

Gina looked at her daughter in a way that seemed to say, "I hope you are one who is not interested."

Huw said, "New York law requires that everybody on the birth certificate of a child given for a closed adoption agree before it can be unsealed—child and mother, both parents if the father's name is on it. But honestly, Seth, it doesn't matter that much anymore. And it'll matter less in twenty years. There are these open-access DNA websites that adoptees can go to and find any biological relatives that might be out there, people who have uploaded their own DNA profiles. First one was an outfit called GEDmatch. You may not find your biological parents, but odds are decent that you'll find some random third or fourth cousin. Then some online genealogy, and you may be able to find what the State of New York won't tell you."

Huw Griffiths had founded a successful company that developed websites for independent schools and other non-profits. He knew his way around the cyber world.

As they were about to leave, Gina asked Ludington if he would like to hold her daughter. Perhaps they thought he might need to practice baby holding. The child stirred when he had taken her in his arms. She seemed to be fragility incarnate, weighing nothing in his arms, though her father had proudly declared that she had been "7 pounds, six ounces" at birth and now, at three weeks old, was "almost eight."

"Seth," Gina said, "We love her so. She's all we ever wanted. She's the most wanted child there ever was."

The babe opened her eyes at this declaration from her mother and looked directly at Ludington. Held in her infant gaze, Ludington thought of the bones in his ash pit. What arms had held them when they stirred, if they had ever stirred? Had that child been wanted, maybe loved—or not? Had the child been named or perhaps baptized? And what in God's name had happened?

# Chapter Twenty-Three

*Sunday, April 7—The Fifth Sunday in Lent*

L udington took the child from her mother's arms for the baptism. He did so clumsily as he had little experience with infants; baptisms were few at Old Stone. He arranged her across the crook of his left arm, his right hand free to dip into the water in the font and wet the little forehead that had a faint reddish flame mark above the nose. Common enough in fair children, he understood. It would fade in time. Sophia's parents had eagerly told him so when he met with them in his study late Saturday morning for the pre-baptism meeting. They assumed he had noticed it then, though he had not. As Ludington touched the fuzz on the child's nearly bald head with his wet fingers and spoke the name of the Trinity, he dared to trust that this invisible mark would never fade. Her name was to be Sophia, Sophia Lucy. She returned his gaze soberly, without a hint of a smile, as if she knew what he was really thinking about as he looked down at her.

After he had baptized Sophia—the child quiet in his arms, water running down her face—he turned from the parents to the congregation and said, "This child is now received into the holy, catholic and apostolic church. See what great love the Father has for us that we should be called children of God."

He caught Fiona's eye as he finished speaking. She was seated where she always sat when not traveling, three pews back on the pulpit side. Ludington

126

saw a tear run down her cheek. She smiled at him; he smiled weakly back, then turned quickly toward the child's parents behind him. Sophia's father stretched out his arms for his daughter, the longed-for child they had named Wisdom and Light.

Ludington greeted worshippers at the door after church as he usually did. He had been right about the wolves-in-sheep's-clothing sermon. Some people had heard it politically, a few to their pleasure, others to their displeasure. When Harry and Georgia came through the line, he yanked up his pulpit robe and fished out the baggie containing the black plastic comb Dolores McCrae had mailed to the church and slipped it into the extended hand of his Clerk of Session.

He and Fiona made a quick pass through the coffee hour in the Social Hall under the Sanctuary. Like most ministers, Seth Ludington disliked coffee hour. The same people cornered you every week. Fiona, a minister's child and more of an extrovert, was inured to them, even enjoyed them. She was engaged in a conversation with a gaggle that included Sophia's proud parents and grandparents, all hovered around the child, asleep in an elaborate SUV of a stroller. Seth caught Fiona's eye and gave a nod aimed at the door. She raised an index finger that said, "In a minute."

They walked hand in hand up the stairs from the Social Hall to the lobby entrance that emptied onto 82nd Street. Felix, the church's sexton, was seated at the small desk near the lobby door. The venerable ecclesial office of sexton had morphed over the centuries and come to mean "general handyman, janitor, and building manager" rolled into one.

"How's the manse renovation coming, Reverend?"

"Just getting started, Felix. Building Department's coming in two weeks. It's going to be quite the project, I'm afraid."

"Well, I gotta tell ya, Reverend, nobody's happier than me that you guys bought the place. Looking after that old barn, on top of keeping up the church—too much. It was always one thing or another over there. Busted faucets, clogged toilets, fuses blowing, leaky roof. Used to be some weeks I was in the manse more than here at the church. All yours, Reverend. But it's a great old house."

As he and Fiona walked over to Lexington and up to the Lex Restaurant, he wondered who the sexton was 50 years ago. He must have been in the manse as much as Felix. And there had doubtless been days, even weeks, between one tenant moving out and the next moving in. Van der Berg will know, he concluded.

Nero greeted them as warmly as ever and ushered them to the back-corner table that he did his best to keep open for them every Sunday. He brought a glass of wine for both without asking. The house cab for Seth—quite nice for a house wine—and a sauvignon blanc for Fiona.

She was in a bubbly mood. "What a doll that little Sophia is. All that blond fuzz, the cute little flame mark. I had one when I was a wee bairn, you know. Gone now, except when I get upset. And not a peep from her in church."

"They'll be great parents."

"And Seth, seeing you with a child in your arms. Made me weepy it did, just lovely."

He merely said, "That's one."

Nero was hovering a few feet from their table, hands behind his back. No pad or pencil. He always took orders by memory.

They both ordered chicken Milanese, which was almost a salad—chicken breast pounded very thin and tender, breaded and sautéed in a little olive oil, then covered with fresh greens and circled with little plum tomatoes sliced in half. It was one of their regular Sunday lunches.

When Nero had withdrawn to the kitchen at the back of the narrow restaurant, Fiona took a sip of her wine, set down the glass, looked at Seth, and said, "I'm so ready, my love. Let's have a baby. I want to be a mother. I want you to be a father." She paused, took not another sip, but a great gulp of her wine.

Seth looked at her, then down the length of the restaurant to the large window that gave onto Lexington Avenue and at the parade of humanity marching north and south, so many of the faces looking anxious or vacant. So many people, he thought. So many of them miserable.

The conversation that ensued followed the same pattern as its predecessors. He mentioned his anxiety about a world that was warming, dirty and crowded. He rehearsed her demanding job and travel schedule. They both half knew that these concerns were mostly a ruse to cover his fears about fatherhood, an unease that she suspected was rooted in his experience of his own father's love—a bit calculated and transactional, almost—but never quite—unconditional.

She responded with the same counterarguments. "The U.N. has generous parental leave policies, and I talked to Fritz about cutting back on travel."

Fritz was her Austrian direct supervisor. Then she said, "And Seth, ye know full well we can afford a whole clan o' nannies."

Her Scots accent always thickened with passion.

Finally, she turned her guns toward that gnawing sense of inadequacy that ate at him, and launched into a strategy of praise, "You're gentle. You're always wanting to experience the unexperienced. It's a facet of that relentless curiosity of yours. Fatherhood will be new. You so care about right and wrong, to see justice done. More than me, even. Any child will be blessed to have you as a father."

"Let's talk about this after Easter, Fiona. You know how much I've got on my plate right now." He looked down at the chicken Milanese Nero had just set before him.

"Not that plate," he said, making a weak stab at humor to defuse the conversation.

"You know what I mean. The ash pit."

"Don't you play that card, Seth. If it's not that, it's always something."

They picked at their meals in silence. Seth could see the flame mark appearing, slowly, faintly, on Fiona's forehead.

After lunch, she went back to the house, he to his study at church. He phoned van der Berg to ask who had been the sexton when she first started attending Old Stone.

"A fine Puerto Rican gentleman. He served as our sexton for many years, till he died. He died rather young, in the 1980s it would have been. Such a tragedy. I got to know him a bit. Devilishly handsome he was. In a Latin way, that is. His name was Jorge Perez, but some of the old-timers called him George. He and Harry were very close. You might talk to him. Why do you ask, Dominie?"

"Well, it occurred to me that a sexton would have had access to the house when it was a manse and the church looked after it. And the place must have been empty for some time before and after the McCraes. And there would have been the summers, weeks, a month maybe, when ministers were away on vacation. Old Stone has always been generous with vacation time—as long as it was in the summer when everybody's gone."

"I suppose you're right about this, Dominie. I think we perhaps have yet another investigatory lead, as they say."

Ludington ended the call and immediately phoned Harry Mulholland at home.

Harry and Georgia generally went out with friends for brunch after church, but Ludington figured they'd be home by now. Harry had a cell phone, but preferred to use his landline. His Apple 6S frustrated him. Coverage was often poor among the concrete towers of Manhattan.

"Seth, fine sermon this morning. Wolves in sheep's clothing. Not hard to guess what's been on your mind these days."

Seth told him what occurred to him when Felix had confessed how happy he was not to have to bother with the manse any more. "The sexton would have had access, essentially private access, in the days after the Cunninghams and before the McCraes and then after the McCraes and before Phil Desmond moved into the place. And in the summers when either of them might have been off on vacation somewhere. Harriet said that you and the sexton back then were friends. Hate to say it, but I need to know."

The silence on the phone was so long that Ludington finally said, "Harry, you still there?"

"Seth, we need to talk, I mean in person, not on the phone. Can you meet me at Jacques? Say at six."

"Sure, Harry, of course."

The line went dead.

# Chapter Twenty-Four

*Friday, February 14, 1969*

Sally Wilcox had phoned Harriet van der Berg nearly a week earlier. "Harriet, please, I can't go alone. Would you go with me? You're a member of that church. I don't want to sit alone, all by myself."

"I am not a member, not as yet. We have been attending for some months and do intend to join. And, Sally, though he was a member, I did not know the man. I would feel rather a voyeur showing up at his funeral."

"If you're with me, people will understand."

In the end, the Lindsay's Blizzard had postponed the service, which ended up being rescheduled late in the morning of Valentine's Day. Harriet waited for Sally in front of Old Stone Church, wrapped in her old upstate parka. Sally arrived by cab, one of the bulbous Checkers. The car's door swung open, and Sally Wilcox emerged, ascending and then descending the Everest of snow piled at the curb, holding fast to a "No Parking" sign to steady herself.

She looked terrible. They had not seen each other for a few months as Sally had made excuses whenever Harriet phoned about getting together for one of their lunches. The girl now seemed larger than ever, even draped in a long, belted trench coat. Her face was blotchy, her eyes red. She wobbled over to Harriet and threw her arms around her friend.

"How can I ever thank you, Harriet? I had to come, I mean, I just had to, but I could never have done it alone."

The church was half full, maybe a hundred people. Harriet noted to herself that funerals for the young—and to Sally and Harriet, 39 still seemed rather young—are generally well-attended. It mattered little how well-loved the decedent was; if you were not old, you generally had enough survivors to fill the pews.

They sat halfway back on the left, the pulpit side of the sanctuary. Oscar Cunningham's family was on the other side of the center aisle, in front of course, directly under the lectern. Harriet and Sally scanned the family pews, both of them silently guessing at which individuals were which. Van der Berg picked out a couple in their seventies, a man and woman seated in the second pew back, who she thought were probably Oscar Cunningham's parents. Next to them was a woman in her forties, probably an older sister.

In the front pew along the center aisle was a strikingly beautiful woman in a black suit—Chanel, Harriet guessed—and a pill-box hat. No veil to hide her exquisite features. She sat rigidly upright, staring at nothing. Next to her, Harriet saw a teenaged boy in a blue blazer too small for him, his head buried in his hands.

The service was short and mechanical, conducted by an Associate Minister from the Brick Church, Old Stone's nearest Presbyterian neighbor. The Scripture readings were predictable, though perfectly appropriate. The minister obviously did not know Oscar Cunningham, as the brief eulogy that he embedded in his generic funeral meditation was much the same as the newspaper obituary. No family or friends rose to offer remembrances. It was blessedly over in thirty-five minutes.

Harriet and Sally went downstairs to the Social Hall for the reception—coffee, tea, and cookies. Catered, Harriet guessed, not made by friends or by the Women's Association of the church, though two of its members had been corralled to pour.

The beautiful woman, obviously Oscar's widow, stood alone, greeting the mourners who had formed a line of sorts. Harriet watched them, appraising them as colleagues from his Wall Street world and maybe some old private school friends. She saw no one she recognized from church.

Mildred Cunningham—Sally had told her the woman's first name—shook hands with all who approached her with their condolences. One quick shake for each, then she pulled her hand away. She did this without a scintilla of emotion, neither warmth nor sorrow. She's just doing her duty, Harriet thought to herself.

The teenaged boy, clearly the son—"young Oscar," Sally called him—had retreated to a folding chair in the corner of the room where he slouched, mopping his reddened eyes with the too-short sleeve of his jacket. A woman whom Harriet guessed to be his aunt finally pulled up a chair next to the boy and put her arm around him. He collapsed into her, his curved back pulsating with silent sobs. Harriet saw as Mildred watched this scene, and also saw as she quickly looked away, her exquisite face unaltered.

Sally whispered to Harriet, "I want to say something to his parents."

Harriet, not a mourner, felt she had no place offering condolences. She said, "And to Mr. Cunningham's widow, of course."

"I don't think so," Sally snorted.

She turned, crossed the room to Oscar's mother and father, and shook hands with both, doubtless telling them how much she had appreciated the opportunity to work with their son and what a fine attorney he had been.

The reception, brief and awkward, was emptying in a mere half hour. As Harriet and Sally retrieved their coats and prepared to leave, Sally jerked to attention and nodded in the direction of Mildred Cunningham as a woman, a mere girl too young and small for the mink coat that encased her, approached the widow. She had waited to be one of the last of the mourners.

Sally said, "The receptionist I told you about. Little twit."

The girl stood in front of Mildred, hands buried in her coat pockets. Mildred did not extend her hand either. Emotion animated Mildred's face for the first time, but it was neither sorrow nor appreciation; it was something closer to fury. Their voices were gradually rising, finally becoming loud enough for Harriet to overhear the last of Mildred's words, "You have the nerve to be here too, you dumb little bitch."

The two women separated as they left the church. Harriet walked home. Sally said she had an errand to do before taking the subway back downtown.

# Chapter Twenty-Five

*Sunday, April 7—The Fifth Sunday in Lent*

Ludington spent the afternoon in his study catching up on emails and worrying about the sermon for the next Sunday. It would be Palm Sunday, properly "Palm and Passion Sunday," the schizophrenic Sunday before Easter. You could go either way in a sermon—waving palms and the joyous parade into Jerusalem, or the horrific passion that lay in wait.

He texted Fiona to remind her that Harry wanted to meet him for dinner. She responded with a terse "Okay." She was still angry.

Café Jacques was Belgian, which meant dozens of beer choices and mussels done in as many ways. Happily, it seemed that *steak-frites* had migrated north from France as an alternative to the assortment of *moules-frites* that were the place's specialty.

Harry had already arrived and gotten them a table in a quiet corner. He was in one of his closet full of Harris tweed jackets and regimental ties. Ludington guessed he had not changed clothes since church that morning, though if he had, the man would have doubtless donned a jacket and tie for dinner with his pastor.

He nodded at Ludington as he sat down at the small table across from him. "Thanks for coming, Seth."

"Of course, Harry, of course. You okay?"

"Sure, just need to talk. Talk in person."

The waiter arrived just as Mulholland leaned forward in his chair, a movement that was often a harbinger of speech for him. Like most people who guarded their words, their fewer words garnered closer attention.

Mulholland ordered his *moules-frites "marinieres"* style, which the menu explained meant in chardonnay, garlic, and parsley. "And a Diet Coke, please."

Ludington thought to himself that most anything, even rubber bands, would taste wonderful in chardonnay, garlic, and parsley. He ordered the *steak-frites,* "Medium-rare to medium, please, and a lager, whatever you recommend."

Ludington knew a bit about wine, nothing about beer.

When their drinks came, Harry tapped the rim of his tall glass of Diet Coke and said, "Seth, did you ever notice that I don't drink? Alcohol, I mean?"

"Well, yes, I suppose I did."

He looked Ludington square in the eyes and said, "I'm an alcoholic, Seth, a recovering alcoholic. I've been sober for almost forty years, but it's still one day at a time. I go to meetings, usually twice a week, Florida and here, never the ones at Old Stone, though I really don't know why. No shame anymore. Habit, I guess. I hope you're okay with your Clerk of Session being an ex-drunk."

Ludington made all the right listening noises, even reached across the table to lay a hand on top of Mulholland's. The man didn't pull right away, but let Ludington's hand lay on his for nearly a minute as he continued.

"Let me tell my story, Pastor. I've told it often enough at meetings. I started in high school, grass and beer. Then not so much grass, none in college or at the academy, but lots of booze, all the time. I hit bottom early, thank God. Georgia was a lousy enabler. Told me she was leaving if I didn't quit. And she would have. That and the two DUIs, one when I was still walking a beat, the other after I was promoted to homicide. The precinct covered them up, but the captain told me one more, and my career as a cop was over. My first AA meeting was on December 23, 1980. Christmas was rough that year. I lost most of my cop friends. Wasn't drinking with them anymore."

"Harry, you know I hold you in the highest regard, just now even more so. I mean, for the courage to go through recovery and for sticking with it all these years. And for telling me, though I'm not sure why now...tonight."

"There are two more chapters in this story. When I tell you the third one, you'll understand.

"If sobering up was chapter one, here's chapter two. The third step in recovery—you know there are twelve steps in AA—the third step is 'Made a decision to turn our will and our lives over to the care of God as we understand Him.'

"When I got to that step, I was twenty-eight years old. I hadn't been in a church since high school except for our wedding. I'd stopped praying. When I bottomed out that winter, the winter of 1980, I was a mess. It was a slow slog back to sanity, not easy. Seldom is.

"They told me to turn my life over to the care of God as I understood him. I understood Him as I had been raised here at Old Stone. Seth, that winter I had nowhere to turn except—well—to Jesus. Sounds hokey, but that's how it was for me. I prayed, and when I prayed, I prayed to Jesus. All I had to do was ask. Here I'm sober almost forty years, happily married to the same woman, a condo in Florida, and the damn Clerk of Session, would you believe. You know that most alcoholics are nervous around clergy, expect judgment, I suppose."

"Not from me."

"I guessed as much. So that's chapter two. Chapter three, well, chapter three is Jorge Perez. You discovered he was the sexton back in the late '60s and early '70s, the time frame for the bones. I'm guessing Harriet told you. In fact, he was the Old Stone sexton for a long time, till a few months before he died. He died in 1994. He'd just turned fifty-one. Died of cirrhosis of the liver, waiting for a transplant. I was his sponsor, I mean at AA. We all have one, you know. I was his sponsor for ten years, his ten sober years, the last ten years of his life. Dried out and then died of cirrhosis anyway. Not fair. Like Georgia says, 'The only fair is the state fair.'"

Ludington made more listening noises. Harry was not looking for conversation, only an ear.

"Anyway, Seth, we became very close, Jorge and I. Most sponsors talk with their sponsee almost every day. You get close, you inevitably get close. I want to tell you, Jorge Perez became one remarkable human being after he got clean, that is. Became a sponsor himself. Tutored little kids up at P.S. 171. He actually joined the church, joined formally, and sat himself in the narthex in the back, right by the front door, every Sunday. Sat in his own folding chair with a Bible and a hymnal. Still "Mr. Smooth," but now it was real. Even took to wearing neckties."

That memory evoked the first smile Ludington had been given in this conversation, not that Mulholland much adorned his words with them.

"But Seth, the earlier Jorge, 'George' back then, the one who was using, he was a different story. So, this is chapter three. He was one wild ass of a kid—booze, drugs, and not just grass, petty crime. He told me some of this himself, but he was one of those "let-it-all-hang-out" types at meetings. He liked to be the center of attention, and he got it at AA, telling the crowd "old Jorge" tales that would curl your hair. And they were true, mostly. Anyway, this was the old Jorge, and he was the one who was sexton when the manse was empty, I mean both before and after the McCraes. It's a miracle the guy never got fired. He did the work, and like I said, he was such a sweet-talker. Point is, he would have had access to the manse. He was responsible for seeing that the place was maintained. The Jorge I came to love would never have done what somebody did for those bones to end up in your ash pit. No way, ever. But I can't say that about the old Jorge."

Ludington's trip to Philadelphia and his conversation with Moze Washington had reminded him of how the horror of Viet Nam and the draft had hung over the heads of young men in the late '60s and early '70s.

"Harry, you didn't go to Vietnam, and it sounds like Perez didn't either. You were the right age."

"I wasn't quite the right age. I was a year too young for the lottery, thank God. But Jorge was a few years older and exactly the right vintage. He got exempted because he was legally blind. Actually, blind in the right eye—the 'right' eye in both senses of the word. Right because it was that one, and right because it was the one that got you exempted. Can't aim a gun if you're right handed and blind in that eye. You'd notice it only if you looked at him really close. Didn't keep him from wearing that eye patch when he wanted to look like a pirate. Gave it up later, fortunately."

The waiter arrived with their dinners, Harry's *moules* in a little galvanized metal bucket, Seth's New York strip on a sizzling-hot plate, their *frites* piled in paper cones.

"Let's eat, Seth. Then I have something I need to give you."

They turned down dessert and coffee, the waiter cleared their table, cleaned the tablecloth with a crumber, and announced he'd be back with the check. As he left, Mulholland reached to the floor beside his chair, picked up his tatty old leather briefcase, and set it on his lap.

"I visited Jorge every few days in the months before he died. He died a brave death, by the way. At peace with the injustice of it all. And he believed. A few days before he passed, he gave me a file, all his personal papers. There was no family here in the states, not a soul. He said he wanted me to have it. Some legal stuff, a will, a stack of letters he'd kept, and a diary. Some in Spanish, some in English. There was almost no money to leave to anybody. The little he had had gone to the church. Anyway, there could be something there—in the letters, maybe the diary. A lot of people in recovery keep diaries. Knowing Jorge, it's doubtless pretty candid. I never looked through the stuff. No reason to, not until now. I'm going to give it to you. I'm pretty conflicted about it. Anonymous really is anonymous. But Jorge is gone, and this stuff could maybe be important."

Mulholland reached into his briefcase and fished out an envelope. He reached into it and pulled out a thin pile of papers and a small red book labeled *"Diario."*

So, go through this stuff, Seth, and see if there's anything there."

He worked the papers and the diary back into the envelope and slid it across the table to Ludington.

Mulholland looked his pastor square in the eyes, paused, and said slowly, "If Jorge Perez had anything to do with this, I want you to remember he's dead. I know you have to know, and I guess I want to know, but let's just leave him dead, okay?"

# Chapter Twenty-Six

*Sunday, September 14, 1969, evening*

T he day had unfolded delightfully—cool in the morning, bright and
warm by the afternoon, one of those New York days when it's hard
to know exactly how to dress.

"Harriet dear, I think I must have left my coat at church. I know I had it
on this morning when we left. It's not here. I must have left it in the pew. I
do recall taking it off. You helped me."

Margaret Whitaker was standing in the entrance gallery of their apartment, staring into the front closet as if the missing coat might suddenly
decide to appear.

"You can fetch it in the morning, Margie."

"I'm not sure the church is open on Mondays, and I'd like to have it for
tomorrow."

Harriet knew that Margaret had just bought it at Bloomingdale's and was
eager to show it off at work. She worked in fashion after all, and the new
coat was decidedly fashionable.

"Harriet, let's take a little walk and see. The high school youth group is
there till 7:30, so somebody'll be at the door to let us in. And it's such a
pleasant evening. We won't get many more like this."

They arrived at the 82nd Street door to the church parish house at 7:20.
Harriet pushed the door buzzer, and they both peered through the glass
door so that whoever was minding it might see that they were no threat and

139

admit them.

George Perez, the young sexton stationed at the lobby desk, looked up, waved a hand, and rose from his desk to let them into the lobby.

"You are very late for church today, ladies. Late for youth group too."

To underscore his wit, Perez flashed a smile, a row of perfect white teeth set off by his olive complexion. His coal black hair was slicked back into a near pompadour that might have been fashionable north of 96th Street, but looked nothing but Latin in Yorkville.

Harriet thought to herself, "My, he is a handsome one, if you're so inclined."

"Good evening. George," Margaret said. "I think I left my new coat in the sanctuary this morning. Is it okay if we take a look? I know where the lights are."

"No problem, ladies. At your service. I'm here till the last of the kids leave." He actually bowed ever so slightly before he returned to his desk.

When they were in the hall leading to the sanctuary and out of his earshot, Harriet whispered to Margaret, "Rather an Eddie Haskell type."

Margaret flipped on the bank of switches inside the sanctuary door. Even with all of the lights fully on, the room was dim and moody. They walked to the center aisle and down to their regular pew, eight rows back on the lectern side. There lay Margaret's coat, precisely where she had taken it off and neatly folded it that morning. She sidled into the pew, fetched it, and lay it over her arm.

Harriet saw Margaret's head turn toward the rear of the church just as hers did. They had both heard the unmistakable sound of someone weeping—softly, but loudly enough to hear.

They looked at each other, nodded agreement, and walked quietly toward the very back pew. A young girl was crouched forward, her face in the palms of her hands. She was either weeping or praying, perhaps both. She heard the women approach and looked up at them through reddened eyes.

Harriet and Margaret sat down in the pew with her. Harriet almost asked if anything was the matter, but caught herself before the words came out. The answer to that question was obvious.

She asked an equally predictable question, "What's the matter, dear?"

The girl shook her head and put her face back in her hands. Harriet understood adolescent angst well enough, recalling her own not so terribly long ago.

"Well, they'll be locking up in a minute. Can we walk out with you?"

The girl's head jerked up. "Not while he's still here. I can't leave till he's gone."

"Until who's gone?" Margaret asked.

The girl returned her blotchy face to her hands and mumbled through them, "Him. I can't let him see me like this."

Harriet put a hand on the girl's shoulder. The girl took a hand from her face and pushed it away.

Harriet said, "Margie, sit here with her. I'll go tell George he can go home and we'll let ourselves out."

Harriet walked out of the sanctuary and through the hall that led to the lobby where George Perez was stationed at his desk. As she was about to go in to tell him that he could leave, she saw one of the youth group kids sitting on the sexton's desk. The two young men were alone in the room. The rest of the high school kids must have already left. The kid laid something in George's outstretched hand. He slipped the kid something in return. Harriet could not see what they had exchanged. The kid then slid lithely off the corner of the desk and walked toward the exit door.

George called after him, "See you next week, Holly." The kid, dressed in blue jeans and a hooded NYU sweatshirt, turned back to George and smiled. Holly, maybe 17 or 18, was a boy. Harriet did not know him.

George slipped whatever Holly had given him into his pants pocket as Harriet entered the lobby. He heard her, turned, and offered another of his winning smiles.

"Margaret and I would like to merely sit in the church for a moment, if you don't mind. We'll let ourselves out."

"No problem, Miss van der Berg. The door locks automatic. Just be sure it's closed tight." His English was barely accented.

He rose from his desk, donned the leather jacket that was draped over his chair, and left the building.

Harriet returned to the sanctuary to find Margaret muttering "There, there" to the still inconsolable girl.

Harriet sat down and said, "Everyone else has left. Can we walk you home?"

The girl's head jerked up. She turned away from Harriet and Margaret and began to slide away from them toward the side aisle. When she reached the end of the pew, she turned back to the two women and mumbled, "Thanks." She rose and dashed out of the sanctuary.

"Who is that girl?" Margaret asked.

"Eleanor Westerberg. Jim and Ruth Westerberg's older daughter. I met them, I mean the whole family, at the Rally Day coffee hour last month. Such a fine family.

"So, who do you think she didn't want to see?"

"I'm not sure, but there were only two people in the lobby, and that's where she had to pass through."

# Chapter Twenty-Seven

*Sunday, April 7—The Fifth Sunday in Lent*

Fiona was sitting at her laptop in the kitchen as Seth walked through the door after his dinner with Harry. She looked up at her husband and offered the barest whisper of a smile, a signal that her anger at lunch had cooled, not to cold, but perhaps to lukewarm.

She said, "How's Harry? What did he want?" Nodding at the package he clutched, the one Mulholland had just given him, she asked, "And what's in the envelope?"

Seth loved his wife for her ravenous curiosity, probably because it partnered so congruously with his own. It was one of the many ways they fit with one another. When they drove anywhere together, they simply had to stop at every roadside historical marker. They both had to know what once happened at this spot in the world. Would that they moved in synch on the question of children.

"Well, my dear," he said, "The plot thickens. Cliché, I know, but it does, and it just did."

"Sit down and tell me. I'll fix tea." America had converted Fiona to coffee in the morning, but tea still reigned after noon.

Ludington had already told her about his visits to Dolores McCrae in White Plains, Philip Desmond in Philadelphia, and the miserable Mildred Cunningham around the corner. He had also brought her up to pace with the story Moze had reluctantly told him about Rachel Ruvenstein and the young Desmond.

He said, "And you were there this morning when Harriet told me about the church sexton back then, guy named Perez, said that he would have had a key to the manse. He would have had access whenever the house was empty—between ministers and in the summers when they were away. Anyway, after Harriet mentioned the name, I asked Harry about Perez. He went all quiet and summoned me for dinner."

"And?" Fiona was setting the kettle to boil and stuffing loose tea into a tea strainer. She loathed tea bags. "Floozies," she called them.

"Harry knew Perez well, really well. He was the guy's AA sponsor for years, until he died in fact. They were in recovery together. I had not guessed Harry was an alcoholic. Short of it is that Harry said the sober Perez was a genuinely decent man. Even joined the church. Harry obviously came to like him. But the not-sober Perez, the one circa 1970, was a different story. Harry didn't exactly say it, but he made it sound as if the guy was capable of anything back then. Harry seemed reluctant, in fact anxious, about telling me any of this, but he did. So, he must have his suspicions. He's a cop, remember. He's seen it all. Not a naïve bone in Harry Mulholland's body. Anyway, this means we have a fourth cluster of people who could have been in the house and could have used the fireplace in the late '60s and early '70s—Cunningham, McCrae, Desmond, in that order—and now Perez, in between all of them."

"Well, that does rather thicken the plot. So, that packet? Papers of some ilk, I assume. Did Harry give them to you?"

"Yes. He was with Perez when he was dying, In the mid-'90s it was. The man had no family here on the mainland—he was Puerto Rican and Dominican—so he gave Harry his little pile of personal papers. Harry said there was a will, a few letters, and a diary. The will left everything—not much—to the church."

Seth opened the envelope and gently slid the contents onto the kitchen table. Fiona set a steeping teapot, two hefty white china mugs, and a pitcher of milk she had heated on the kitchen table and sat in the chair opposite her husband.

The will was not there. It had doubtless been probated and filed. There were five hand-written letters—correspondence from the age before email—and a small red leather-bound book labeled *"Diario."*

They tackled the diary first. Perez had clearly started to keep it when he embarked on his journey into sobriety. The first entry was dated "3 Enero, 1985." "January 3rd, '85," Fiona translated.

The entries were not daily, in fact, there were no more than a couple dozen in the entire book, which spanned a decade. Perez would go for weeks, even months, without writing anything and then fill half a page several times in the same week. The earlier entries were entirely in Spanish; the later ones were mostly in Spanish, but often with a curious admixture of English words and phrases. Fiona translated easily. Her Spanish was near-native and of the New World variety.

"They're mostly about his recovery, Seth, about AA. He had a few slips. This one from late 1985 talks about Harry helping him back after one of them."

She read, aloud and in Spanish, the short entries written in Perez's large but tidy hand. She translated those that she thought might be of interest to Seth. "Here's one about his mother coming to visit. He says she's *euforica*—euphoric—about his getting sober."

Fiona said that the deeper into the diary she read, the more self-examining the entries grew. They mostly examined what had obviously become painful memories that the man held onto like hot coals in the hand, memories of the old Perez, the man he named "George." She noted two entries that admitted to having stolen from the church, several about his drug dealing. She observed that his rhetoric was increasingly confessional in tone, almost in the liturgical sense, like the prayers of confession printed in the Sunday worship bulletin for the congregation to recite. Indeed, many of the entries seemed to be addressed not to the diary, but to God.

One jolted Fiona as she read it aloud in Spanish. It was dated "8 Febrero, 1994". "February 8th of '94," Fiona whispered as if the date needed translation.

"The year he died," Seth said. "Harry said he died in '94. He was waiting for a liver transplant."

Fiona translated the entry. Most of it was in Spanish, but lapsed into English here and there. "I stole from the people who accepted me, the people who loved me. I sold drugs to their kids. And it wasn't just money and drugs. Such a betrayal! But more than anything, I am so very sorry about E. I took advantage of her. I know she regrets it. I wish I could carry the burden for both of us. And it hurt him, too. It all comes back to me in church when we do the Prayer of Confession. After we say the words, the minister always says that God forgives. I suppose I believe that. It's me that's the problem."

Fiona set the diary down and looked at her husband. I wonder if he ever forgave himself. And I wonder who or what 'E' was."

They turned next to the letters. Three were from his mother in San Juan. They were short, offering news about the weather and her sister's ill health, all ending with profuse expressions of her pride in her son for "stopping the liquor" as Fiona translated it. One was from Harry, a short note telling Perez how pleased he was that he'd joined Old Stone. It ended, "This place loves you, Jorge, it really does."

The fifth letter was a mere note, a card fashioned from a folded piece of pink construction paper. On the cover, someone had written with a gold marker in a careful and flowery script, all caps, "TE AMO." "I love you," Fiona translated, though Seth knew that much Spanish. Inside, on the right side of the card, was the note itself. "Yes, I really do, *te amo*, so much *amo*. But I don't know what to do, George. Please, please, let's meet and talk. We have to talk soon. All my love, Eleanor."

Seth looked at his wife. "Eleanor...there's only one Eleanor around Old Stone that I know of. Can't imagine it, though."

# Chapter Twenty-Eight

*December 27, 1984*

The Brick Church was three long blocks west, nine short ones north, and a universe away from Old Stone. "New York neighborhoods change at a corner," so thought Harry Mulholland as he and George Perez rounded 82$^{nd}$ Street and leaned north up Park into a cold headwind blustering down the avenue. Park was a wide canyon of mid-rise apartment buildings, most of them pre-war and still very desirable places to live, all defended by uniformed doormen peering out of toasty lobbies. The snow that had fallen earlier in the day lay on the brightly-lit evergreen trees erected in the avenue's median for the holidays.

Mulholland had agreed to meet Perez at Old Stone and walk with him up to Brick for what would be his first AA meeting. George had told Harry he didn't want to walk into the meeting alone. Mulholland could understand that. He was himself four years clean and remembered his sweaty discomfort sitting in the same overheated room in the basement of Brick Church only four Christmases earlier, garnering courage to say for the first time, "Hi, I'm Harry, and I'm an alcoholic."

Three days earlier, after the Christmas Eve Candlelight service at Old Stone, Mulholland had found Perez unconscious at the foot of the steps leading up to the front doors of the sanctuary. It was not clear if he had passed out and then fallen, or had knocked himself out in a tumble down the stone steps to the sidewalk.

Mulholland had seen that Perez was drunk—yet again—when he and Georgia arrived for the service at 9:30. Mulholland knew that Perez was a heavy drinker who had somehow managed not to get himself fired from the church sexton job. He was a long-time employee, generally got the job done, and was masterfully ingratiating. Mulholland guessed that after the Christmas Eve service had begun, Perez had scurried to his little sexton's office in the basement and drunk himself from mildly to severely intoxicated.

His fall resulted in a head wound to his brow, just below the hairline. Like most such wounds, it bled dramatically. The crowd that gathered around him could not rouse him, so they called 911. This occasioned an equally dramatic ambulance, siren blasting down 82nd Street, a three-in-the-morning diagnosis of mild concussion, and a two-day stint in New York Hospital on York Avenue.

Harry had known George from church for the last fifteen years. He decided to visit him at New York Hospital late Christmas Day. He sat down next to the man's bed which was raised to a sitting position, looked Perez in his blackened eyes, and said, "George, you're going to die. You keep it up, you'll die."

They say you can't catch a drunk. They run too fast. But George Perez was too tired to run anymore. He turned his bandaged head to Mulholland and said, "Okay, boss. I guess it's time."

Walking together up Park two days later, Harry said, "George, you don't have to talk today. Just listen. When the time comes, you simply tell your story, the truth. Maybe next time or the time after that, whenever you're ready."

The room in the basement of Brick Church was fuller than usual, maybe twenty people. The holidays are a challenge for alcoholics and druggies—parties, seasonal excess, the general sense that it's "a time out of time" when you might do what you wouldn't do "in time." So, you go to an extra meeting. The regulars were there, plus a number of faces Mulholland didn't recognize. They got coffee. Perez loaded his with three sugars and a spillover of milk. They sat next to each other in the circle of metal folding chairs, waiting for things to begin.

The chairman cleared his throat and said, "I'm Jim, and I'm an alcoholic. Let's say the Lord's Prayer together." This was a routine that often started meetings. He followed it with a reading from the *Big Book* and the day's reading from *One Day at a Time.* Harry knew the man slightly. He was good at this, well-spoken, a major Wall Street banker with a Park Avenue home address, a place on the water in the Hamptons, and an ex-wife who had ended up with all the same.

He then asked if anybody had "topics to discuss, something they were dealing with they wanted to talk about."

Harry had decided that he would say something that night. He didn't speak at every meeting, but he wanted to set George at ease. He waited until several in the circle had spoken, then after a moment's silence, said. "I'm Harry, and I'm an alcoholic." He talked about a phone call he had gotten late the day before, the day after Christmas, from a fellow cop inviting him to join the boys that night at Finnegan's Wake for a couple of beers. He had said no. He confessed to the group that he missed drinking, but that he missed his drinking friends more.

He finished by saying, "When you get sober, you find out who your friends are. That's all I've got for tonight. Thanks for listening."

He was startled when George said, "I'm Jorge, and I guess I must be an alcoholic." His hedging introduction evoked a few chortles and knowing nods. "I gotta thank my old buddy, Harry Mulholland, for dragging me along tonight."

He then launched into his story, soon rather too much story. He began with a stepfather who smacked him around before going back to the DR. He talked about pinching beers from the fridge at thirteen, then about selling purloined booze and dealing grass in East Harlem during high school. He said he discovered vodka at seventeen—quick, and almost odorless to teachers who got in your face and asked questions. He talked about confrontations with his mother, now back in San Juan with her sister. "She totally gave up on me. Can't blame her."

His veritable autobiography advanced to the job he had gotten at Old Stone Church when he dropped out of high school his senior year.

"They took a chance on me, a kid from East Harlem, and I screwed 'em royally." He turned around and glanced at Harry behind him. "I mean, I drank on the job. Not all the time, but most of the time. Drank on the job for the last fifteen years." He then unfolded the tale of his tumble down the church steps on Christmas Eve, the concussion, New York Hospital, and Harry's visit. The man had a gift for personal narrative. "They treated me like a human being. I did the work, mostly, but I screwed 'em."

Perez hesitated for a moment. He was clearly past discomfort and enjoying the attention, enjoying it rather too much.

"I took stuff from the church. I don't mean just loose stuff, you know. Mostly petty cash in drawers that nobody missed. But it was worse than that. I did stuff, and I took stuff, took some stuff that can't ever be paid back, not ever. I hurt people, hurt 'em bad."

He turned to look at Harry. He did not smile at him, nor did Mulholland smile at him.

The room was clearly growing uncomfortable with this overly long and too disclosive tale, as uncomfortable with it as Perez was thrilled in the telling it. Harry saw the glances being tossed around the circle.

Cross-talk is discouraged at meetings, but he knew he had to stop Perez before he went too far.

Mulholland stood. "I'm Harry," he said for the second time that evening, "and I'm an alcoholic. I'm a member of the church George works for, and I want you all to know that we love the guy and that we'll stand by him."

He threw an arm around Perez, gave him a sideways buddy shake that clearly meant "Shut up, Perez."

A few more of those at the meeting spoke, the last a woman who said, "George, it's good to have you here."

After a silence lay for a good minute, the chairman said, "So, okay, let's close with the Serenity Prayer."

All the circle save Perez mumbled together, *"God, grant me the serenity to accept the things I cannot change, the courage to change the things I can, and the wisdom to know the difference."*

*  *  *

The two men walked east on 92$^{nd}$ Street toward Park, now moonlit and as quiet as New York streets ever are. Perez would turn north to his walkup in East Harlem, Mullholland south to his apartment in the 80s.

At the corner, Perez broke the silence. "Where does that prayer come from, the one you said at the end?"

Mulholland happened to know the answer. "A minister wrote it. A theologian. Guy named Niebuhr. He taught at some school way uptown. You like it?"

"I did. But I think 'knowing the difference' can be pretty tough."

"Yes, it can, George. Yes, it can."

"You know, Holly, let's make it 'Jorge' from now on. I'm gonna go back to 'Jorge.' New me, new name. Actually, old name."

# Chapter Twenty-Nine

*Monday, April 8—The Twenty-Ninth Day in Lent*

Harriet van der Berg did not normally come into church on Mondays for her unpaid job. For that matter, Seth Ludington did not usually come in on Mondays for his paid job. But neither was surprised to find the other there on this Monday. He wanted to know what she knew. She wanted to know what he knew.

They had last discussed what van der Berg had taken to calling "our case" the previous Friday. They had talked but briefly on the phone Sunday afternoon when van der Berg named Jorge Perez as the sexton who had served Old Stone in the relevant time frame and agreed that the man would indeed have had access to the manse.

Van der Berg rose from her chair when Ludington arrived at her office and followed him into his study without being invited to do so. She sat herself in the chair opposite him across his expansive desk, her back straight, and said in a rising tone, "Well?"

"Several 'wells' to explore, Miss van der Berg. All deep. I phoned the Rachel Ruvenstein you found. She's *en route* to the Caribbean, but we have a meeting scheduled on the 15th when she gets back to New York. I confess to having represented myself as a potential real estate client."

"Good for you, Dominie. One must sometimes prevaricate in pursuit of truth."

"Proverbial ends justifying the means, I suppose. Wobbly ethical reasoning."

Leaning forward, van der Berg asked, "And Mildred Cunningham and her son? You visited her Saturday, did you not?

"One miserable woman. She said little beyond her litany of complaints. I suppose chronic complaining offers an illusion of power to someone like her, someone who feels they've been crushed by life. You judge everything negatively, you set yourself over it all. But I did manage to purloin a handkerchief from her, hopefully, sodden with her unhappy DNA. And I'm having lunch with Oscar Junior today. He was actually eager to meet. Curious. I'll see what there is to see and try to snag yet more Cunningham DNA, some related to Oscar Senior this time. Then both samples will be off to Harry ASAP. And speaking of Harry, God bless him... I gave him a call Saturday to see what he could find out about Oscar Senior's death. He called the Nassau County cops and begged an accident report. They sent it, and he read it to me. He guesses it could well have been a suicide. Lots of single-car accidents are, and this one looks like it might have been one of them."

"You have been busy, Dominie."

"Ah, Miss van der Berg, not even close to done. Last night Harry and I had dinner. The minute I said 'Perez' to him after church, he wanted to talk. Last night he told me that the Jorge Perez of 1970 was one loose cannon of a man, ethically speaking. He said that he and Perez became very good friends later, but it was obvious that Harry wouldn't put anything past the guy when he was younger."

Ludington had decided to keep AA and the alcoholism factor to himself.

"And Harry gave me some of Perez's papers, letters, and a diary that Jorge gave him right before he died. Fiona and I went through them last night. A cryptic entry in the diary points to a romantic relationship—perhaps one of many—with someone the diary names only as 'E.' And then there's a desperate adolescent love letter signed 'Eleanor.' It was obviously a relationship that the mature Jorge came to regret deeply."

"Ah, yes, 'Eleanor,'" said van der Berg. "Dominie, while you have been sleuthing, I have been both remembering and, would you believe, consulting my own diary. Did you know that I am a lifelong diarist? Well, since I was fourteen."

"Can't say that I'm surprised." Ludington knew that if van der Berg were anything, it was self-disciplined.

"Yesterday afternoon, after you inquired about Jorge Perez, I retrieved my diaries from 1969 and 1970. I found two most interesting entries. One mentions both Perez and an Eleanor."

Van der Berg said that she had recorded the events of the evening she and Margaret had found a weepy teenager named Eleanor Westerberg in the back pew of the sanctuary, reluctant to leave the church until there was no one to pass by in the lobby.

"And as I read my entry for that day, I vaguely recalled the event. One does remember moments in life that are heavy with passion. Emotion etches memory."

"Indeed, Miss van der Berg."

"And I kept reading. Reading one's own diary is a memory-quickening experience, Dominie, though sometimes I must say it is rather discomfiting. One does do and think some rather silly things, especially when younger. Anyway, you'll recall that I told you I was present at Oscar Cunningham's service. Not that I really knew the man; I went with my friend Sally at her insistence.

"Well, it seems I recorded an experience of that day, one equally laden with emotion, but this one anger, not fear. This is the other diary entry of interest that I discovered. Sally and I were present at the reception after the service. I told you I had attended the service. My diary noted that sharp words passed between Mildred and the receptionist from Oscar's firm. She was there, rather surprisingly. She approached Mildred toward the end of the reception and said something to her. I didn't record what; I'm not sure I even heard her words. But I did record Mildred's response in my diary. Excuse my directness, Dominie, but she called the girl, ahem, 'a dumb little bitch.' As I read the words in my diary, I think I remembered. I remembered that she spoke those words quite loudly, right in our Social Hall. I mean, I gasped. I recall gasping. One hardly forgets such words spoken in church."

"I can easily imagine the woman I met Saturday saying something like that."

"Dominie, my father used to say that alcohol and age make us more into the person we really are. He was a teetotaler. But he lived to ninety-three and did become increasingly contrary."

"I pray that age doesn't inevitably amplify our true natures, Miss van der Berg. We're in deep trouble if it does."

"Perhaps you are a Calvinist after all, Dominie."

Ludington answered with a grimace and said, "Back to the distraught Eleanor you and Margaret encountered in the sanctuary. Could your Eleanor be the only Eleanor I know of in this congregation—Eleanor Johnson? Don't know that I've met her, but she and her husband are pictured in the church directory. More to the point, could it be that she's the 'E' in Jorge Perez's diary and the 'Eleanor' who pledged him her love in a little note the man kept for twenty-five years?"

"Oh, that weepy young girl was indeed Eleanor Westerberg, now Eleanor Johnson. Eleanor is an uncommon name. I ran a computer check of our membership roll when I arrived this morning. She is Old Stone's sole Eleanor. And I do recall that Jorge was at the lobby desk that night and that she told us she was loath to leave until the coast was clear. I really don't know her. She is rarely in worship. The church roll lists a country home up in Millbrook. She and Henry—that's her husband—doubtless retreat there most every weekend. Those country homes are the devil's own tool. They still do pledge to Old Stone, however. I doubt she remembers me and Margaret as the two ladies who found her so despondent that evening in the sanctuary."

"Well, I'll call her. I'll ask her to meet. Another parishioner I'm eager to get to know better. And perhaps a bit of DNA might be at hand."

Van der Berg smiled broadly at that and rose from her chair. "I'll fetch her contact information for you directly."

She returned with no fewer than three phone numbers for Eleanor Johnson. One was a 212 area code number labeled "home." One was an 845 area code, doubtless the Millbrook place, and the last was a second 212 number noted as "work." No cell number on file.

Ludington thought to himself, "She's got to be late 60s and still working. Good for her." He dialed the 212 work number. A chipper voice answered, " Yorkville Women's Clinic, how may we help you?"

Ludington was jolted into a moment's silence. He was vaguely familiar with Yorkville Women's Clinic. It offered counseling to pregnant women, reproductive care, pregnancy tests, and of course, abortion services.

After his hesitation, he asked to speak to Eleanor Johnson. He was transferred, and she picked up and said in a soft voice, "This is Eleanor."

Ludington rehearsed his lines about being the newish minister eager to meet his flock. She confessed to being an absentee member, noting their weekend retreat outside the City, but said she would be pleased to meet the new pastor of her New York church.

"Tomorrow, perhaps," Ludington said. "I'm happy to come down to the clinic." He was Googling the agency as they spoke. Their offices were nearby.

Eleanor Johnson, nee Westerberg, agreed happily. "Ten o'clock okay for you, Rev. Ludington? I'd love to show you our offices and maybe talk to you about our work here."

# Chapter Thirty

*Monday, April 8—The Twenty-Ninth Day in Lent*

L e Grenouille had been on Seth and Fiona's list of must-visit restaurants since they'd moved to the City. It was French, multiple tiers above mere bistro, pricey and stubbornly snooty, staffed with waiters in suits and ties who could pass for bankers. Like most Midtown restaurants, it was stuffed with the business lunch crowd from noon to two-thirty.

He arrived at the restaurant at 12:15, a few minutes early. He had walked to the 86th Street Lexington Line station, taken a local 6 train to 51st, and walked the two blocks over and one back up to the restaurant. After a year in New York, Ludington was still learning the complexities of computing travel times around the City.

The sober *maître d'* greeted him just inside the door with a curt and vaguely pretentious *"bonjour, reservation?"* The second word could have been English or French.

"Under Cunningham, I believe."

"Ah, yes Monsieur Cunningham. He has not yet arrived. Follow me, please."

The man bowed slightly to Ludington, turned on his heels, and led him to what was surely a prime table in a quiet back corner of the restaurant. He pulled the chair out for his customer, took the folded linen napkin off the table, opened it with a snap, and handed it to Ludington after he had taken his seat.

"I am sure monsieur Cunningham will be here momentarily. He is always quite prompt. Can I get you anything to drink while you wait? Would you prefer tap or bottled water?"

Ludington said tap was fine and that he would wait to order anything more.

Oscar Cunningham arrived at exactly 12:30. He approached the table where Ludington sat waiting, hand extended, and asked, "Rev. Ludington?"

Ludington rose to take his hand, but before he could say anything, Cunningham continued, "It's such a pleasure to meet you. Thank you for coming all the way down here for lunch. I'm sorry I'm late."

Which he was not, of course. The man's mannerly deference surprised Ludington. Oscar Cunningham, Jr. was a distinguished-looking 60-something, approaching handsome, graying at the temples. He was dressed in a perfectly cut gray flannel suit, conservative, but set off with a jaunty blue Vineyard Vines tie bedecked with little lobster traps. Ludington felt underdressed in his blue blazer and knit tie. It was Monday, his day off, and he had chosen not to wear his clerical collar.

Cunningham began the conversation by asking how Ludington was settling into life in the City and how things were going at Old Stone. After Ludington answered with the predictable bromides about transitioning to life in New York, Cunningham inquired about family. Ludington told him about Fiona and her U.N. job that had led them to the City. He then edged into their recent purchase of the manse and the impending restoration project.

"They tell me at church that you and your family once lived in the house. That your family bequeathed it to Old Stone."

"My father bequeathed it, to be precise. I was a kid—fourteen—when my dad died."

The waiter arrived at this promising turn of the conversation and asked if the gentlemen were ready to order. Neither of them had looked at the menu. Ludington picked his up and began to scan it. It was in French, but blessedly with an English translation under each item. Without looking at his menu, Cunningham ordered in straight-up English, "The cheese soufflé with a frisee salad."

Which sounded perfect to Ludington, who said, "Exactly the same."

Cunningham smiled and said to Ludington, "And how about a glass of wine? I usually don't at lunch, but this is singular."

Ludington never drank at lunch either, save for Sundays after church, of course.

"Why not?" he said.

Cunningham consulted the encyclopedic wine list perched on the table and ordered. "Two glasses of the *Poully-Fuisse,* please, the *Les Brules,* 2014."

He looked back at Ludington as the waiter marched off and said, "The place is a little stuffy, but the food is to die for."

As their meals arrived, Ludington was jolted when Cunningham asked him if he might say grace. Prayers before restaurant meals were unheard of in New York, though if he and Fiona were feeling feisty, they would occasionally do so—just to be counter-cultural. He prayed briefly, thanking the Creator for the goodness of the earth without mentioning eggs or lettuce specifically, as well as new friendships, also in general, without mentioning himself or Cunningham.

Over very fine cheese soufflés and salads—the latter served second—they spoke of their jobs. Cunningham was a partner in a Midtown law firm specializing in international law, so he was eager to hear about Fiona's U.N. work as a human rights lawyer. He asked where Ludington was from and then inquired about Old Stone Church.

After Ludington spoke of his Michigan youth and outlined the diminished state of the Old Stone congregation, the scaffolded steeple, and the church's challenging finances, Cunningham said, "I was confirmed there when I was twelve. A couple years before Dad died."

"Tell me about your father."

Cunningham spun his wine glass at the stem between his thumb and index finger, quarter turns this way and then that. "He was a very complex man. I always understood that, even though I lost him when I was young. Two memories, especially, rise to the surface. First, he was a wonderful father to me. He had a big career, but he somehow managed to carve out time for his son. And he would do the things with me that I wanted to do, not what he wanted to do. Mostly then, it was baseball. He got me into one of the Central Park Little League teams. He never coached, but he was at every game I ever played. I was shortstop. Not a bad player. Dad was an embarrassingly loud and ardent parent in the stands. I loved it."

Cunningham smiled at this memory. "When I was about six or so, I morphed into a rabid Mets fan. They were not the right team in that neighborhood. In Yorkville, you're supposed to be a Yankees fan. Maybe my first push-back against convention. Anyway, Dad got us season tickets, and we schlepped out to Shea Stadium for most every home game. Until he died."

"What's the other memory?"

Cunningham took a sip of the *Poully-Fuisse*, leaned back in his chair, and said, "The horror that their marriage became. They fought all the time but seldom loudly, and they tried to keep it from me. They fought with lethal—usually silent—stealth, though Mother was not always so silent. Dad? He just disappeared, figuratively and finally literally. Their relationship became blue ice. No love, though there must have been at some point. I know he "wandered," as they say. I don't know if it was his wandering that so embittered her, or if it was her bitterness that led him to wander. 'Wandering'—such an exculpatory euphemism for philandering and what was doubtless legal harassment. I didn't quite understand all this then, but I came to later. After he died, Mother never stopped harping about what she called 'your father's whoring.' I think he was aching for some love. I know I'm tempted to excuse what was probably some pretty rank behavior toward young women, manipulative and exploitative. A son prone to let his late and lamented father off the moral hook. Whatever, even then, Mother was retreating into her carapace. It's like her suit of armor, lets nothing in or out. It became no love in, no love out."

"I visited her just the other day. Part of my get-to-know-the-church campaign. She does seem to be unhappy."

"I dread my visits. I go every other week. I have to steel myself to do it, but she has no one. She's pushed the world away. I try to love her, but honestly, Seth, it's mostly pity and duty that get me up there."

It was the first time Cunningham had addressed Ludington by his Christian name. He had said, "Please call me Oscar," as they finished their salads.

"I can only imagine how difficult it must be. You are a good son, Oscar."

"Not in Mother's opinion. It was the house that pushed her beyond the pale, though. Dad left her enough money to manage without working, but hardly sufficient to keep up that barn of a place. And he left a trust for my education. But the house went to the church. A last 'gotcha' at Mother? Guilt and a grand act of penance? Who knows. But Mother was furious, beyond furious."

"Your father's death must have been devastating. It was so sudden."

"I thought it was sudden then. But in retrospect, it really wasn't. He'd been dying inside for years. He was probably clinically depressed. I don't know. Not wise to psychoanalyze the dead. But I've come to believe that the accident was probably suicide. I mean, he'd drawn up the new will the week before. And I've seen the accident report."

Ludington said, "The funeral was at Old Stone?"

"Yes. The service itself is a total blur. I do remember the casket. Shiny wood and brass handles. I'd never seen a coffin before. It was closed, of course."

Ludington said nothing, hoping silence might coax more memory.

I do remember what happened afterward. It was unforgettable. Mother got into two fights. Verbal fisticuffs that were almost real fisticuffs. One was down in the Social Hall right after the service. My Aunt Mazie, Dad's sister, had come over to me. I was sitting in a corner, moping, I suppose. She had her arm around me. Then I heard Mother screaming. I looked up and saw her shaking her fist at this skinny girl in a mink coat."

"Your mother must have been terribly distraught."

"I suppose. But not so much about my father's death. More about the house. We went back there after the funeral, after the reception, only Mother and me. I went up to my room, but I hadn't been there long before I heard a

161

commotion downstairs. I went to the head of the staircase to see what was happening. A girl was at the front door, trying to wedge herself into the house. Mother was shrieking at her, yelling at the top of her lungs, pinning her between the door and the frame. I'll never forget her words. 'No chance, whore.'"

Ludington said, "The same girl, the one from the reception, I suppose."

"No. This one was a redhead, big girl. She was in a tent of a trench coat, of all things."

Ludington drank the last of his wine and pressed the subject of the two women whom Oscar remembered from that day, "Do you know who either of those women were? From his office, maybe?"

It was a strange and forward query for a minister "getting to know his congregation" to put to a parishioner he had just met. Cunningham-the-lawyer knew an off-topic and leading question when he heard it, but he answered anyway.

He wrinkled his brow and took a sip of his wine. "I've never told anybody this, but I know who both of them were, always have. One was Dad's admin, the other was the receptionist in his office. I have no idea about either of their names, but I had met them both. Dad had brought me to the office for one of those go-to-work-with-your-parent days, maybe a month before he died. The whole day was a drag. Dad was busy, and I spent the better part of it bored stiff, sitting outside his office with the big girl. I suppose she was his admin, 'secretary' in those days. The other one, the skinny one, brought me a Coke. You wouldn't remember such things normally, but you do remember your mother's outrage the day of your father's funeral. I put it together then, but never said anything—certainly not to Mother—not that she didn't know. Dad was doubtless romancing the both of them, at the same time or serially."

This piece of news fit in with Ludington's suspicions, of course. Oscar Cunningham may not know the name of his father's erstwhile admin, but Harriet van der Berg did.

Cunningham grimaced and said, "On to a happier topic. I said I was planning on calling you when you phoned. I want to ask if Old Stone would please send a letter of transfer for me to First Presbyterian down in the Village. We've been attending there for a few years, Andrew and I, and will be married there this June. We've been together for a decade, and now that it's legal in the state, we want to make it official. First Pres is just around the corner from us. And we have a lot of friends there. We plan to continue to support Old Stone financially. First Church as well, of course."

Ludington had neglected to even check on whether Oscar was still contributing to Old Stone.

"Congratulations, Oscar, and all the best to you both. The Letter of Transfer is no problem. I'll have my admin prepare it this afternoon. Session will act on it next meeting."

"Mother has already declared that she will not attend the wedding. I'd tell you to try to get her to change her mind, but it would be in vain."

Cunningham insisted on paying the bill and promised that he and Andrew might venture uptown and worship at Old Stone one day soon. They parted on the 52nd Street sidewalk, shaking hands, Seth offering more congratulations. Then he patted his blazer pocket and said, "I think I left my cell on the table."

As Cunningham turned the corner and headed down 5th, Ludington went back into Le Grenouille and to their table, which had not yet been cleared. He took Oscar's napkin and used it to pick up the small narrow water class he had drunk from, poured its remaining water into his own, and slipped Cunningham's into his jacket pocket. He felt more than a stab of remorse as he did so. He could not help but like and respect Oscar Cunningham, Junior. As he left the restaurant for the second time, he thought to himself, "Sometimes the apple falls very far from the tree."

He took the 6 train back to 86th Street and walked over to Harry's building. He buzzed his apartment, and Harry came right down, meeting his pastor on the street. Seth gave him the handkerchief he had purloined from Mildred as well as Oscar's water glass, both now safe from further contamination in plastic sandwich bags, those needful tools for DNA-snatching. One was labeled "MC," the other "OC." The first baggie he had given Harry, a week and an eternity ago, had been labeled "LO"—"little one." The one he had given him Sunday after church, holding an old black comb, had been labeled "MM," for Malcolm McCrae.

Seth Ludington had taken to carrying several plastic baggies wherever he went.

# Chapter Thirty-One

*Tuesday, April 9—The Thirtieth Day in Lent*

The offices of Yorkville Women's Clinic were on the third floor of a featureless 60s-era ten-story glass box on Second Avenue in the lower 70s, not far from New York Hospital and Sloan Kettering. There was no door staff. He pushed the button labeled "YWC—Suite 310" on the panel inside the first door. He assumed he was being viewed on a camera. The inside door buzzed to signal it had been unlocked. He yanked it open and took one of the two elevators to the third floor.

The lobby of Suite 310 was slick and modern. There were several black leather Wassily chairs and glass-topped side tables. The art on the walls was contemporary and remarkably fine. The paintings looked to be originals, not prints. The receptionist was a chipper woman whom Ludington guessed to be in her early thirties. She lifted her head and smiled as he approached her uncluttered desk.

She said, "Good morning," with a welcoming smile. She did not say, "Can I help you?" The answer to that question might trespass confidentiality. She simply smiled even more broadly.

"I have an appointment with Eleanor Johnson. At 10." It was 9:40. Ludington knew he was early.

"Of course. She looked at her desk phone, saw a red light, and said, "She's on a call, but I'm sure she'll be free in a bit. Have a seat." She did not ask him his name.

Ludington sat in one of the Wassily chairs, more comfortable than it looked. There were two other people waiting in the lobby, a couple, both young. They were unsmiling, looking intently at hands folded in their laps.

Ludington had spent an hour on the clinic's website the previous afternoon. It was, he judged, well done. Everything was carefully worded, even eloquent. The website said that clients could avail themselves of an in-office pregnancy test, could meet with a counselor, and could even utilize a "decision-making tool" should they choose." The site carefully outlined options available to a pregnant woman. She could choose to give birth and keep the child; the site offered links to local support groups for women electing this alternative. The woman could give birth and place the child for adoption. Yorkville Women's Clinic, the site noted, was not an adoption agency, but could refer women to reputable agencies should she make that choice. Or she might elect to terminate her pregnancy. Such procedures were available at the Yorkville Women's Clinic.

The site also included a note that abortion was legal in New York State—up to twenty-four weeks, nearly the end of the second trimester. That detail had led Ludington to do further internet research on the topic. Abortion had become legal in New York State in early April of 1970, three years before Roe v. Wade. New York was the first state to legalize the procedure. Of course, the infant in his ash pit could not have been legally aborted. It could have been aborted illegally, but such a thing would have been a horror. Tiny as it was, it was too mature, surely beyond six months.

Sitting in a women's clinic and ruminating about pregnancy and childbirth, he was startled by his cell vibrating insistently in his jacket pocket. He fished it out and saw that it was Oscar Cunningham. Ludington had added the name and number to his contact list a few days earlier. He signaled the receptionist that he had a call and stepped out of the waiting room into the hall.

"Oscar, hello."

"Seth, sorry to bother. Can you talk for a minute?"

"Of course, of course. I've got an appointment in ten minutes, but it's fine." This was not a call-back Ludington had expected.

"I enjoyed our lunch yesterday very much, really did. But I have to ask you something. It's a bit awkward, Seth, but I've been mulling it over and need to know. Why in the world are you interested in women with whom my late father may have had affairs? I've practiced law for nearly forty years, and I know when somebody is ploughing around for information."

Ludington was jolted. He started to perspire, something he often did when he was anxious. This was the first person he had visited in the course of his "getting-to-know-the-congregation" ruse who had seen through it. Oscar Cunningham was perceptive, too perceptive for him to deceive any further. But he could hardly tell him everything.

"Well, it's like this. There's a matter of historical concern at Old Stone that I'm checking through. It could involve your father. More specifically, relationships your father may have had before he gave the house to the church." "Historical concern" was a decidedly hazy euphemism for a dead child, Ludington thought as he said it. But it was the truth, though he had framed it in a way that suggested the "historical concern" had to do with his father's bequest of the manse.

Cunningham pressed the matter in that direction. "Is there some question about the will? Is there some other claimant out there? Some offspring of my father's. One of the women my father had relationships with may have had a child, a potential heir that might contest after all these years. Some receptionist or maybe Dad's admin—the big one? Maybe one of them had a child by my father? I mean, I saw her, the admin. She could have been not merely large, but pregnant. But this is so legally unlikely. I mean, this was fifty years ago. The will has been probated. The estate closed. It's a long-done deal, Seth. But if my father had a child by one of them, I want to know."

Ludington worked to wiggle his way out of saying any more than he had to. "Tell you what…my admin, Harriet van der Berg, has been around Old Stone since the flood. I think she was actually at your dad's service. I'll ask her if she might know names. She tends to keep track of these things." He said this knowing full well that van der Berg was at the service and not only knew who one of the women was, but still exchanged Christmas cards with her.

"Seth, is it possible that I have a brother or sister out there? I mean, a half-sibling? If I do, I want to know."

"I don't know." He said this knowing that the man's half-sibling might well rest in the ash pit of the house Oscar had grown up in. "I'll talk to Harriet van der Berg right away."

He was relieved when the receptionist poked her head through the door to the clinic and mouthed the words, "Your appointment."

Ludington told Cunningham that he had to run and promised to phone him back if and when he discovered anything. He went back into the waiting room and saw a woman whom he deduced to be Eleanor Johnson walking down the hall that led to the lobby. She was slender and handsome in a matronly way, her medium-length gray hair pulled back and held in place by one of those velvet headbands no longer fashionable anywhere but on the Upper East Side of Manhattan.

She approached Ludington, smiled, and greeted him with, "Good morning, Pastor." She did not extend her hand, explaining, "I've got a cold, a cold that you don't want to catch. Okay to talk in my office?"

"Of course, of course."

She turned, and he followed her down the hallway past half a dozen doors. A changeable slide-in-slid-out (slide-in-slide-out?) nameplate to the right side of her office door read "Eleanor Johnson."

The office was tiny—eight or nine feet square—and windowless. A computer monitor and keyboard sat atop a small desk, a rolling chair pushed up to it. Two more of the ubiquitous Wassily chairs were in the opposite corner at a right angle to each other. She sat in one of them rather than at her desk. Ludington lowered his lanky self into the other.

He pushed back the lock of dark errant hair, forever falling over his right eye, and said, "Thank you for your time, Mrs. Johnson. I do appreciate it. As I said on the phone, I'm trying to get to know my congregation a bit better. I won't be able to call on everybody, but you've been a member of Old Stone most of your life. Such deep roots."

"Baptized, confirmed, and married at the Old Stone Presbyterian Church," she said with a smile."

"So, you've seen a few ministers come and go over the years."

"Indeed. Mostly I remember Phil Desmond. He officiated at our wedding. We were in the City on weekends back then before we bought the Milford house. And I was active in high school, in the youth group. That would have been late 60s. I didn't go away to boarding school. I went to Spence—through my junior year anyway—so I was here in the City.

"You know that Fiona and I recently bought the manse from the church. We're about to embark on a restoration. It's a bit of a mess, I'm afraid. First thing I did was clean out that fireplace." Ludington paused and added, "Actually, the ash pit under it, down in the cellar. It hadn't been emptied in ages."

Changing the subject, Johnson said, "You don't see Henry and me very often these days, though. We have a country house upstate. We love the City, and we love getting out of it. I guess we love New York partly because we're lucky enough to be able to escape. We're up there almost every weekend."

Ludington said, "A lot of New Yorkers adore the City as they do, seem to relish the rhythm of being in it and out of it."

"We'll probably sell the apartment and move up to Milford when Henry retires. We do go to church there. Little Episcopal congregation. I still have an abiding affection for good ole Old Stone, though. Henry and I were so pleased when you accepted the call to come. We were at the welcome reception after you were voted in, not that any mortal could remember who all was there. Those things are always such a blur. Last time we were there, I have to confess. I recall meeting your wife. Delightful Scottish accent. Do you have children?"

"No, we don't." He almost added, "Not yet." But he bit his tongue before the words escaped. Eager to change the subject, or at least depersonalize it, he said, "Tell me about your job at the clinic."

"I love it. It's a pleasure to have a job that intersects with your personal convictions."

It seemed that they were going to talk about abortion and the labyrinthine questions that circled the topic. The setting rather suggested it. He found that he wanted to have the conversation with this woman, even though he barely knew her.

Ludington said, "I think that the whole subject has become as polarized as anything in our polarized world."

Johnson nodded at this and said, "Actually, the truth is that relatively few people who identify as pro-life would forbid abortion under any imaginable circumstance, say that of a very early pregnancy which clearly threatened the life of the mother. There are extreme voices that would, but they're the hard-core minority. Conversely, there are very few people who identify as pro-choice who would allow abortion in every imaginable circumstance, say a late-term healthy fetus that's no threat to the mother's health. Such terminations are extremely rare, but there are some voices who would permit them, but they're the rather doctrinaire few."

Ludington was listening closely as she continued. "My point was that the question is not simply dichotomous. The media loves sound bite either/or questions, and politicians do tend toward simplicities, so it gets framed that way. There's the first question—' where exactly on the continuum do you draw your line?'" And the second question, just as fraught—"'Do you have a right to draw the legal line in the same place you draw your own personal moral line?'"

Ludington offered no answer to her questions. Nor did he not note that they had once been personal questions for him, if not exactly for him, at least close to him. Not moral abstractions, to be sure.

"Well, Pastor, I must tell you that for me—and I think for most women—it's a radically personal question." As if she'd read his mind, she said, "It's not abstract, some mere theoretical. It's born out of personal experience. Like I said, that's a big part of the reason I work here."

She stood, stepped to her desk, pulled a tissue from a box, and blew her nose.

"Excuse me," she said as she dropped the spent tissue in the waste basket by her desk.

Ludington was jolted by her hints at intimacy implicit in her frank discussion of abortion. He was saved from having to respond when the phone on her desk broke the silence that lay in the wake of her candor. She stood, picked up the receiver, listened, and said, "I'll be right out."

"My 11:00 is here, a tad early. Seth—may I call you Seth?—please call me Eleanor. Thank you for coming to meet a wayward parishioner. Maybe you'll see us at Old Stone one of these days."

"I'll look forward to that, and to meeting your husband."

Ludington opened the office door for her. She turned down the hall to meet her 11:00 client. He half-closed the door, reached into his jacket pocket for one of his sandwich bags, and used it to retrieve the tissue that Eleanor Johnson had just tossed in the waste basket. He stuffed it into his pocket, feeling as uncomfortable doing so as he had the day before with Oscar Cunningham's water glass. He liked Eleanor Johnson, too.

On his walk back up Second Avenue, it occurred to Seth Ludington that he needed to do something he had not done, something he had, in fact, avoided for the past week-plus. He needed to measure the size of the opening in the floor of his fireplace. And he needed to try to measure the length of the skeleton that lay below it in its bed of ash. He had avoided considering the forensic details of the cremation that had almost surely occurred in his fireplace. How was it done? How did the bones come to fall eight feet below?

He went home rather than back to the church. Fiona was at work. He found a carpenter's measuring tape in the kitchen junk drawer and went to the living room. The fireplace was clean. He had not laid a fire since his discovery of the bones, and he had cleaned the fireplace after the last fire some weeks earlier, sweeping it into the ash pit, of course.

He lifted out the heavy cast iron log grate to expose the trap door that lay under it. It was hinged at the rear and opened up in such a way that it could be leaned open against the back wall of the fireplace. Ludington opened it. It screeched and exposed an opening that fell straight into the ash pit below. He measured the opening on the floor of the fireplace. Exactly two feet wide and 18 inches deep. A pyre of paper and wood, perhaps soaked with an accelerant of some sort, might have been laid under the little body with no grate underneath and the ash pit door open so that the post-fire remains, bone and perhaps some tissue, would not have to be retrieved, but could descend untouched and whole to their bed below. Any way he imagined the scene, it was revolting.

He closed the trap door on the floor of the living room fireplace and replaced the grate. He went down to the cellar to open the ash pit. It was the fourth time he had done so. The first was the day of his discovery. Then for Fiona, who insisted on seeing. Finally, to retrieve a bit of bone for Harry's lab guy.

But he needed to know precisely how long the little skeleton was. He steeled himself, opened the ash pit door, sighed at the sight, and then measured. The skeleton, largely but not perfectly intact, seemed to be well under 18 inches from head to foot, though it was hard to tell. He closed the door softly and went into the kitchen to replace the measuring tape. He took out his phone, sat at the table, and Googled "average length of newborns." All the sites agreed on twenty inches for boys, a bit less for girls. The lowest normal for full-term infants was 18.5 inches.

He called Harry and said he would be by in ten minutes. Yet again, Ludington met his Clerk of Session on the sidewalk and handed him a sandwich bag, this one holding a tissue and labeled "EJ."

As he did so, Ludington said, "Harry, Jorge's papers indicated a romantic involvement in the late '60s or early '70s with a woman—a young girl—named Eleanor. Seems it was probably Eleanor Westerberg, now Johnson. I just met her. She is an absolutely delightful woman."

Mulholland stood stock-still for a moment and finally answered, "Yes, she is. She truly is."

# Chapter Thirty-Two

*Tuesday and Wednesday, April 9 and 10—The Thirtieth and Thirty-First Days in Lent*

Ludington got back to the church at 1:00 that afternoon. He told van der Berg about Oscar Cunningham's alarming phone call and suggested that it was time for her to contact her old friend Sally Wilcox. Cunningham might soon be on her trail. He was suspicious, and the man had the resources and contacts to hire a private investigator. That could well open a very large can of worms. It would, Ludington said to van der Berg, be best for her to call Sally and dredge up history before Cunningham did.

As soon as he suggested it, she fished her cell out of her purse, found Sally's number, and punched it without asking a single question. "I understand the dilemma precisely."

Ludington listened to van der Berg's side of the conversation. She assumed an almost girlish tone as she offered her old friend updates on life since they had last spoken, which seemed to have been a decade ago. She then asked mirror-image questions of Sally and listened patiently to answers Ludington could barely hear. The conversation ended with a luncheon date set for the next day. Van der Berg was eager; Ludington assumed that Sally Wilcox led an unhurried life and could make a last-minute lunch date.

"Just like old times," van der Berg had said as they agreed on a downtown diner and ended the call.

"I'll find out what I can, Dominie."

Ludington spent most of the day trying to get a jump on the coming liturgical season—Palm and Passion Sunday, then Holy Week, and of course, Easter. As if you could get a jump on Easter. He was feeling more than a little guilty about how much time his sleuthing was consuming, time cribbed from his duties as a pastor and preacher. It was beginning to look as if the matter of the bones might well come to crisis during Holy Week. He was committed to knowing what he might know by Easter—nine days away—or give up his quest and report the bones to the authorities. The whole thing was unhappily timed in the extreme.

He was treading investigatory water for the day, doing his real job while waiting impatiently for Harry's call about potential matches between the DNA of the bones and that of the series of people who had access to the manse around the relevant period of time. He had passed to Harry to give to his lab guy the one profile he had been freely given, that of Dolores McCrae; the one DNA sample freely offered, that of her husband, the late Malcolm McCrae; and the three he had obtained by stealth, those of Mildred Cunningham, her son Oscar, and Eleanor Johnson. He would have to wait for Rachel Ruvenstein to return from St. Bart's. They would see each other Monday. And he had a plan for a second attempt to storm Philadelphia Theological Seminary in pursuit of a tad of Phil Desmond's elusive DNA.

\* \* \*

Wednesday morning, Ludington had taken a first crack at his looming Palm Sunday sermon. He outlined the short meditation he had been asked to offer at the ecumenical Good Friday service, this year to be held at Yorkville Methodist. It was a traditional "Seven Last Words" service. Assorted preachers from the neighborhood would each read one of the seven utterances the Gospels record Jesus speaking from the cross and then offer a short reflection. He guessed that the thin midday crowd attending the service hoped for brevity. He had been assigned "It is finished." Which it wasn't. Neither the meditation nor the matter of the little bones.

That afternoon, as he still pondered how he might say anything of substance at the Good Friday service in five minutes or less, van der Berg returned from her lunch with Sally Wilcox, exploding with a piece of news.

"Well, Domine, Sally was, in fact, pregnant at the funeral, pregnant by her boss, Oscar Cunningham, with whom she'd had a 'brief dalliance'—that was her term—the summer and fall prior. And she did, in fact, confront Mildred Cunningham at their home afterward, precisely as Oscar Jr. recalls. She was asking for financial assistance. You can imagine Mildred's response. And, Dominie, she did indeed have a child."

Van der Berg could tell a tale well and paused dramatically and triumphantly before she finished it.

"That child was a girl. She raised the child herself as a single mother. That child is now a fifty year old woman, happily married, her nest newly empty, in Summit, New Jersey. She has suggested that her mother move in with them. It seems they have a grand old house with a multitude of spare rooms. Sally plans to do so after Easter."

"Happy news, Miss van der Berg. Well done. This, of course, eliminates her from our pool of suspects, though not Oscar Sr. My hunch is that he enjoyed multiple 'brief dalliances.' There was that receptionist. I think we need to tell Oscar Jr. that he has a half-sister before he initiates his own investigation. He's both suspicious and curious."

"I thought to ask Sally if we might tell Oscar Jr. She was very reluctant, said she wanted to check with her daughter. I offered her the use of my phone right there at lunch to call the daughter. It seems the daughter had always known she was a 'love child.' Sally actually used that antique term. The daughter had always known her father had been married to someone else. She took the news with surprising equanimity. She told Sally that she had always rather hoped she had a sibling. In fact, Sally said she sounded pleased. It seems Sally had always been honest and told her that her father was her boss and that he had died in an automobile accident before her daughter was born. But Sally had never mentioned a half-brother. I rather think she had willfully forgotten that little fact. Anyway, I explained to her that if we didn't tell Oscar, he'd probably find out himself. Of course, I didn't mention your role in this."

Van der Berg gave him the name, address, and phone of the daughter in Summit. He would have to phone Oscar Jr. with the news and do it soon. He wondered whether Oscar Cunningham would be as pleased to hear the news of a hidden sibling as his half-sister had been.

# Chapter Thirty-Three

*Thursday, April 11—The Thirty-Second Day in Lent*

On his walk to the church the next morning, Ludington began to ruminate about his impending Easter sermon, a looming ten days away. He promptly put the thought aside. It felt presumptuous to plan the proclamation of the Resurrection before the fact, before even the Crucifixion. You were supposed to be surprised.

Adding to the pressures of the season was his decision to attend a Phil Desmond retirement event that evening in Philadelphia. He had gotten an invitation in the mail three days after his last visit. Moze Washington would be there, and he wanted another conversation with the man, a conversation about the Phil Desmond and Rachel Ruvenstein of fifty years ago. It was also a second chance to snag some Desmond DNA. He had booked a ticket on the 4:00 Acela.

But on this dark morning when he should have been scribbling sermon notes, he sat in Harriet van der Berg's little office holding the large Flat White he had picked up at Starbucks on the way to church. He had gotten her a small cold brew, no milk. They both understood that he was stalling before he went back to his Palm Sunday sermon, but there really were details to be reviewed.

"Here is how I understand matters, Dominie. We know that four clusters of persons had access to the manse and your fireplace in the time period in question."

Harriet van der Berg, Ludington reflected, was one of those people with a gift for consolidating complexities into their rationally conceivable constituent parts. Maybe they had taught her such skills at the Katherine Gibbs School, though he guessed this charism came naturally to the woman.

Setting down her coffee on her bare desk, she said, "Firstly, in chronological order, the Cunninghams. We know Oscar Senior to have been a philanderer, but we now know that Sally was not the mother of the bones. Her child is quite alive. But we can surmise that there were other affairs that may have resulted in an unwelcome birth, the receptionist in the mink, for instance. We can guess that Oscar Cunningham could have been under the kind of emotional pressure that might lead one to take one's own life. We know that Mildred was and is an embittered woman, perhaps psychologically unsound. What if her husband's illegitimate child were left on her doorstep? What might she have done? Horrific to consider. Or perhaps she was capable of making a lamentable decision should she have found herself with child."

"But Miss van der Berg, from your memory of her at the funeral, she was not pregnant, at least not very, when her husband died."

"Quite true, Dominie, but she might have been pregnant earlier, I mean much earlier."

Ludington nodded in agreement. "Unlikely, but it's conceivable that the child could have died years earlier. But that's only imaginable if no ashes were swept into the ash pit atop the bones from that time until the summer of 1970 when the *Life* Magazine and the copy of the *Times* were burned. We have DNA samples from both her and her son who carries some of his father's profile. They'll tell the story. And the story could be the root of Mildred's anger."

"Secondly," van der Berg said, "we have the McCraes. Dolores has volunteered her DNA profile, and we shall soon know if she's related to the bones, unlikely as it seems, given her willingness."

"And," Ludington said, "we have the comb of the late Malcolm McCrae."

"Precisely so, Dominie, but as I recall, the man, Malcolm McCrae, was a stiff and upright little gnome and one blessed with precious little hair to comb. I can guarantee that there were no whispers of clerical infidelities at the time, and there would have been whispers. And, of course, Dolores was right there in the manse all the while."

"Unlikely again," said Ludington.

"Thirdly, there is Jorge Perez and—extraordinary as it seems—Eleanor Westerberg. She was a mere child at the time, though it does appear she was hopelessly enamored of Jorge and felt herself to be in a crisis of some kind. He was just the kind who would turn a silly young girl's head. That eye patch, oh my. Such a fetching rascal."

"And fourthly," said Ludington, adding van der Berg's pretentious"-ly" to the ordinal number, "We have Phil Desmond. I failed to snag any of the president's DNA last week, but I'll see him tonight while he is wining and dining and depositing DNA about. I also have my appointment with Rachel Ruvenstein next Monday. She will, I hope, drink coffee, or perhaps tea. I'll do my best to see to it."

Harriet van der Berg reiterated her skepticism and then sang another refrain of praises to the Rev. Philip Desmond. Ludington took his coffee into his study to fortify himself for engagement with the unfinished Palm and Passion Sunday sermon waiting in his computer.

The Palm Sunday sermon was as finished as his sermons ever were by 3:00. He hailed a cab on Second Avenue and was at Penn Station in plenty of time to catch his 4:00 train. While on the train, in a nearly empty car, he made the phone call to Oscar Cunningham. He did not know whether the news he had would be welcome or unwelcome.

Ludington called the man's cell rather than his office number. "Oscar, I have some news. Well, it seems your suspicions have been borne out. My admin did recall the name of your father's secretary. In fact, they were—and are—acquainted. Your father was in a relationship with her, just as you guessed. And she was pregnant, and she did have a child. That child is now a grown woman. She lives in Summit, and Oscar…she knows about you. She's okay with it if you want to be in contact."

The line was silent for a good ten seconds. "Oscar, are you still there?" Reception on trains could be iffy.

"Yes, still here. At least, I think I'm still here. I guess I'm not exactly shocked by this news, Seth, but it's a bit of a jolt."

"I have her contact information, if you want it."

More silence, then, "Why not?"

\* \* \*

The Acela had him in Philadelphia by 5:15. He arrived at the Seminary in time for cocktails and hors d'oeuvres. This event, he knew, was Desmond's penultimate retirement fete, smaller and more exclusive than the everyone-invited bash scheduled for the day after commencement a month hence.

Ludington cruised the huge tent that had been set up on the seminary's grassy quad for the evening, a glass of surprisingly nice cabernet in hand. He knew a number of people there from his Philadelphia days. They asked polite and predictable questions about life in New York, his leap into parish ministry, and the lovely Fiona. Smiles, pats on the back, and good wishes, and he'd move on. Schmoozing, Ludington had come to understand, was a ministry skill they did not teach in seminary. You had to learn it on the job.

He caught a glimpse of Moze Washington chatting with a couple in a back corner of the tent. Ludington accepted a cucumber slice with goat cheese and a sprig of dill from a smiling server, just the kind of fussy canape that his parents always served at their cocktail parties. Thinking he'd much sooner have a pig-in-a-blanket, he headed toward Washington. Moze was solo by the time he reached him. Their greetings were perfunctory. They had seen each other only a few days earlier.

"Back in Philly for a bit more of your sleuthing, Seth?" The question was not asked teasingly, but with earnestness.

Ludington grimaced and raised his wine glass to tap the one Washington held.

"I found Rachel Ruvenstein. Seeing her Monday."

"And what exactly do you plan to say to the woman?"

"First, I'll ask her for a guestimate of my brownstone's market value. Then we'll see where it goes from there. Maybe some DNA."

Washington gave his head an incredulous shake followed by an eye-roll.

"Moze, it needs to be done. I need to know. The truth needs out. The bones cry for it."

"I suppose. What's the saying? Reconciliation follows truth."

"Moze, what else do you recall about the two of them that year? And what about the summer after Phil came to Old Stone? I just learned that he and Penny didn't get married till September. He was in the house alone for three months."

"I remember the wedding, Seth. I was his best man. Martha's Vineyard, right after Labor Day. Quintessentially Waspy affair. It was conspicuous, to say the least."

"Anything else you remember, Moze? Anything at all?"

Washington looked into his wine glass as though he were scanning tea leaves or entrails for a portent.

Finally, he spoke, "The last time I saw her, saw her and Phil together, was our last semester, winter or early spring probably. It was outside Stuart Hall—Old Ugly—at Princeton. He and I were coming down the steps after some class or another. Rachel was waiting for us, for Phil, to be precise. He peeled off to talk to her. I couldn't hear, but it was an animated, angry conversation. You know, arm-waving and finger-pointing on her part. He tried to hug her, but she pushed him away. She stomped off toward the train station to catch the Dinky to Princeton Junction, I'd guess. Then she turned back to Phil, pointed at him—like Prophet Nathan pointing at David after the Bathsheba business—and yelled the only word I heard—'hypocrite.'" You don't forget that word when it's spoken on a seminary campus."

"What did Phil say?"

"Nothing. He didn't want to talk about it, ever."

Washington and Ludington sat next to each other, just feet from the head table, for the dinner—airline chicken on a bed of kale—and the speeches, heartfelt and too long, that followed dessert.

Desmond was the last to speak. He began with thanks, of course. Thanks for all those in attendance, thanks for the opportunity to serve Philadelphia Theological Seminary for the last ten years, thanks for all the support offered him over those years. He thanked the trustees and the faculty, the staff, and the students. It was the predictable retirement speech.

Then Phil Desmond departed from the set liturgy. Ludington saw that he was not speaking from notes and had a sense that what followed was spontaneous—off-script, spirit-driven, heat-of-the-moment candor. He spoke slowly and deliberately, slurring a word every few sentences. Perhaps the wine, Ludington thought.

"You all understand that theological schools have to offer two kinds of education. On the one hand, we're professional schools, plain old trade schools, if you will. We teach women and men skills—how to do stuff. How to counsel the confused, how to write a sermon, how to conduct a funeral, how to officiate at a wedding, how to moderate a committee meeting, how to balance a budget. Seminary is training school. No getting away from it.

"On the other hand, we are an academic school. We teach the head. We push our students into the depths of theology—reasonable thought about God. We lead them into Biblical interpretation—how to carry ancient, sometimes inscrutable, texts across the chasm of time and figure out what they might mean for today. We push them into history, the history of the church especially, whether they want to go there or not. The past matters because it made us. We do all this at Philadelphia Theological because faith and reason are neither rivals nor foes. They complement each other, the one leading the other deeper into truth, elusive truth. So, seminary is also school for the mind. No getting away from it."

This academic dichotomy was more or less familiar to everyone under the tent. They would have guessed that Desmond would end it here, with two hands—this one and that one. He paused, drank first from his water glass, and then took a sip of wine.

He was not finished. "There is a third hand." He paused again, smiled, and said, "I know, the metaphor gets feeble at this point. Indulge me. On the third hand, seminary is school for the heart. I went to seminary fifty years ago for one reason and one reason alone. I was dodging the draft. I hated the war, and as much as the war, I hated the idea of getting killed in it. Not all of you remember the 4F deferment. If you were clergy or even studying to be a minister maybe, you got out of the draft during Viet Nam. When I went off to seminary, I'm not sure that I had a God bone in my body, at least not one I knew about. I'd put up with the church my parents dragged me to, and by my sophomore year in college, I had decided it was all BS. But I went to seminary just to avoid Viet Nam. It was either seminary or Canada. But here's the thing, once I was in seminary, I actually had to go to class to stay in seminary. If you never go to class, you do tend to flunk out."

There was a titter of laughter at this last, then the hush of hard listening. Desmond had his audience by the leash.

"An inch at a time, it changed me. Not only the wisdom—yes wisdom—I heard, but the love and the acceptance, the great grace of it all. I didn't go to seminary because I had faith. I found faith in seminary. What I encountered in seminary, the great story that is the Christian faith was—surprise, surprise—congruous with my experience of life. It suddenly all fit. It made sense of me and my life. My senior year, they held the draft lottery. Low number, you went to Nam unless you had a 4F or a doc who said you had flat feet. You drew a high number, and you were okay. No need for flat feet or seminary. That December, I drew 328. I was safe, but it never occurred to me to drop out. I was hooked. And here I am."

Desmond scanned the silent tent, chuckled to himself, and said, "God moves in mysterious ways her blunders to perform." Then he sat down.

The crowd that pressed congratulations on the man permitted neither Ludington nor Washington to get close to him. But Desmond had moved away from his seat at the head table. Ludington had watched him lick the fork he had used to finish off his carrot cake and observed him set it carefully atop the empty plate. He sidled over to Desmond's seat, pulled a sandwich baggie from his pocket, and used it to lift the dessert fork from the plate on which the president's carrot cake had sat. Again, Ludington grieved at having to do such a thing. He suddenly respected Philp Desmond even more than he had before this evening.

* * *

183

Halfway home that evening, just as the Acela slipped past Princeton Junction, Ludington's cell vibrated. He was half asleep, and it jolted him to awareness. As he dug the phone out of the chest pocket of his blazer, he hoped it was Fiona. It was Harry Mulholland.

"Seth, I know it's late, but I know you'd want to know right away. Lab got to me an hour ago. None of the samples you've snagged are a match for the bones, not Dolores McCrae's profile, either. No surprise there. Seth, I'm sorry about this. Dead end, I guess. Dead ends plural."

He thanked Harry and reached down to make sure Phil Desmond's desert fork was still in his pocket.

# Chapter Thirty-Four

*April 14—Palm and Passion Sunday*

Ludington had vacillated much of the week about what direction to carry the Palm and Passion Sunday sermon. As its name implies, the day itself vacillates. It shifts moods between the triumphant entry of Jesus and his rag-tag band of followers into Jerusalem five days before his crucifixion—the Palm part and then arching forward to the suffering and death later in the week—the Passion part.

Ludington had first thought to preach human changeability, positing the probability that some of those in the crowd who waved palms and sang happy "hosannas" on Palm Sunday as Jesus passed by were also in the crowd that cried out "crucify him" to Pontius Pilate a few days later. But he could not imagine how to make such a sermon edifying, much less pleasing to the congregation of Old Stone, clutching palm fronds they had been handed by the ushers upon their arrival. Mortal fickleness may be a reality, but would be a downer on Palm Sunday.

So, he had settled on preaching irony, yet again. Ludington had always thought that irony drove the whole of the Christian story, a conviction that was hardly his alone. So, he wrote a Palm and Passion Sunday sermon that began with the irony of Christmas—the long-awaited One born not to some Caesar, but to an unwed peasant girl, and born not in a palace, but a barn, and laid to sleep his first night, not in a regal cradle but a feeding trough. He moved on to the irony of Jesus's message—"blessed are the poor in spirit," "the first shall be last," "do not lay up for yourselves treasures on earth." Ludington winced as he typed that last line from the Sermon on the Mount, but included it anyway. He then noted the irony implicit in the stripe of the followers Jesus gathered around him—rustic fishermen, a tax collector of questionable reputation, and, most scandalously, women.

He peaked the sermon with the Palm Sunday parade, slathered in irony as it is. The Messiah's entrance into Jerusalem had long been imagined as a grand military procession, phalanxes of victorious troops led by the Chosen One mounted on a noble steed. Instead, he would preach, we get a rabble of Galilean peasants led by a Messiah perched on a borrowed donkey, sandals dragging in the dust. He pushed the sermon forward into the darkest irony of all—the coronation of Good Friday with its crown fashioned of thorns and cruciform throne. "This ironic faith of ours," Ludington concluded the sermon, "turned the world upside down. And you know what, from that perspective, it all starts to make some sense."

Chesterton had said something like that, he recalled, but he couldn't find the exact citation online, and his congregation would doubtless wonder why he would quote a mere writer of detective fiction in a sermon. Odd, Ludington thought, that G. K. Chesterton should come to be remembered as the author of the Father Brown mysteries, his quirky theological and sage political writing largely forgotten.

Come Sunday, Ludington preached the irony sermon, even though he knew the congregation had heard the likes of it several times before over his year-plus with them. The sanctuary was not full, but there was less unoccupied oak than on most Sundays, indeed, a number of unfamiliar faces were peppered among the pews. As he finished the sermon, one of those faces caught his eye. Cara Lundberg was sitting halfway back, alone at the center aisle end of a pew. She saw that he saw her and smiled up at him, but barely. She held his gaze till he turned away and descended the steps out of the pulpit.

She made sure that she was the last person in the greeting line after the service. Like most ministers, Ludington stood in the narthex after worship to shake hands and exchange pleasantries. Occasionally, sermon comments were tendered. Sometimes he picked up news about somebody in the hospital who needed a visit. He had seen Cara herself holding back, standing in the center of the sanctuary's center aisle and letting others pass so she might have a private word with the minister.

She looked him in the eyes and said, "I see you have an open announcement time in your church, after the sermon, and before the prayers. Anybody can stand up and talk about what's troubling them, what you should pray for." Ludington had inherited the practice from his predecessor. He disliked it. The same people stood up and talked—occasionally an uncomfortable length—about the same ailing great aunt week after week. He planned to end the practice as soon as he could get away with it.

She said, "I think I might make a little speech next Sunday. And bring the proof along, copies to pass out to the congregation." Then she handed him one of the little prayer cards she had taken from her pew. There was no prayer request, but a rather different kind of request. As Cara walked out the door and onto 82$^{nd}$ Street, he read what she had written in the card's blank space. "$5,000 a month, paid quarterly. See you next week—maybe or maybe not. Give me a call."

He ripped the card into small pieces and stuffed them in his front pocket. He thought to himself that this was a modest amount as extortion demands went. He wondered if she realized how easily he could afford it.

Shaken as he was, Seth made an obligatory pass through Coffee Hour in the Social Hall. He found Harry waiting for him near the tea end of the serving table. With nary a word, Ludington looked to see if anyone was watching as he discreetly passed Desmond"s carrot cake fork, swathed in its baggie, to the retired detective. Mulholland said only, "I'll tell him to hurry it."

Seth spied Fiona engaged in a conversation with a studiously tiresome occasional attendee who seemed to be an expert in all things. Ludington smiled at the expert, laid an arm around his wife's shoulder, and reminded her that they had a luncheon reservation at Lex in twenty minutes.

She rested her hand on the one of his draped over her shoulder and said, "Lovely, but let me finish hearing Dexter's thoughts on brownstone cladding repair." She was so good at this. He turned away and whispered, "That's one," just loudly enough for her to hear.

When he had phoned van der Berg the Saturday morning before—at 8:30 no less—to tell her about Mulholland's call and inform her that none of the DNA samples they had obtained so far, nor Dolores's volunteered profile, were a match to the bones in the ash pit, he had asked her to join Fiona and himself for lunch after church the next day. He could hear the disappointment—even alarm—at this news in her voice as she agreed to come. Not only had their efforts gotten them exactly nowhere, but the field of suspects had been narrowed to precisely where van der Berg did not want it to go. He had told her that he had snagged Phil Desmond's dessert fork and would give it to Harry in church the next day. She already knew he was slated to see Rachel Ruvenstein on Monday.

"Perhaps," she said before hanging up, "We should have let sleeping dogs lie."

Ludington knew that sleeping dogs could not always be left to lie, but said nothing to van der Berg except, "Lex at 1:00."

Nero greeted them as warmly as ever, said, "I save your table for you," and led them to the quiet banquette in the back corner of the narrow restaurant. They knew the menu well enough not to need to look at it. Fiona ordered the grilled salmon, Seth his regular chicken Milanese, and van der Berg nothing but a Caesar salad, no chicken or salmon. No wonder she was so rail thin.

"Wine?" Nero asked.

The three of them answered, "Yes," in immediate unison. It was that kind of a day.

When Nero had filled their glasses, van der Berg said, "You preached irony, Dominie. Indeed, irony seems to hang over us. I mean, all this effort, and nothing comes of it."

Ludington said, "Irony sees things as they are, but if irony goes to rot, it becomes cynicism."

All three of them knew that cynicism was a way of viewing the world that led to soul death. All three of them also knew that Desmond's DNA, and hopefully, Ruvenstein's as well, were to be checked for a match in the next days. Van der Berg did not want to speak of this, and Fiona thoughtfully said nothing about the obvious, so Seth recounted the details of the Philadelphia retirement dinner Friday evening. He told them of the jolting confession that Desmond had made in his after-dinner speech—coming to seminary faithless for no other reason than to dodge military service, and then finding both faith and vocation in spite of his initial motivation.

"Ironic it was," Ludington said, taking a sip of his cabernet, "but not at all cynical. When Desmond sat down, you could hear a pin drop in that tent. And then someone started to clap. In no time, he got a standing ovation. He deserved it. My regard for the man is deeper than it ever was. Such radical honesty is winning, especially when directed at one's self."

Fiona, twirling her glass of sauvignon blanc by its stem, said, "Yes, it is. But he kept that a very big secret to himself for a long time. Maybe there are others."

"Well," van der Berg sniffed, catching the implication of the observation, "There are secrets, and then there are secrets. I watched Philip Desmond as he served Old Stone for nearly two decades. In spite of where we stand in our unhappy investigation, I cannot believe that he would ever have had any connection whatsoever with your ash pit."

"Nor can I," Seth said. "Nor can I. But what else can we do?"

"Seven days, Seth," said Fiona, "Building inspectors seven days from today." He knew only too well that it was not only New York City building inspectors who had issued seven-day threats.

# Chapter Thirty-Five

*Monday, April 15—The Thirty-Fifth Day in Lent*

L udington drank three cups of coffee, one more than he usually allowed himself. He needed fortification for another round of clerical dissembling. He found some comfort in van der Berg's circular casuistry, her reassuring reasoning that "prevarication is sometimes necessary in the pursuit of truth." He had lied on the phone to Rachel Ruvenstein, whose typically Jewish last name could not but call to mind the bald clarity of the Ninth Commandment. He was now about to lie to her again.

She arrived at the manse at 10:00 sharp, knocking not on the lower landing door to the kitchen where he sat, but at the formal front door at the top of the brownstone's grand entrance stair. He dashed up the inside steps to the main level, unlatched the door, and greeted a svelte woman in a dark blue Chanel suit holding a tattered leather briefcase. Worn briefcases, he knew, were in vogue among New York executive types, much more so than slick new ones. Ludington guessed that they were prized because they suggested that their owners also had provenance.

"Ms. Ruvenstein?" he said with a rising inflection.

"The same," she answered.

"Come in, please."

She stepped into the entrance gallery, her realtor eye immediately scanning both that space and the expansive living room beyond. Ludington wondered if she had been in the house before—forty-nine years ago. If so, she betrayed no hint of familiarity.

Looking then to him, she said, "Rev. Ludington?" She moved the briefcase to her left hand and extended her right.

Her hand was small, lost in his, but her grasp firm, strategically professional, and accompanied by a quick shake.

Rachel Ruvenstein was of medium height and slim, her finely chiseled features freshly tanned in St. Bart's. Her riotous coal-black hair was worn long, parted in the middle, pulled back, and held more-or-less in place with a gold barrette. Ludington figured she had to be 72, but she looked a decade younger. He had no doubt that Rachel Ruvenstein would have been a stunning twenty-two-year-old.

She took charge, as Ludington guessed she generally did in life, walking past him into the living room.

"Gorgeous space," she said of that room. "It looks untouched, quite original."

"Oh, the house has been touched over the years, and not always kindly, but this room is much as it was in 1918."

"So," she said as she took a notebook out of her briefcase before setting the latter down on the floor, "Give me the tour."

Ludington squired her through all five floors of 338 East 84th Street, top to bottom, liberally pointing out each of the catalogue of shortcomings that D'Amato, his hired inspector, had discovered a mere 26 days earlier. Those 26 days seemed a lifetime.

"But she's got good bones," Ruvenstein countered. Like ships, Ludington thought, old houses often invite feminine pronouns.

They ended up in the cellar, where Ruvenstein made more extensive notes, suggesting politely that "the utilities need some updating." A gross understatement, but realtors know never to insult their clients' houses.

Ludington wandered casually over to the ash pit door. "This is an interesting little feature," he said. "It's an ash pit. There's an opening in the floor of the fireplace in the living room, so you can sweep the remains of fires down here instead of having to clean out the fireplace in the living room. I actually cleaned out the ash pit a few weeks ago." He waited for a reaction.

"Not an uncommon thing in townhouses of this era," Ruvenstein said. Then she asked, "By the way, does the fireplace work?"

"It does indeed. We use it often, and it was obviously well-used over the years." Ludington thought it time for some more aggressive fishing, if fishing were ever aggressive. "When I cleaned it out, I found more than ashes. I mean stuff that had been half incinerated in it over the years. I came across a *Life* magazine cover. It was from the summer of 1970."

Ruvenstein had turned her attention to the fuse box on the wall opposite the ash pit. "I don't know the last time I saw an actual fuse box. You have an unspoiled treasure in this place. So much potential." With that comment, she moved quickly toward the door that led from the cellar into the kitchen.

Ludington followed her, saying to her back, "I made a copy of the inspection report we had done. Would it be helpful?"

"It really would. Can we talk for a minute? I've got a question or two."

"How about I get us a cup of coffee? We can sit here in the kitchen. I'll fetch a copy of that report. It's upstairs in the living room."

"Would you mind grabbing my briefcase? I left it by those pocket doors between the living room and the gallery."

Pocket doors that, stuck in their pockets. [?], were all but invisible. She missed nothing. When Ludington returned with both the report and the briefcase, he found Ruvenstein tapping away at her smart phone.

"Just looking for some comps in the neighborhood. My office has a listing for a townhouse on 81$^{st}$, totally renovated, though. It's my listing. Reverend Ludington, how did you come to call me? I'm interested. I mean, my office is over in Carnegie Hill."

Ludington braced himself to tell a half-lie. "My admin found you. She did a little internet research and saw that you had that listing nearby. Thought you'd know the neighborhood."

He set the kettle to boil and took two cups from the cupboard. Ruvenstein had not responded to his question about coffee, but would hardly decline if he went to the trouble. He had more tales to tell about the erstwhile manse and more questions to ask Rachel Ruvenstein.

She said, "So, let's see if I have everything straight. You and your wife bought this place from your church, and you're planning to renovate and then perhaps sell. And you'd like an informal idea of what it might be worth. You understand I'm not a licensed appraiser, so any thoughts I'd offer are worth exactly what you're paying for them."

Which was nothing, Ludington thought to himself. This is one direct and to-the-point woman.

"Can I ask you how much you paid for the house?"

She was tactfully silent when Ludington told her, then said, "Renovated well, you will get at least that out of it, doubtless more."

Ludington sat down opposite her at the kitchen table and said, "Before we bought it, Old Stone Church had owned the house for 50 years. It was willed to the congregation back in 1969. Then a string of ministers lived here for half a century." He rattled off a few of the names of the more recent clergy to have lived in the manse, as if nostalgically, then said, "But the longest occupant was a guy named Desmond. Lived here for nearly twenty years in the '70s and '80s."

Ruvenstein looked Ludington square in the eyes and said nothing. Her eyes offered not a hint of recognition.

He pushed down the plunger on the coffee press and poured them each a cup. "Milk or sugar?" he asked.

She shook her head, whether in response to his question or to clear her thoughts, Ludington could not discern. Finally, she said, "No, black."

"Like I said, Phil Desmond was here in this house for nearly twenty years, from the early summer of 1970 to the late '80s. He was a Princeton Seminary grad, rambunctious character back then. Anti-war, I mean anti the Viet Nam War. May have even got himself arrested at the Democratic National Convention in the summer of '68, or so I heard. I know some of this because I used to work for his roommate. Anyway, Desmond flew straighter and higher later in life. Became something of a Presbyterian rock star. Ended up President of a seminary down in Philadelphia."

"Good for him." Ruvenstein looked at her over-sized boyfriend-style wristwatch and said, I really have to get moving." She slipped the notebook into her briefcase and said, "I'll get back to you in a few days with some numbers. Potential value will depend on how far you go with the renovations, so I'll have to give you quite a range. But I'm not sure I'm the person to handle the sale, if you decide to put it on the market. I mean, I focus on Carnegie Hill."

"Don't you have that listing down on 81st?"

"Well, yes, but Yorkville is really not in my wheelhouse. I could suggest another agent in our office."

He let her out the kitchen door, retrieved a large baggie from a kitchen drawer, and turned it inside out to pick up Ruvenstein's empty coffee cup. He would bring it to Harry later that morning.

As he closed the baggie, he thought to himself that this was the last of the string of DNA samples he would have to purloin. The field of suspects, a field that was bounded by a time frame of access to a fireplace 49 years ago, had narrowed itself to this most unlikely pair. But how completely impossible and consummately unhappy it seemed. Phil Desmond was so candid and credible and, well... impeccable. Rachel Ruvenstein had been utterly unfazed by the house. But then she was obviously a fine actress, stone-faced as she'd been at his mention of Phil Desmond, a man he knew she knew, even if it had been fifty years ago. Was she merely embarrassed to explore the memories of a college infatuation, or was there more to the lie of her silence?

# Chapter Thirty-Six

*Wednesday, April 17—The Thirty-Seventh Day of Lent*

"Dominie, you know that I am a woman of faith, but I fully credit the conclusions of science and, of course, reason. Indeed, it is because of my faith that I trust human reason and science. God, you understand, has created an orderly and predictable universe and endowed us with the wits to understand something of its workings."

Ludington knew that Harriet van der Berg's three-sentence incursion into the precincts of natural theology was occasioned by what he had just said to her as they sat across his desk from each other. It was late on the Wednesday afternoon of Holy Week, four days shy of their looming deadline. He had told her that he expected the results of the DNA samples he had filched from Rachel Ruvenstein and Philip Desmond—a coffee cup and a dessert fork, respectively. He had said he expected them today or tomorrow. Van der Berg was struggling to reconcile herself to what they might be about to learn. They had been pressed into this corner—discomforting for both of them—because all the previous samples had come back negative for a match to the bones. Van der Berg's vaunted reason and trusted science seemed to be pushing the conclusion of matters in a direction neither wanted it to go.

"I am no happier about this than you, Miss van der Berg. But who knows? It could be that we draw another pair of blanks and that all our assumptions about timing and the access to the manse and the fireplace—perfectly reasonable as they appear—are somehow mistaken."

Van der Berg sighed, shook her head, said, "I do hope so, Dominie. We seem to have opened Pandora's proverbial box," and retreated to her office.

Ludington rushed through his final work on the two little meditations he was slated to offer in the next days—one the next day, Maundy Thursday evening, at Old Stone, and the other at Good Friday's ecumenical Seven Last Words service. His Easter sermon was still no more than scattered thoughts. He hoped to return to it Friday afternoon, incongruous as it seemed to contemplate Easter on Good Friday. He had to attend to his real job, though his thoughts were more focused on finding answers that seemed just beyond reach.

It was time to go home to Fiona, but he decided to check his email first. He was a compulsive email checker—hourly on either his phone or laptop if he could get away with it. He recalled a retired pastor once telling him that in his forty years as a minister, nothing had changed his work like the advent of email. "For better and for worse," he had added. This was probably true for the work of many people other than clergy.

Ludington brought up the email page on his laptop and saw that there was nothing fresh in his Gmail inbox. Old Stone was too small an operation to afford its own server. Its several employees—himself and the part-time musician and sexton—all relied on personal email accounts. Van der Berg had set up a second personal account for herself for church-related emails.

He was about to close his laptop and head home when he noticed that there were a pair of inbox emails indicated in his iCloud account. That account was a mystery to him. He did not recall ever setting it up, nor did he give the address to anyone, nor—to his knowledge—did he send emails from it. Yet the occasional random email landed there anyway. This happened so seldom that he almost never thought to check. Ludington chalked it up to the fickle gods of the internet.

He opened the iCloud account and discovered a two-email chain on which he had been cc'd. He went to the earlier of the two and found an email dated April 2. It was from Harry to a recipient noted only as "Lou" at an NYPD email server address. Attached to that email from Harry was the Ancestry.com profile of Dolores McCrae. This was the profile that van der

Berg had forwarded to Mulholland to get to his guy—obviously "Lou"—at the NYPD forensics lab. The text of Harry's email read merely, *"DNA profile I called you about attached."* Deliberately or otherwise, Harry had copied Seth on that first email. It had landed unaccountably in his iCloud inbox two weeks earlier.

The second email was dated ten days later, April twelfth. It was from "Lou" at the NYPD server, sent to Harry's address, but again Ludington had been copied. "Lou" must have hit "reply all." It was brief. *"All later samples submitted, as well as that profile, negative. None match the first one you gave me."* The "first one" would have been from the bones. This was the news that Mulholland had communicated to Ludington in the phone call he received on the train coming back from Desmond's retirement fete in Philadelphia. "Lou" then specified the details of this disappointing news in a column listing each of the DNA samples Ludington had given to Mulholland to pass on. Each was noted by the initials he had written on its baggie when he gave it to Harry:

"Ancestry.com profile—negative." That was, of course, Dolores McCrae's.

"MC—negative." That would be Mildred Cunningham's handkerchief.

"MM—negative." That would be Malcolm McCrae's comb that his widow had volunteered.

"OC—negative." That would be Oscar Cunningham Jr.'s water glass.

Naturally, results from Desmond and Ruvenstein were not noted in this email. Harry had not passed them to this Lou until later that week, days after Lou had sent this message. Desmond and Ruvenstein were doubtless still being analyzed.

But it suddenly occurred to Ludington that something was missing. He had given Harry the tissue he snagged from Eleanor Johnson's wastebasket on April 9th. It should have been analyzed by the time his lab guy sent this email late on the 12th.

Without thinking it through, Ludington replied to the latter email with a short query, *"What about the sample labeled EJ?"* Again, and still without thinking it through (so often the sin that bedevils email), he hit "reply all." His question would go to both "Lou" at the lab and to Mulholland. It occurred to him that this might have been a mistake. "Reply all" can be a perilous click.

He got up and poked his head into van der Berg's office to see if she was still there. She was. He sat himself on her spare chair as she said, "About to head home, Dominie?"

"In a minute." He told her about the emails he had come upon in his iCloud inbox and the curious fact that there was no mention of a DNA sample from Eleanor Johnson.

"No EJ," he said. "Simply not there. I mean, Harry would have certainly given him Eleanor's by then. And even if the lab guy had not yet done the analysis on hers yet, he could hardly have said, *'All samples submitted are negative.'*"

Van der Berg, her steely mind driven by the logic of the matter, laid out the painfully obvious conclusion. "Harry may have not submitted Eleanor Johnson's DNA sample for some reason. You must consider that he could be protecting her, or perhaps guarding the memory of George Perez. You know how very close they were to one another. I must say that I utterly despise the very thought of this, as I do that of any connection of this matter to Philip Desmond. But we must go where reason leads us, Dominie."

Ludington returned to his study, sat in his chair, sighed deeply, and phoned Harry Mulholland's cell. No answer. He left a message, "Harry, it's Seth. Call me ASAP." Unlike Mulholland, he did not make the four letters a word. Then he dialed the Mulhollands' landline. Georgia picked up on the first ring.

"Seth, glad you called."

"Georgia, is Harry there?"

"He's not here, pastor. The oddest thing happened about twenty minutes ago. Harry was on the computer, and all of the sudden, he yelled out, 'Oh crap.' You know him, Seth. He never uses scatological language. Then he grabbed a jacket and stomped out of the apartment. I asked him where he was off to, but he didn't say a thing."

Ludington said, "Have him give me a buzz when he gets back."

He went home and sat restlessly with Fiona before their cold fireplace, each with a glass of wine they barely touched. He told her the whole story. He said that he was worried about Harry. But worry was only the half of it. Seth was forced to wonder if Harry was somehow involved with the bones himself. But how? And if he was, why did he encourage Seth to get answers? Was it so he could control the investigation? And keep himself out of trouble? Ludington was beginning to suspect that he might have been used, manipulated, in this whole investigatory foray into DNA snatching. Even worse, Ludington feared that he may have been betrayed by a man he loved and respected. His worry was soaked in anger.

He called the Mulhollands' landline again and asked Georgia to let him know when Harry got in. Ludington could tell that the woman was distraught. Sitting with Fiona and fidgeting with his phone, he dialed Harry's cell every 20 minutes. He stopped leaving messages after the third call.

At 9:30, Fiona said, "This is pretty worrisome, Seth. I'm going to go sit with Georgia. She must be sick with fear, there in that apartment all alone."

"And I'm going to look for Harry," he answered.

Assuming the worst, namely that Mulholland had, in fact, deceived him and had not passed on Eleanor Johnson's DNA sample to the lab, and assuming that there was an old and dark reason for not doing so, and assuming that Harry had realized he had been found out, Ludington went to the one place he feared Harry might return to in a crisis.

Ryan's Daughter was on 85th between First and Second. When Harry had told him about his addiction and recovery, he had mentioned that the bar had been his veritable second home for years. Ludington reasoned that if the man were to have a late-in-recovery slip, Ryan's Daughter was where he would likely fall.

It was an unpretentious place, unapologetically Irish, small, dark, and almost intimate. Guinness on tap, of course, as many free potato chips as you could manage, no kitchen. Ludington had walked by it any number of times, but had never been inside.

The place was quiet on a Wednesday night, but not empty. He went to the bar and was approached by the single bartender on duty. "What can I do for you, Father?" Ludington suddenly remembered he had his clerical collar on.

"I'm looking for a friend. Late 60s, medium height, natty dresser. Tweed sport coat, probably in a necktie Would have been alone."

"You mean Holly Mulholland?  Hadn't seen the guy in an age, but I remembered him.  Came in late this afternoon, ordered a Guinness, sat, and stared into it for an hour. Then he paid up and left. Never touched his beer."

"He didn't say where he was going, by any chance?"

"Never said a word, except for 'Guinness.'"

# Chapter Thirty-Seven

*Wednesday April 17—The Thirty-Seventh Day in Lent*

Ludington walked the neighborhood for four hours following his visit to Ryan's Daughter. He poked his head into a blur of First and Second Avenue watering holes, most of them now packed and noisy. No Harry Mulholland on the streets of Yorkville or in any of its remarkable assortment of taverns.

He phoned the Mulhollands' apartment again at about 11:00. Fiona picked up.

"Harry's not here," she said without his asking. "Seth, I gave Georgia an Advil PM and ordered her to bed. I think she's asleep, finally. She was in a state. When do you file a missing person report in this country?"

"Not sure, but I think they usually want you to wait a day." He then told her about Harry's visit to Ryan's Daughter and his own walking tour of the neighborhood.

"So, he didn't drink? That's so good. But Seth, where can he be?"

"I have one more thought, my dear. Let me check, then we call the precinct and file a report. Either way, I'll call you back in a bit."

Ludington unlocked the Parish House door of Old Stone Church and dashed to the security system panel ten feet inside the building to turn off the alarm. It had to be done within sixty seconds of unlocking the door. He discovered that the system had already been disarmed. He distinctly remembered setting it when he had left to go home late that afternoon.

Several people had keys to the church and knew the alarm code—van der Berg, the organist, the sexton, and the clerk of Session. He turned to the left, toward the sanctuary. One of the pair of heavy oak doors from the lobby hallway was cracked open. The sanctuary lights were off. He decided not to turn them on.

Ludington entered quietly and went to the front of the room, all the way to the foot of the chancel steps. He then walked down the center aisle toward the rear of the sanctuary. It was dark, but there was barely enough light finding its way through the stained glass from the streetlights on 82$^{nd}$ for him to see.

Harry Mulholland was sitting in the last pew, hard against the center aisle. He was staring ahead, dressed in his predicable Harris tweed jacket. Unpredictably, he had taken off his necktie and draped it around his neck. He did not look up at Ludington, but moved in a few feet to give his pastor a place to sit next to him.

"You found me, Sherlock," he said, still staring straight ahead.

Ludington sat down next to his Clerk of Session and said, "First thing we do is phone Georgia. She's worried sick. You want to do it, or do you want me to?"

"Would you do it?"

Ludington dialed Fiona's cell. She picked up immediately. "Fiona, I'm with Harry. He's okay. He'll be home soon. Tell Georgia he's fine, that we just need to talk, Harry and me."

She asked no questions, guessing that Harry was listening. As Ludington slipped the phone into his blazer pocket, Harry reached into his jacket. He withdrew a plastic baggie containing a tissue, and holding it between his index and middle finger, offered it to Ludington, again without looking at him.

He said nothing except, "Damn email."

Ludington did not take it, but said, "Let's talk first."

Mulholland said, "I've been sitting here for five hours. Thinking mostly, praying some. I've decided you need to know. I mean, the whole story."

Ludington said nothing. People were more likely to talk into silence, just to fill its emptiness.

"I told you about Jorge. His drinking and the drugs. Me helping him get clean. Made myself quite the hero."

Mulholland looked at Ludington for the first time and shook his head, almost imperceptibly, a movement he punctuated with the barest guffaw that mocked his virtue.

"Back then—I was in high school, he was working for the church—we were drinking buddies and drug buddies. Grass mostly, sometimes more. He was also my dealer, everybody's dealer. And he had a key to the manse. We'd hang out there sometimes—that spring after the family that gave it to the church moved out and before the McCraes moved in, and then later in the summer when they were away on vacation. Shared a six-pack or two and more than a couple of joints. I think we may have shared more than beer and grass."

Ludington remained silent and nodded his head ever so slightly, just as he had been taught in a counseling class in seminary. "Listen way more than you talk," the professor had said.

Jorge and me...and Eleanor Westerberg, we were a trio. Called ourselves the 'unholy trinity.' Not sure who came up with that. I pray it wasn't me. We messed around a lot when we were drinking and doing drugs. Know what I mean by messing around? She and I, we slept together a bunch of times. I was young and horny and dumb and high. No excuse. I'm pretty sure she slept with Jorge too. It was the wake of the summer of love. No excuse, but it was in the air."

"Then, after that junior year, come the fall of our senior year, she was simply gone. Didn't come back to Spence. I bumped into her father on the street one morning that winter and asked where she was. He said something like, 'You got a lot of nerve, Mulholland. Stay away from her.' Then he turned on his heels and walked off. I was dumb, but not that dumb. I figured she might have gotten pregnant. When girls did back then, they tended to disappear. I think Jorge could have been the father. I know I could have been the father. A year later, she went off to college, or so I heard. When I dried out and started back at Old Stone, I saw her a couple of times, married with little kids. I said nothing. She said nothing. We just looked past each other. Point is this, Seth, there's a chance those bones in your ash pit could be my child. Or Jorge Perez's. I swear I know nothing about what happened in your fireplace or how they got there, but I know it's possible. I've known it was possible since you first told me three weeks ago."

Ludington looked toward the chancel at the front of the sanctuary. He could make out the cross, but barely. He felt sorrow and pity, generously seasoned with hot fury.

All through his confession, Mullholland had been holding the baggie that contained Eleanor Johnson's snotty tissue. He again moved to pass it to his pastor. This time Ludington took it.

"So, here's what we do, Seth. Tomorrow we go visit my buddy Lou in person. You know who Lou is. You give him this, and I spit into one of his little sample tubes. I've decided I gotta know. I know you have to know. And the bones need to know."

"Yes," Ludington thought to himself, "the Little One needs to know."

# Chapter Thirty-Eight

*April 18—Maundy Thursday*

Ludington pulled up to Harry Mulholland's building on East 84th Street at 8:30 sharp the next morning. He had walked Harry home just before midnight the evening before and then waited in the lobby for Fiona to come down. He hadn't had to wait long. Fiona had left the apartment as Harry walked in the door, not wanting to be witness to whatever conversation was about to unfold between errant husband and worried—now livid—wife, wide awake in spite of Advil PM.

Mulholland had to yank twice to open the old Volvo's stubborn passenger door. He did not comment on the vehicle, a signal of how distracted he was by the errand they were on. People almost always had something to say about Ludington's car when they first met it.

Mulholland said, "The lab's in Queens, Jamaica. I'll give you directions. Actually, Lou's going to meet us at a breakfast joint down the block. I called his cell this morning to tell him we had a couple more samples for him. If it's only me visiting, he's been fine with meeting in the building. The two of us might raise questions. I got a hunch he's reaching the end of his rope with this, Seth. He pushed back on this visit."

"What have you been telling him, Harry? Did you have some kind of a story? I mean, when you gave him the bone fragment and then my parade of what were obviously involuntarily submitted DNA samples?"

"Well, I powdered the little bit of bone you gave me from the ash pit.

205

Tapped it with a hammer right in the envelope, you know, to disguise what it was. Lou could maybe guess, or test it for tissue type, but I told him that it was just matches we'd be after. I said I was working on a "paternity matter for a client." Close to the truth. A lot of retired cops do private work."

Ludington let the two implications of Mulholland's misdirection and their impending visit with Lou sink in. The first was the suggestion that his presence in the company of Harry would surely make. Lou would doubtless assume that he—the Rev. Seth Ludington—was "the client" and thus either the *"pater"* in Mulholland's paternity case or, as was more likely, that he was not the *"pater"* and suspected somebody else was. Ludington was relieved that he had chosen not to wear his clerical collar on this Maundy Thursday foray into deepest Queens. His second concern was over what this Lou would think when his old buddy Harry Mulholland offered to submit his own DNA sample for testing.

That later worry was allayed when, half-way through their trip as they were crossing the Queensboro Bridge, recently dubbed the "Ed Koch Queensboro Bridge." Ed Koch had been a remarkable mayor, Ludington mused distractedly, but the bridge's new name was laden with far too may syllables. When traffic slowed to a stop as they worked their way onto the bridge, Ludington saw that Mulholland had placed an open plastic bag in his lap and was carefully clipping his fingernails and letting the trimmings fall into the open bag.

Seeing that Ludington was eyeing this operation, Mulholland said, "Decided I didn't want to spit into one of Lou's tubes right in front of him. That would really wave a red flag. You can label this sample whatever you want. Anything but 'HM.' You know, but he doesn't need to."

He handed the baggie of nail clippings to Ludington who managed to slip it into his jacket pocket to join the other, the one Mulholland had given him the night before containing Eleanor's Kleenex. Every member of the "unholy trinity" was now in his blazer pocket, except for the late Jorge Perez.

Ludington dropped Mulholland off at the diner Lou had suggested and went in search of a parking spot. He ended up in a structure and got to the restaurant to find Harry and Lou sitting across from each other in a back booth engaged in what appeared an uneasy conversation for two men who were supposed to be old buddies. Ludington sat down next to Mulholland, who introduced him to Lou as "my friend Lud." He had been called that in junior high school and despised it. No other explanation for his presence was offered. Ludington surmised that none was needed; he was obviously "the client." With Ludington present, the mood in the booth cooled even more.

Mulholland offered no last name for Lou. Lou, Ludington noticed, had pocketed the security badge he normally wore around his neck. Ludington could see the red lanyard emerging from his shirt pocket and still draped about his neck. Lou looked to be mid-fifties, skinny with gray hair in a buzz cut, dressed in a lab coat. The guy radiated techno geek. Ludington was surprised he didn't sport a pocket protector.

Mulholland said, "We have two more samples for you, Lou. Last two, I promise." He looked at Ludington, who reached into his jacket pocket and retrieved the two baggies. "We're in a big hurry, Lou. Trial is Monday, so we gotta know—like tomorrow. Sorry."

"The trial," Ludington knew, was not a paternity case or a nasty divorce, but the advent of a crew of DOB inspectors at 338 East 84th Street at 9:00 AM the day after Easter, an event that would doubtless be a trial of sorts. Ludington imagined that Mulholland had often had to tell strategic lies as an NYPD detective. He seemed to have groomed a talent for it.

Lou was radiating skepticism. He looked down at his coffee mug and then launched into an exposition of the complexities of DNA analysis, a lecture that sounded like he was dodging the real issue: "You got your Y-DNA analysis, and your mitochondrial, and then your autosomal. I'm doing autosomal for you, of course."

Then he went straight to the point, in a whisper, "This is one very odd paternity case you got yourself into, Harry. Some of the samples are *mater,* not *pater,* female, you know. That's strange, very strange, for a paternity case, isn't it, Harry? And I'm guessing that the first sample you sent me, the alpha sample, was powdered bone. Bone, Harry, bone. Bone suggests somebody's dead. Really odd paternity case."

He sucked air in through his teeth, looked away, then back at Mulholland. He was still whispering. "This looks deep, Harry, way deeper than I want to go. Harry, I always thought you were a straight cop, but this is it. I'm out." He pushed the two baggies Seth had set on the table back across the Formica to Ludington. "No more. But I will tell you that those last two samples you brought in, they were both negative for a match."

He pulled a tattered notebook out of his jacket pocket and opened it. "The two samples that were marked 'PD' and 'RR,' neither of them was a match to that first one."

The news of these two non-matches jolted both Ludington and Mulholland, especially the latter. Desmond and Ruvenstein were unrelated to the bones. The field of suspects they had assembled, defined as they were by time and access to the manse, had just been narrowed—or so it seemed—to the ""unholy trinity,"" one member of which was the Clerk of Session of the Old Stone church, presently seated next to its pastor. Both men successfully covered their alarm at the implication of Lou's latest back-door analysis. Both men clearly understood what this seemed to mean; neither said anything.

"Lou, can you at least give us the profile of that first sample, the one we're trying to match?"

"You mean the powdered bone, Harry?"

Lou slid out of the booth, stood, and pulled his ID out of his pocket and let it drop around his neck. He began to walk away, but after two steps turned and said, "Tell you what, I'll give it to you on a thumb drive. No more email. It's too risky. I guess I owe you something after all these years. And I do want to trust you, Harry, I really do. Pull up on the corner of Jamaica and One-Fifty in twenty minutes."

\* \* \*

Double-parked at that corner, Ludington watched in his rearview mirror as Lou walked fast down Jamaica Avenue. He saw him look over his shoulder not once, but twice. Harry cranked the Volvo's passenger window open as the man approached. Without a word, Lou gave him a legal-sized envelope with a small lump the size of a thumb drive. The exchange felt like a drug deal, not that Ludington had ever been party to one. Mulholland passed the envelope to Ludington without looking at it. As Ludington slipped it into his jacket pocket, he noticed the word "GEDmatch" scrawled on the front of the envelope.

There was nothing to say on the drive home to Manhattan. In the cold silence that sat between them as they passed through the grimier regions of Queens, Seth Ludington's memory was suddenly jogged by the word "GEDmatch" scratched on the envelope in his pocket. He had heard it somewhere before. His mind slowly wended its way back to his conversation with Huw and Gina Griffiths the day before he had baptized their adopted daughter. Huw had said that closed adoption didn't quite mean what it once had. There were now ways that an adoptee might ferret out birth parents, even ones who wished to remain sealed and unknown. What had Huw said? Ludington recalled the gist of it. *"There are these open-access DNA websites that adoptees can go to and find any biological relatives that might be out there, people who have uploaded their own DNA profiles. First one was an outfit called GEDmatch. You may not find your biological parents, but odds are decent that you'll find some random third or fourth cousin. Then some online genealogy, and you just may be able to find what the State of New York won't tell you."*

Ludington dropped Mulholland off at his apartment with a curt farewell, returned the car to the garage, and walked the ten blocks to Old Stone, arriving just before 11:00. As he stepped into van der Berg's office, she looked up and said, "Dominie, Ginny Grimes is back in the hospital. Her husband called. She had another one of those mini strokes. She's up at Mt. Sinai."

If Howard Grimes phoned the church with this news, it meant that Ginny—and Howard—wished a pastoral call. Ginny Grimes, in her mid-'70s, was a member of the Session and as hard-working and supportive an Old Stone member as imaginable. A visit to Mt. Sinai was clearly called for, and it would need to be made that afternoon.

Ludington sat down in van der Berg's spare chair. "This is her third one, isn't it? I'll run up there in a minute. Miss van der Berg, I do have some happy news—at least it's news I believe you'll find happy."

Ludington told her that neither Philip Desmond's nor Rachel Ruvenstein's DNA samples had proved a match to the bones. Van der Berg managed to say nothing, but the look on her face fairly broadcast, "What did I tell you?" Ludington then rehearsed the obvious, that their search was narrowed to the unlikely Eleanor Johnson and, presumably, Jorge Perez. Ludington planned to say nothing to her about Harry Mulholland—not last Wednesday evening, not his confession in the Old Stone sanctuary, not the clipping of his fingernails in the passenger seat of the Volvo, not the lab guy's refusal to do any more DNA analysis.

Ludington retreated to his study and called Huw Griffiths' cell. He picked up on the second ring. "Huw, I've got a pastoral issue you can maybe help me with. When we met that Saturday before Sophia's baptism, you said something about how adoptees, I mean ones from closed adoptions, might find their birth parents without having to unseal a birth certificate."

Ludington knew he was prevaricating with a good friend, giving him the impression that his "pastoral issue" involved an adoptee searching for his or her birth mother or father.

"I remember that you said something about websites they could maybe use to find relatives."

Huw, the consummate tech nerd, was more than willing to help with a pastoral issue involving adoption and the internet. "Like I said, there are these open access sites out there that adoptees might use to find biological family. Commercial ones, of course. But the pioneer was the one called GEDmatch. Couple of guys in Florida started it about ten years ago. They've been gathering profiles from people who've done Ancestry.com or 23andMe, or any one of the outfits that do your ancestry for you with a DNA sample that you send in. Usually, you automatically give permission for your profile to go public unless you say you don't want it to, so GEDmatch has managed to collect something like a million profiles in one online place. Their idea was to help amateurs doing genealogy and adoptees trying to find birth parents. But that proved to be the tip of the iceberg. Pretty soon law enforcement was using it. They've closed a bunch of cold murder cases, and IDd some John and Jane Does. Last year, it's how they got the Golden State killer out in California. Uploaded his DNA from a crime scene, found relatives of the guy, and then tracked him down from there."

Ludington was stunned by Huw's revelation. It suggested that his serial DNA collecting could well have been needless. He and van der Berg could have uploaded the profile of "Little One," the bones, to one of these sites and looked for relatives—if any, and however distant—three weeks ago. Perhaps none would have surfaced. The odds of finding anybody might have been slender, but it would have been the obvious first step. But even more disconcerting was Ludington's suspicion that Harry Mulholland—a bright man and professional detective—had probably known about GEDmatch all along, and had not told him. That he had not told him because he feared there was a chance it would lead Ludington to Perez...or to him.

Ludington managed to say, "This is great, Huw. Thanks. I think it could be a real help."

He ended the call and left his study to head up to Mt. Sinai, but not before he parked himself opposite Harriet van der Berg in her little office. She turned to him and raised her eyebrows in a way that asked, "Why aren't you on your way to the hospital?"

"Miss van der Berg, I have an idea." Without mentioning Huw Griffiths or the word Lou had written on the envelope containing the thumb drive, he told her what little he knew about open access DNA websites. He specifically mentioned GEDmatch and how adoptees can hunt for relatives and then do genealogical research and perhaps find parents. Then he said, "So, Harry's lab guy gave me the DNA profile of the bone."

He reached in his jacket pocket and extracted the envelope with the thumb drive.

"You've been digging deep into your family tree, Miss van der Berg. So, let's give it a try. You upload the profile of the bones to this GEDmatch thing and see if there might be some shoe-string relative lurking out there. You never know."

As he handed her the envelope with the thumb drive, he explained how slim the odds were, telling her that he understood that there were a mere million profiles on the GEDmatch site. "This is a country of 330-million, you know. But if you should find even one match, then perhaps you could apply your acumen in genealogy."

He mentioned nothing of his guess that Harry had kept quiet about this tactic weeks earlier. Ludington presumed that van der Berg might conclude as much. After all, Harry Mulholland was a retired homicide detective, even if a technologically dated one. But he didn't feel it was his place to implicate his Clerk of Session.

Van der Berg was typically unintimidated by either the task he suggested or the odds of its success. "Dominie, I have never heard of this GEDmatch, but I am a paid member of several genealogy internet services. You go to Mt. Sinai. I shall be 'on it' as they say."

She was clearly pleased with this new investigatory tangent. Ludington went into his study to change into a dog collar for his visit to Ginny Grimes. A clerical collar greased the wheels in hospitals.

As he was on his way through her office, van der Berg looked up from her computer and declared, "I'm on it, Dominie. By the way, I am representing myself as a young adopted boy searching for my lost parents. If clergymen can prevaricate in pursuit of the truth, so can their secretaries."

Most Old Stone members lived in the neighborhood of the church and ended up at the nearby New York Hospital when it came to that. Mt. Sinai was farther uptown, between Fifth Avenue and Madison in the upper 90s into the 100s. Ludington took a yellow cab to the Madison Avenue entrance and grabbed a gyro from one of the food trucks lined up nearby. He asked for extra tzatziki sauce and ate the sandwich on the street. He found Ginny Grimes in a private room on the tenth floor. Her husband was with her, as was a daughter who had driven down from Connecticut. The stroke had been minor, "a TIA" the daughter named it. But there was worry in the room. Though its effect was negligible, it portended the possibility of worse in the future. Ludington prayed before he left, all of them hand-in-hand, Ginny included. "It's all so fragile," he thought to himself as he left the hospital.

The bleakness of Ludington's mood, darkened by Harry's betrayal and an encounter with human frailty, was lightened by a text that pinged just as he was exiting one of Mt. Sinai's excruciatingly slow stop-at-every floor Sabbath elevators. He looked at his phone. It was from Oscar Cunningham. "Met my half sister yesterday. Coffee shop in Summit. She and her husband may attend our wedding." Then—very odd for a Wall Street lawyer—a smiley face. And not only a smiley face, but a selfie of a smiling Oscar Junior and a woman, also smiling, who bore a remarkable resemblance to her half-brother. Ludington smiled back at his phone.

# Chapter Thirty-Nine

*April 18—Maundy Thursday*

Ludington had work to do in preparation for the Maundy Thursday Communion Service at 6:00. He had to set the Communion Table, review the liturgy, and go over his meditation once more. No time to go home and return and still do what had to be done.

The crowd would be small, he knew. One of his predecessors had discontinued the venerable tradition of a special service on the night before Good Friday. Ludington had convinced the Session to revive it a year earlier. Only twelve people had come that first year. A theologically significant number, but discouraging nonetheless. This year he had decided to have the little congregation sit not in the long narrow nave, but in the small elevated chancel at the front of the sanctuary. It was where the choir would sit if Old Stone had a choir. The chancel would provide a more intimate setting, Ludington hoped. Of course, this meant that he could not preach from the pulpit. The little congregation would be behind him if he did.

By 6:00, twenty people had found their way into the chancel of Old Stone Church, all a bit disoriented at the new seating arrangement, but pleased and intrigued to be "up front," facing each other across the stone chancel floor. Georgia and Harry Mulholland were the last to arrive, looking as lugubrious as both the liturgical occasion and the recent turn in their lives suggested. Ludington thought he knew Harry Mulholland well enough to assume that the man had probably told his wife everything, or maybe most everything. Georgia's demeanor seemed to indicate that he had.

Ludington offered his brief reflection without notes. "This night remembers several things," he began. "It recalls—and re-enacts—the last meal Jesus had with his little band of followers. It remembers that awkward moment when he insisted on degrading himself by washing their feet, work consigned to slaves in that day. And, of course, it remembers Judas's betrayal and Peter's denial. But the Fourth Gospel, John's Gospel, also remembers the words—the great many words—that Jesus spoke that night."

"One of the many things Jesus said to his disciples that night were the words 'mandatum novum.' Yes, Latin. I don't speak Latin, you don't speak Latin, and Jesus probably didn't speak Latin. John's Gospel recorded Jesus's words in Greek, and then the Greek got translated into Latin, and we get this mandatum novum. By the way, the 'maundy' of Maundy Thursday is derived from the first of those two words. So, I suppose you might properly call today 'Mandatum Novum Thursday.' Those two Latin words mean 'a new commandment.' They are the first words—in the Latin—of the verse from John's Gospel I read to you a moment ago, John 13:34. In English, it reads, 'I give you a new commandment, that you love one another.'"

Ludington's meditation unfolded, but briefly, to focus on two of the words in that verse, a verse, he said, "that puts two words in the same sentence and is perhaps the crescendo of Jesus's teaching—the words 'love' and 'commandment.'" When speaking about the first, "love," Ludington slipped as close to poetry as he dared; "The love that Christ enacted and invited us to live was like a slip of lily planted in the cold blood and steel of Roman power, a delicate bud sown in the unapologetic brutality of the ancient world. Even today, that love is still such a delicate thing."

When speaking of the second word, "commandment," he said, "This love is no mere feeling. It's not some capricious emotion, unwilled and unchosen, that comes upon us like a sickness and retreats on its own. This love is something we choose to do or not to do. It is an act of will. It has been commanded." He stressed that word. Then he said, "We can choose to obey, or we can choose to not obey. Life hinges on a great many choices, none more than this one."

As he uttered those last words, he happened to glance at Harry and Georgia just as she moved her hand to the left and lay it on his. Perhaps his wife was ready to forgive. Perhaps she did not know the whole story. Ludington knew more of it, and he did not think he was quite ready to forgive.

It fell to him to tidy up after the service. Winifred Grimes, one of the scant Maundy Thursday crowd, entered the little vestry and asked if she could help. Winfred was a soft-spoken grandmother from St. Croix in the Virgin Islands. Ludington loved to listen to her speak. The accent was so graceful, as was what she usually had to say, minimal as it generally was. This evening, as is the custom after a Maundy Thursday service, she said nothing at all as she put away the flagon and the chalice used for communion. She knew exactly where everything went. When they finished, Seth said to her, "Can I walk you home, Winifred?"

She declined the offer, "No, but thank you, Pastor. It's just a short block."

She headed east down 82$^{th}$ Street. Ludington walked west. Cara Lundberg was standing on the corner of Second Avenue, obviously waiting for him.

"Well?" she asked in a rising tone that made the word a question.

He kept walking past her, about to turn north up Second toward his home. As he had at the Lexington Social, he refused to answer her.

She grabbed his elbow to pull him around toward her and looked directly at him. She was tall, but not as tall as him, so her gaze was slightly upward. "Look at it this way. I have information. Information has value—in this case, especially to you. I am willing to sell it to you. Simple financial transaction. Maybe I'll see you Sunday, you know, at announcement time. You have my cell."

# Chapter Forty

*August 28, 1999*

Seth had thought he might take his dad's boat out into the big lake, but changed his mind. The Tartan 37 was set up for single-handed sailing—power furlers on both the main and the jenny, as well as self-steering, but the wind dying and the waves churned up by all the power boaters out in the lake on the last Saturday in August would mean they'd be bouncing around, sails flapping above them. Sara had said she'd like to go for an evening sail when he had called, but she wasn't much help on the boat. And she tended to sea sickness. Anyway, all he really wanted to do was down a few beers with her and see where things went. He had picked up a couple of six-packs of Molsons at Cenzo's.

He had gotten out to the boat about seven-thirty. He had always thought that *Interlude* was a poor excuse for a boat name. His mother had chosen it. The vessel, one of the grandest in the harbor, was moored on the south side of the channel that ran down the middle of Pentwater Lake. His dad kept a Zodiac with an outboard at the Yacht Club, not the closest spot to their mooring, but really, it only took five minutes to get out to the boat. Seth had left the dinghy's oars at the Yacht Club, as he often did. No way he would need them. The Honda two-horse always started on the first pull.

It was ten o'clock and just getting dark when he finished his seventh Molson and saw Sara waving from the Village Marina. It was closer to their mooring than the Club, so he usually picked her up there after she got off her shift at the Landing. They first had met at the restaurant on Memorial Day Sunday, three months earlier. She had waited on him and Chip when they had gone there for lunch. Chip was a frat brother who had stopped on his way from Ann Arbor up to Charlevoix, where his parents had their summer place. They had both flirted with her, and she had flirted back. Chip was gone the next morning; Seth was there for the summer.

He didn't feel the least guilty about the romance that followed. He and Trish had been an item at Michigan for going on two years, but she was off for a Junior year abroad come fall. Both of them had tacitly agreed to let things cool for a year. Then they would see what they thought come their senior year when she was back in Ann Arbor after the year in Spain. Or at least, that's how he understood it. Seth had never considered following her to Barcelona or doing his own junior year somewhere exotic. Not because he loved Ann Arbor so much, he just never got around to applying to the program. Not getting around to things seemed to be his style. He was fine with that.

Both he and Chip had decided that Sara-from-the-Landing was the most gorgeous thing little old Pentwater had to offer. She was dark for someone with the last name of Lundberg, but blued-eyed, tall, and slender, with a swimmer's body. Seth was "summer people" of course, and Sara was a "local," a social chasm that only people raised in tourist towns fully understand. But the two of them had managed to bridge the chasm in the space of a few weeks in early June. The privacy of a Tartan 37 with a roomy v-berth in the forward cabin helped.

Seth tossed the empty beer can down below into the cabin and climbed down the stern ladder and into the Zodiac. He gave the engine a pull, untied the painter, and headed to the village dock where Sara stood waiting. She was pacing, wearing the same distracted look that she'd fallen into over the last few weeks. So unlike the devil-may-care attitude that he had always liked about her. He could see that she had not changed out of the black jeans and white blouse she wore for the dinner shift at the Landing. She usually changed into something fresh whenever they planned to meet, changed in the women's room at the restaurant, often into the cut-offs that Seth told her flattered her legs. But she looked pretty good, even in work clothes with ketchup stains.

She climbed gracefully into the rubber dinghy and sat with her back to the bow, facing Seth, as he twisted the throttle to the fast position and headed back across the channel to the *Interlude*. She smiled at him, but said nothing. It was a challenge to talk over the noise of the little air-cooled outboard. As he tied the Zodiac to the stern of the sailboat and killed the engine, he asked, "So, how was work?"

Her answer was always more or less the same, not that he was much interested. "Place was a zoo. People lined up out onto Hancock Street." He vaguely respected Sara for working over the summer after finishing high school. She was saving up to go to Grand Valley State, she said. She had been accepted, having graduated near the top of her class at Pentwater High. But there were only seventeen kids in her graduating class. She had been hurt when Seth had pointed out that the top of a class of seventeen was no big deal. He was just glad that he didn't have to wait tables all summer to cover tuition and room and board at Michigan, not that the possibility of actually having to do so had occurred to him.

He let her climb aboard first. He steadied the Zodiac as she did so. He always let her go up the boarding ladder before him. Good manners, and he enjoyed the view. She was sitting in the cockpit, leaning forward, making no move to change out of her grimy waitress outfit. "You want a cold one, Sara?"

She shook her head. He went below and fished another Molson out of the boat's refrigerator. He opened it, took a swig, and went back up to the cockpit. He sat next to Sara and went to drape his arm over her shoulder. She moved away and said, "Seth, we need to talk." And then she began to cry, softly, just tears, not sobs.

"What's wrong, Honey." His father called his mother that, and he had fallen into the habit, both with Trish and now with Sara.

She stood up in the cockpit, steadied herself on the locked wheel, and said, "What's wrong is that I'm pregnant."

Seth said the first thing that came to him. "That's not possible. You're on the pill."

"I am now. But not at first. I went to the doctor. She says I'm ten weeks. I had guessed. She confirmed it."

He stood, but did not reach to take her hands, nor did he try to hold her. "Well, we'll get it taken care of. No problem."

"Seth, I'm Catholic. Are you forgetting? We don't do that." Now the tears burst into sobs. She went around the wheel and moved toward him. He backed away and sat down on the cockpit berth.

He look up at her and said, "Well, it's your choice."

"No, Seth. It's our choice. It's our baby. Yours and mine."

"Are you sure?" he asked.

"Yes, I'm sure. How can you say that after what we've had this summer? Seth, you said you loved me."

He could not remember having said any such thing, but then a guy sometimes forgets himself.

She sat down next to him on the berth. He edged away. She said, "Seth, we could always get married."

The thought of marriage was so far wide of anything he could imagine that he actually laughed. Years later, he would remember that. He would always recall that he had laughed.

"You entitled bastard." She said the words loudly enough to carry across the water.

"I may be one of those, but I know I'm not both. I have my father's eyes." It was the eighth Molson talking.

"Take me back to the dock, Seth. Now. I want off this boat."

"Calm down, Sara. How about a beer? Take the edge off."

"Seth, I'm pregnant. I want to go home."

"Okay, okay, your choice."

He climbed unsteadily into the Zodiac, almost letting it slip out from under him. He set the throttle to start and pulled the starter cord. Nothing. He checked to make sure the tank valve was open. It was. He tried again, and then again, but the engine refused to start. He opened the fuel filler cap and peered inside. It was dark, and he couldn't see much, but decided the thing was out of gas. He remembered that it had burped a couple of times coming out to the *Interlude*.

He looked up at Sara, standing at the top of the boarding ladder, and said, "No gas."

"Well, row the damn thing then."

"Sara, I left the oars at the club."

He climbed back aboard *Interlude* and saw that Sara was taking off her jeans and blouse. "I'll swim, then."

"Your choice." He knew she was a strong swimmer. She had told him she'd swam freestyle for the rec program's team up in Ludington. They had sometimes gone swimming off the boat after sex. She was a better swimmer than he was.

She did not dive into the lake, but lowered herself off the stern ladder into the still water, all without a word of farewell. He saw that she was easily holding her clothes above her as she side-stroked away from the boat, heading across the channel toward the village dock. Seth sighed, downed the last of the Molson, lay down on the cockpit berth of *Interlude,* and fell asleep in spite of the roar of a powerboat coming down Pentwater Lake, way too fast for a no-wake zone.

* * *

The Oceana County Sheriff phoned Seth's parents' cottage the next morning at nine. Sara Lundberg's father had called them the night before—actually early in the morning—worried because their daughter had not come home from work. They had called the Landing first, but nobody had answered. The Sheriff told Seth's father that he had just phoned the restaurant and had talked to the manager. She had assured them that Sara had left after her evening shift the night before. "You might want to check in with the Ludington kid," she had said, unbidden. The whole staff knew that she was dating Seth Ludington. "Yes," she had told the Sheriff, "he would sometimes pick her up and take her home after work, but other times she came to work in her dad's truck. But as often as not," she added, "they would relax on his

221

boat for a while after her shift was over. Everybody knew about it." She had managed to say the word "relax" without a hint of irony. The Sheriff ended the phone conversation with Seth's father, saying, "I'll need to come by and have a talk with your boy, Mr. Ludington."

Later that morning, the Sheriff found Sara's father's Ford F-150 parked on Fourth Street around the corner from the restaurant. He was at the Ludington cottage by noon. Seth had just gotten back home, having slept the night aboard the *Interlude*. He told the truth in his interview with the Sheriff, most of it anyway. Yes, he had picked Sara Lundberg up at the Village Marina after she finished work. "It was about 10:00, I think." They went out to the boat. "We thought maybe we'd have an evening sail." But they had gotten into a bit of a fight, and Sara said she wanted to get home. He couldn't get the motor on the inflatable started, so she swam ashore. "It's only a hundred yards. She's a strong swimmer." He did not mention the eight Molsons, falling asleep in the cockpit, or what their quarrel had been about. When the sheriff pressed him about their fight, he said, "Just stuff. You know how it is."

The divers found the body late that afternoon. The autopsy revealed not only drowning, but wounds—probably not fatal, but certainly enough to render her unconscious—across her upper back, doubtless caused by a boat's propeller. It also revealed that she was almost three months pregnant. The Sheriff assured the Ludingtons that this last detail was not the kind of thing that would routinely be made public.

The Lundberg family was given the full autopsy report and soon threatened to sue. The Ludington family lawyer brought up from Detroit assured Seth and his parents that the girl's family had absolutely no case, but that they could certainly disclose the pregnancy, and that it would all add up to some very unpleasant publicity. So, the lawyer visited the Lundbergs in their home in Crystal Valley armed with a meaningless non-disclosure agreement and a checkbook. Seth never knew how much his father had paid for their silence. He never wanted to know.

# Chapter Forty-One

*April 19—Good Friday*

S eth Ludington was exhausted when the morning of Good Friday dawned light and airy, the precise inverse of his mood. He decided to sleep another hour and drink rather too much coffee. He did not get to Old Stone till almost noon.

"Well," Harriet van der Berg said, swiveling her chair to face him as Ludington entered her office, "We seem to have found something, Dominie. I uploaded—such a curious verb—uploaded the DNA profile of the bones to this GEDmatch website. There is no charge to do so, by the way. And there was a match, just one match. His name is 'Patrick Sean O'Hearn.' Very Irish, doubtless RC. But I emailed him. GEDmatch requires an email accompany each profile. They ask for a name also, but permit you to use a pseudonym should you choose. At any rate, I emailed this Patrick Sean O'Hearn, telling him—how did I phrase it?—telling him that I knew of a possible family member distantly related to him. Would he be interested? Dominie, he replied immediately. I told him I'd love to speak with him, and he replied again, this time with a phone number. I thought you might wish to place the call yourself. You are so gifted at these matters."

Seth wondered if she meant gifted at dissembling. But he said, "I'll call. I'll call right now."

She gave Ludington the number, and he retreated to his study. He phoned O'Hearn on his cell so that Old Stone would not come up on the man's caller

ID. The voice that answered was young. Ludington saw no reason not to introduce himself with his real name—minus the "reverend," however.

"I'm doing some genealogical research, not into my own family, but I'm trying to plot the genealogy of a person born in 1969 or 1970, a person connected to a Presbyterian church in New York City. The DNA of this person indicates that you are related, though perhaps very distantly. It's historical research I'm doing." True enough, Ludington thought as he said it, but hardly the precise truth.

Patrick Sean O'Hearn said, "Yeah? So, I'm taking this genealogy class in college, doing the family tree thing. It's totally wig, what you find out when you start poking around the fam. I'm a freshman at Holy Family. Anyway, I uploaded my profile onto GEDmatch, and I was hoping for something, maybe a call like this. What's the name of this person who's my relative?"

"That's the thing," Ludington said. "I'm not sure. I'm doing my own digging, too." This was vague and obviously invited clarification that Ludington was reluctant to offer, so he immediately said, "Do any of these names show up in your family tree: Cunningham, McCrae...Perez... Mulholland...Westerberg...Desmond...Ruvenstein...? Like I said, the person I am trying to trace could be related to a minister, a Presbyterian minister, or connected to somebody related to the church. They may have one of those names, probably lived in New York City."

"My whole family is like totally Irish and super Catholic. My uncle is a priest. And as far as I know, the whole family is from the Philadelphia area, ever since they got off the boat. All the O'Hearns are Catholic, officially, anyway. He paused for a moment and then said, "Except maybe for some relative of Mom's. I remember her saying something once about 'a lost Protestant back there in the O'Hearn family tree.'"

"Do you have a name for your 'lost Protestant,' Patrick?"

"Well, no." But O'Hearn was growing more than a bit intrigued. He was eager to be helpful, if for self-serving reasons. "This could be the perfect edge for my family tree project—an actual Protestant in the O'Hearn family. Almost as good as a Native American. I don't know what the person's name was, I mean the Protestant one Mom told me about, but I can call her and ask. She doesn't like to be called at work. She said she's going to church at noon and then coming home. I'll call her then and get back to you. Are you over in New Jersey? You got a Jersey number."

Ludington, who had gotten his first cellphone while in seminary at Princeton, decided not to disclose his location, and merely said, "That would be great. Sooner the better."

"No problem, man. I'll get back to you later this afternoon."

# Chapter Forty-Two

*April 19—Good Friday*

L udington told van der Berg about his conversation with the kid from Philadelphia with the absurdly Irish name and his promise to call back with the name of a possible Protestant in the family tree he was tracing for a college class. She listened intently, then fairly shouted at Ludington, "Dominie, look at the time. It's 12:30 I seem to recall that your Good Friday Service with the Methodists is scheduled for 1:00, is it not?"

"Ugh," sighed Ludington. He rose, went into his study, retrieved his black pulpit robe and the text of the meditation he had prepared on the sixth of the Seven Last Words—all four double-spaced pages of it—and set off on the five-block hike to Yorkville Methodist Church.

Yorkville Methodist was on East 86, sandwiched between a pair of mid-rise apartment buildings with which it shared side walls. This meant that its sanctuary, set in from the street as it was, received no natural light. Ludington had been in it once before and had thought it made Old Stone's sanctuary look bright and airy by comparison. Perhaps it was a fit choice as a worship space for Good Friday.

The pattern of traditional Seven Last Words services was familiar to Ludington. The cross at the front of the sanctuary of the church was draped in a black shroud. The two rows of art deco chandeliers had been dimmed, offering just enough light for good eyes to read the words in a hymnal.

A string of local Protestant clergy would read their particular assigned words—sentences actually—that Jesus had spoken from the cross. Then the congregation would sing a hymn, and the same minister would offer what was supposed to be a brief reflection on the words from Scripture he or she had read. In the letter that Ludington had received two weeks earlier outlining the service and its rubrics, the word "brief" had been both set in italics and underlined, suggesting that infractions of the brevity guideline had occurred in previous years.

Seven earnest sermons and seven turgid hymns sung by a very small and elderly congregation not inclined to sing, all set in a dour space, portended a grim several hours. As Ludington sat through it, awaiting his penultimate turn, it occurred to him that perhaps the agonizing liturgy was designed to help worshippers experience something of what Jesus experienced on the cross.

His word, the sixth, was, *"It is finished."* In his preparatory study, he had learned that the words would probably be better translated, *"It is accomplished."* It was after 2:00 by the time his turn came. It was clear that the faithful little congregation was itself quite ready to be finished. A few people had begun to leave. Ludington shortened his already brief meditation, sat down, and looked at his Shinola Runwell. Less than four minutes—brief by any standard. Unhappily, the preacher assigned the Seventh and last Word, *"Father, into Thy hands I commend my spirit,"* had interpreted "brief" quite differently. By the time he finally finished, there was almost no one in the church save the seven preachers and the organist.

Ludington got back to Old Stone, still in his dour Good Friday mood. He opened the door to van der Berg's office to find her impatiently waiting for him, her chair swiveled to face the room's entrance rather than her desk. "Has Mr. O'Hearn been in touch?" she asked the moment he darkened her door.

"Not yet." He wandered into his study to consider his Easter sermon when his cell vibrated. It was Patrick Sean O'Hearn, as promised.

"Sir, he said in a questioning tone. It's me."

"Thanks so much for getting back to me, Patrick. Were you able to talk to your mother?"

"Yep. My Prod relative was my great-grandmother. She was named Ann Moore. She was from Harrisburg, Mom said. She married my great-grandfather, that would be my mom's grandpa on her mom's side. He was named James Walsh. So, he was my maternal great-grandfather. That's how they say it in genealogy class."

Ludington was disappointed. Neither of these names, neither Moore nor Walsh, was related to anyone they were guessing might be connected to the bones.

"Mom says Grandma Ann wouldn't convert, and it was a huge scandal back then. Go figure. Mom said that she lived and died a Congregationalist. Never went to church, though, not even to Catholic church with her husband on Christmas and Easter. She was 'one stubborn lady,' mom says. They couldn't even get married in church, not in either of their churches. Got married at the courthouse, mom says. Oh, she also said that the family, I mean the Moore family, was, like, uber-prominent in Harrisburg. Do you think there's a connection to your person, the one from New York you're trying to trace?"

"None of the names are familiar, Patrick. I really don't think so. I mean, there would seem to be some sort of genetic connection between your family and my person, but I don't know what it is. I've got more digging to do."

O'Hearn was not greatly disappointed. He had found at least one Protestant in his Irish Catholic family, a discovery that he surmised would make his genealogy project a tad more intriguing at Holy Family College. Ludington said he'd get back to him if he was able to figure out the link. The kid thanked him, Ludington thanked him back, and they hung up.

Ludington found van der Berg restless in her cubicle. He told her about O'Hearn's call, and the universal and resolute Irish Catholicism of his clan save the "lost Protestant in the family tree," one Ann Moore of Harrisburg.

"Well," van der Berg said, "That's not nothing. Moore is not a name we know. But it's a place to begin."

"How unlike you to let a double negative escape your lips, Miss van der Berg. But it may be just the place to begin some genealogical sleuthing."

"And that is my métier, Dominie—genealogical research, that is to say."

He suspected she had used the affected French term to atone for the double negative.

"I have been ferreting around into my upstate Dutch family for many years now. This will be familiar territory for us."

It was generous for her to say "us," Ludington thought. He knew nothing of genealogical research. He had never wanted to poke into his own family tree. He suspected the earlier of them to have been rascals at the least, robber barons at worst, and that the latter of his ancestors to have been among the more sluggish of the idle rich. "I'm not really sure I want to know any more about the Ludingtons than I already do," he had told Fiona when she had asked what he knew of his family history.

Van der Berg turned to her computer and Ludington to his study where he planned to broach his Easter sermon yet again, odd as it was to consider on Good Friday. Unable to focus, he finally wandered back into van der Berg's little office about 4:30, pulled up the extra chair and sat beside her. She was pecking away on computer keys and wiggling her mouse like a teenager. Ludington had always been taken aback by the woman's computer skills, so unusual for a person her age. Many an old New York secretary, even ones as superlative as Harriet van der Berg, had never quite managed the translations from shorthand, Dictaphones, and typewriters to computers, email, and the internet. She had obviously done so with alacrity and singular success.

"Your friend Patrick had this right." She pointed at her screen which displayed an official looking document that had been filled out in a fluid and delightful longhand.

Ludington said, "You seldom see handwriting like that these days."

"So true, Dominie. More's the pity. It's the application for a marriage license issued in Dauphine County, Pennsylvania in 1934 for one Ann Seely Moore and one Roger James Walsh. Doubtless Mr. O'Hearn's lost Protestant great-grandmother and her scandalously Irish R.C. husband. Such marriages were not done in those days."

As Ludington waited, leisurely sipping the last of his cold coffee, van der Berg slowly traced the multitude of issue from that marriage down to the present, a present which included one Patrick Sean O'Hearn, born in Philadelphia in 2000.

She leaned back in her chair and said without looking at Ludington, "No one in this branch of the O'Hearn family seems to have had any connection with any of our suspects. None even have New York connections."

Another forty minutes and she had discovered that all three of Ann and James's children had been baptized at Immaculate Conception BMV Roman Catholic Church in Harrisburg.

"BMV?" van der Berg asked.

"Blessed Virgin Mary," he answered. She raised a Protestant eyebrow at that, and began to scroll around to show Ludington the proof of the three R.C. baptisms on her screen.

He stopped her. "I believe you, Miss van der Berg. Ann may have been a resolute Congregationalist, but she obviously lost the baptism battle, if she even fought it."

He returned to his study and another hour of vain consideration as to how he might preach Easter. He was back in van der Berg's spare chair at 5:35.

She was working so intensely at her computer that she did not even look up at Ludington as he came into her office, much less offer a greeting.

"Oh, you're back, Dominie. I am so glad you have returned. You will not believe what I have discovered, not that I understand what this discovery may mean. It's rather confusing."

She turned at last from the computer screen to look at Ludington. "I traced Ann Moore's family sideways and then down. Do you understand what that means?' She asked this question in a teacher voice, a tone Ludington might have resented in another context. But in this context, she was the expert and he the pupil. "It means I looked for siblings and then their descendants." She said again, "And you will not believe what I have discovered."

"I looked for siblings, brothers and sisters to this Protestant woman, Ann Moore. I discovered that one of her sisters, a Genevieve Moore, married a man—are you ready for this, Dominie?—named Rufus McCrae in 1929.

McCrae. Can you believe it? McCrae."

Ludington pulled up the spare chair and sat close to van der Berg. She directed him to the screen. They stared at her discovery in tandem. He was again amazed at how adept she was at this.

"And I discovered that this Rufus was a Congregationalist minister and that he and Genevieve had six children." She asked Ludington yet again, "Are you prepared for this, Dominie?" With that preface, she brought up another page on her computer.

She pointed proudly at the monitor. "You will see that one of those six, the oldest, was named 'Malcolm.'" Van der Berg touched the name on the screen. "He was born in Radnor, Pennsylvania in 1930. When I discovered this, Dominie, I called out, *'Bingo!'*, not that I have ever played that Popish game. It's simply what came out of my mouth in my excitement."

She turned to Ludington and smiled triumphantly.

Ludington was stunned. He finally said, "Well, first off, how many 'Malcolm McCraes' born in 1930 into a clergy family can there be? Not many, doubtless just one, and the DNA connects him to the bones."

"Precisely, Dominie. Patrick Sean O'Hearn and the bones are third cousins. They share great-great-grandparents. Both descended from the parents of Ann and Genevieve, he through the former, the bones through the latter. Malcolm was Genevieve's son. As to how Malcolm is related to the bones, well…that we can only guess. But he is…somehow."

They both fell into silence, pondering the confusion elicited by van der Berg's discovery.

Finally, Ludington voiced what they were both thinking. "But, we know for certain that Dolores McCrae is not the child's mother. We know for sure she's not related to the child in any way. Her DNA profile proves she couldn't be. There's no way I can imagine that she could fake it."

Van der Berg completed their second shared thought. "And Malcolm's DNA was not a match either. The DNA sample from his comb, the one that Dolores sent us. It was not a match to the child either."

Ludington sat silent another moment, folded his hands as if in prayer, and whispered, "Miss van der Berg, Dolores McCrae said it was her husband's comb."

"Yes, but Dominie, even if she deceived us and Malcolm is related to the child, even if he's the father, who in the world could the mother have been?"

At 6:00, a baffled Seth Ludington bid an equally confused Harriet van der Berg a good evening and set off on his three-block walk home. The cold gloom with which the day had dawned had happily yielded to a cloudless azure evening. The afternoon sun, welcome as it was, was theologically inappropriate for Good Friday, had warmed the sidewalks that were suddenly redolent—as they often were on such days—of dog urine.

As he rounded the corner unto 84th he saw that Orsolya Tabor was at her late afternoon station in front of her five-story walk-up, directly across from his house. Ludington did what he rarely did and deliberately crossed to the north side of 84th. He paused as he came near her. She was perched on the top step of the concrete stoop leading up to the front door of her first-floor apartment. Seated where she was, and Ludington standing on the sidewalk, they met each other eye-to-eye. A paper cup in her hand, she quickly stubbed out her half-spent cigarette and flicked the butt into the open garbage can in the trash crib to her left. Perfect shot.

The evening was growing chilly enough for her to have donned a coat, today a pink suede motorcycle jacket that somehow worked with her pile of bottle-blond curls and black polyester tights, an ensemble comically young for her 75 years, though in New York it hardly turned heads. Very little did.

"Good afternoon, Orsolya." They had ostensibly decided on first names some months before, though she never spoke his, always addressing him formally and deferentially.

"Hello to you, *Tiszteletes*. Such a fine day for Good Friday. It should be a storm today, like the first one, don't you think?"

"It seems it often does rain on Good Friday, but of course Good Friday is always in the spring, and it rains in the spring. But I must say, I do like my Easters to be sunny."

"Did you have a service today at your fine church?"

"No, we had a joint service with some other neighborhood congregations. It was at the Methodist church up on 86th."

"I went to my Hungarian church. I like the old hymns that I know. Not so many peoples there today. Not so many Hungarians in Yorkville now. They all moved to the suburbs."

"You must have seen a great many changes in this neighborhood over the years."

"Oh, goodness, yes. So many changes. Some good, some not so good. You like some wine, *Tszteletes*? You finish your work for the day, right? And Mrs. *Tszteletes*, not home yet. No work for you till Sunday. I have some very nice bull's blood for you."

Ludington said, "I would love some. He didn't say, "a glass," as he assumed it would arrive in a paper cup. He lowered his lanky body to the top of Orsolya's stoop, his long legs descending three steps lower. The woman, he remembered, was a watcher. And she was sharp. Maybe, he thought to himself, she had seen something of interest across the street fifty years earlier. Just maybe.

Orsolya retreated inside and returned quickly with a paper cup filled to the brim with the dark inky-red wine Hungarians call "bull's blood." She had refreshed her own cup as well. She sat herself down next to him, easily he thought, given her age.

She raised her cup to him, and he lifted his, the two touching, both spilling a bit.

"*Egeszegedre,*" she said. "Means 'you be healthy.'"

"And to you as well," Ludington replied, not ready to tackle the Hungarian toast.

He took a sip, she a gulp. He nodded to his house, the former manse across the street, and asked, "Were you here when the family that owned our house before the church got it lived there? I think they were named 'Cunningham.' Do you remember them?"

"A little I remember. I was just married. We were living here, upstairs. Mostly the yelling I remember. Not a happy family. Not so much fighting between him and her, mostly her screaming all the time. Screaming at the mister and at the boy. In the summer especially, when the windows were open, you know. No AC yet. My mama and papa never yelled like that.

They fought, yes, but no yelling. Alphonse, he never yelled at me. But I yelled at him... sometimes. He was German, needed yelling." She chuckled, then smiled at the memory of her husband, and took another gulp of wine.

Ludington was eager to coax more memories from her. "Do you remember the young Hispanic man who took care of the house after the church got it? He was named Jorge Perez."

"Oh yes. What a rascal, that one. Too pretty for his own good. Wore a—what you name it?—a thing over his blind eye sometimes. Like a pirate in the films. But later, before he died, he would come over and shovel the snow from my steps and sidewalk. He would do this when he finished cleaning snow for the church. He would not take money. He said, 'What goes around comes around.' Died too young, God bless him."

"And the ministers who lived here all the years the church owned the house. You got to know them?"

"Oh yes, a little. I remember the Desmonds. He was a golden pastor. He is my age, you see. And Mrs. *Tiszteletes* and the pretty little girls. I watched them grow up. Such a nice little family.

"What do you mean, 'golden pastor?'"

In the Hungarian church, we say some pastors are golden. The best ones—kind and wise and visit the old ladies. Maybe you will be golden, *Tszteletes.*"

Ludington took a sip of his wine and wondered whether he had golden in him. Then he offered the question he had been saving, the one he really wanted to ask, "Do you remember the minister before Desmond? This was the first minister to live in the house after the church got it. His name was McCrae, Malcolm McCrae. His wife was named Dolores."

"Was that their names? He was the in-between minister, I think. How do you say it?"

"Interim."

She nodded and said, "I don't think he was so golden. He and his wife, they were very private kind of peoples. Quiet, not so friendly. No visitors, not even church peoples. Sometimes the young people on Sunday nights, that was all. It was the two of them in that big old house all alone, no children."

She raised her cup to indicate Ludington's home.

"One visitor I remember. There was the girl, the girl who came to visit for a while, toward the end almost every day."

Ludington's interest was immediately piqued. "What do you remember about her?"

"It was so long ago, *Tiszteletes,* but I remember she was young, maybe still a teen-ager. So shy. I would wave, and she would look down at the sidewalk. But when the lady or the *Tiszteletes* himself opened the door for her to come in, there was always very nice friendly hello, sometimes a little hug even, no kisses though, but nice. 'Warm' you say in English. This was strange for them, so I remember. They were not so warm. And this girl, she was pregnant. I remember this because I was pregnant with my Bertalan then. It was spring. Bertie was born in June, June 1970. When you are pregnant, you notice pregnant everywhere. You could not see the pregnant when she started coming, but you could see it toward the end, just before they left, right before the golden pastor came."

Ludington downed the last of his bull's blood in a gulp. He wished Orsolya a good evening and crossed the street to his house. As soon as he was through the kitchen door, he phoned van der Berg, told her what Orsolya Tabor had remembered, and asked, "Are you up for another trip to White Plains tomorrow? It will doubtless be even more unpleasant than the last."

# Chapter Forty-Three

*April 20—Holy Saturday*

Seth had told Fiona over a late dinner at Elio's the night before about both the genetic connection between the bones and Malcolm McCrae that van der Berg had traced and Orsolya's revelation to him on her front stoop. He had also told her that he and van der Berg would be making a return trip to White Plains to see Dolores McCrae.

"It'll inevitably be a confrontation," he had said over after-dinner espressos and a shared piece of tiramisu. "I'm not looking forward to it, though I am very much looking forward to having this thing done. There's no way to get there except through this thorny little thicket with Dolores McCrae. I mean, she's an old woman, Fiona. Whatever happened fifty years ago—crime or no—it revolts me. It's so sad, but not merely sad. It had to have been horrific."

They got home about 9:30, both exhausted. Seth asked Fiona to sit with him at the little table in the kitchen. He told her about Sara. About her pregnancy, about her drowning—another "horrific." He told her about him falling asleep drunk—or maybe passing out—in the cockpit of his father's boat. He told her about the hush money his parents had paid her parents. And he told her about Cara. "She's here in New York. She wants money." As he unfolded the tale, he did not varnish it, presenting it as if it were but an example of warped adolescent judgement. He spared no detail, ruthlessly outing the secret that he told her was corroding his soul. He had borrowed the image from van der Berg. It fit.

His wife was grim with anger, mostly because he had not trusted her enough to tell her before. "Seth, we've been married for a decade. And you couldna' be honest with me about this?"

And she told him that she could not but be disappointed in him for what he had done—and not done—twenty years ago. They talked together at the little table for an hour. She finally ended the conversation with a sigh, "Well, Seth, all I know is that person in the boat is not who you are now. Thank God." They went up to bed very late, but neither found sleep until nearly two in the morning.

Fiona wakened her husband at 7:30. She sat up in the bed, looked at him, recalled all that last night had brought to them and what the day before him held. She simply said, "I'll make coffee." She didn't use the word "forgive," indeed she never would, but the offer to make coffee implied as much.

Ludington picked up van der Berg in front of her apartment building at 9:30. The doorman opened the passenger door with a single and mighty jerk, by now acquainted with the old Volvo's sticky door. Van der Berg got in the car, managed the seat belt on her own, and gave her French twist a pat to see that all was in order. She was unsmiling and made no comment—not on the car, not about the bright April weather, not even regarding their impending call on Dolores McCrae.

When he had spoken with van der Berg late the prior afternoon, just after his conversation with Orsolya, they had agreed to make their second call on Dolores McCrae a surprise visit. If they phoned in advance, Ludington worried, she would refuse to see them and alert the retirement home staff not to admit them.

Ludington hoped an early visit would increase their odds of catching Dolores before her lunch and whatever Saturday afternoon activity—bridge, canasta, old movies—Westminster Gardens might schedule to lure residents out of their rooms. He also hoped an early start would maybe get him back to his study in time to finish up the decidedly unfinished Easter sermon he was to preach the next day. It was all so curiously and inconveniently timed—death and detection in the midst of Lent and Easter.

As they crossed Central Park, van der Berg gazed out the car window at the riotous forsythia draping over the stone walls on either side of the 86th Street Traverse. She made no remark on this vernal loveliness, rather said, "If only we had known three weeks ago. I mean, if only we had known about GEDmatch. Dominie, do you think Harry knew—knew and said nothing to you? If so, it will be an interesting experience for us to spend a week on a tour bus in Scotland with him, will it not."

"It will indeed. And yes, I think it's possible that he knew, though I don't know for sure, I mean absolutely sure." In truth, Ludington was sadly confident that Harry had indeed known when he first suggested his pastor undertake weeks of circumlocutious sleuthing. But Ludington decided to sequester his suspicions from van der Berg, hoping he might spare the church's Clerk of Session some fraction of van der Berg's legendary wrath. A dollop of doubt about what Harry knew—and when—might dilute the woman's anger. He had not spoken to Mulholland since their drive back from Queens on Thursday. He was himself still furious with his Clerk of Session. One angry friend was enough.

"Had we known, you would have been spared all those little getting-to-know-my-congregation visits, Dominie. You would have been spared your serial prevarications and all that tacky DNA collecting."

"Life," Ludington said, deciding to shift the conversation to generalities. "Life is a trail of had-I-knowns. I mean, we're always stepping into whatever comes next without quite knowing what it is. You simply have to start off and go, without knowing for sure where you're going. You have to make left turns because you can't turn right. You're on the road, and—what is it they say?—the road becomes the teacher. You know only by going, Miss van der Berg. You generally can't know that much about life—certainly not everything—unless you actually go."

"Humm," was all van der Berg said, and that dubiously.

Miss van der Berg, "Have you heard the little parable of the centipede?"

"No, I haven't."

"There was once a centipede who woke up one morning and thought about walking and then—because he thought about it beforehand—couldn't do it?"

"Well?" she said, waiting for the punch line.

"That's it That's all there is. The centipede couldn't walk when he thought about it. We started this, you and me, our naïve little foray into detective work, not knowing how to walk. We didn't think about it, we just did it."

Van der Berg screwed up her face at this, but said nothing.

Ludington said, "And you must admit that one of our left turns has yielded something of a blessing. Oscar Cunningham is in contact with his half-sister, the only birth family he has in the world besides his lamentable mother. That wouldn't have happened if we had gone the GEDmatch route from day one and discovered the Malcolm McCrae connection first thing."

"Well, perhaps, but had we known, you would not have become furious with your Clerk of Session, a man with whom you must continue to work in the future."

"That's your fourth 'had we known.' And who said I was furious with Harry?"

"I know you, Dominie."

"That book—the Harry Mulholland book—is not yet closed."

Traffic thickened and slowed to stop-start as they neared the onramp to the northbound Henry Hudson. Half of the City was escaping to the country for the Easter weekend. Silence was uncomfortable for both of them as it inevitably drove them to imagine the coming encounter with Dolores McCrae. They both understood that their approach could not be indirect. They would tell the woman what they knew—that the bones in Ludington's ash pit were somehow related to her late husband and that they knew for a fact that a young and pregnant woman regularly visited the manse in the spring of 1970 when they lived there.

Van der Berg broke the awkward silence by changing the subject entirely. "I have always been confused about this today, I mean today, the Saturday between Good Friday and Easter Sunday. What, precisely, is one to imagine our Lord did betwixt His death and resurrection?"

How like her, Ludington thought, not only to deftly redirect the conversation, but to use a word like "betwixt."

"Well, that's an imponderable, to be sure. The Creed says 'he descended into hell,' whatever that may mean. The question has generated volumes of theological speculation over the centuries. Some say 'hell' is a circumlocution, a way of saying that Christ was really and truly dead. Others have speculated that he might have had work to do down in hell."

"What kind of work might that be, Dominie. What kind of work would our Lord do in hell?"

"There's this one quirky tradition named 'The Harrowing Hell.' The idea is that Christ descended into Hell on Holy Saturday and redeemed all the pre-Christian and righteous souls down there, all the good people who had lived and died before Jesus, or maybe lived in remote places where Christianity was unknown, or babies who had died before they got a chance to get baptized. Raw speculation, of course, and a bit edgy, but I like what it suggests about the breadth of divine love."

"Have you ever wondered whether the child in your house was baptized? Have you ever wondered if it had a name?"

"All the time, Miss van der Berg. All the time." In his mind, Ludington was reluctant to name the un-named baby he had found as merely "the bones," or even "the child." He had settled on "the Little One."

They parked in the same spot they had used almost three weeks earlier. The azaleas that had promised to bloom at their first visit had now exploded into red and pink flames. They entered the building by the same door they'd used before, guarded by the same woman at the "Welcome Desk." At Ludington's suggestion, they breezed by the woman with a casual wave and broad smiles.

As they passed, Ludington called out to her, "We're friends of Dolores." He had learned long ago that in hospitals and nursing homes (but not prisons), wearing a clerical collar and striding confidently would get you in just about anywhere you wanted to go.

Ludington rapped softy at the door to Dolores McCrae's unit. It opened slowly. The old woman peered through the crack, saw who was there, and began to close the door. But not fast enough.

Ludington blocked it with his penny loafer and then said through the narrow opening, "Mrs. McCrae, you'd best speak with us. If you don't, the authorities might have to become involved. We'd prefer to avoid that, as would you, I'm sure."

It was almost a full minute before she opened the door. She said nothing, but merely retreated to the living area of her little apartment and sat in the chair to the left of the couch. She held a lacy handkerchief in her right hand. She did not invite them to sit. Her own sitting was all the invitation she offered. Ludington sat closest to her; van der Berg at the other end of the couch. The apartment was as tidy as they recalled from their last visit. The MacBook Air lay closed on the small desk; the door to the bedroom was cracked an inch; the walls were decorated with the same floral still-life prints, all tasteful enough, if bland. There were no photos of family on the walls—an oddity in a retirement home.

Ludington looked the woman in the eye. She returned his gaze. He said, "Mrs. McCrae, you know about the human remains I found in the ash pit beneath the fireplace in my home, the house you and your husband once lived in. You know that they are the bones of a very small infant. Miss van der Berg and I have made considerable effort to bring closure to this matter without recourse to the authorities."

Dolores McCrae was dressed in a dark blue skirt that fell just below her knees and a light blue blouse. A short string of pearls hung at her neck. It was an ensemble that suggested she was going out or expecting guests. She sat stock-still and bolt upright in her chair, holding Ludington's gaze. Van der Berg was leaning slightly forward so that she might see the woman past Ludington.

Ludington continued, "We've discovered that your late husband is genetically related to the child. The connection is unassailable. We have also learned that in the spring and summer of 1970, a young woman—a young woman who appeared to be pregnant—was a regular visitor to the manse."

Dolores McCrae wound her handkerchief tightly around two fingers of her left hand, so tightly as to appear penitential.

She spoke, at last and very softly. Van der Berg leaned forward to better hear her.

"April 14, 1970, was the saddest day of my life, of our life. It's still painful every year. This year it fell on a Sunday, last Sunday it was—Palm Sunday. I never go out on April 14. I stay home and sit. Sometimes I try to read Scripture or *These Days* devotionals, but usually I just sit. It all comes back, of course."

She needed no encouragement to tell the story. Ludington knew she was an intelligent woman and that she understood that telling the pastor of her husband's erstwhile congregation and this blunt woman sitting next to him was infinitely preferable to telling the tale to some police officer or child services worker, either of whom would doubtless take copious notes and file official reports. Then who-knows-what might follow.

"Malcolm," she said, "was a good husband. To many he seemed an unexciting sort of man, plain-looking, an uninspiring sort of minister. But he was passionate about his calling. He always called it that, never merely 'work.' We married the summer after he graduated from seminary and I finished my masters in nursing. We had begun to see each other our senior year at Penn State. He asked me to marry him the day we graduated." That memory brought a hint of a smile to her lips.

"After we were engaged, he went on to Princeton Seminary. I attended the College of New Jersey in Ewing, just down the road. Today we would have probably lived together, but that would have been unthinkable in the 1950s. I always assumed I was his first and only love. I knew that he was mine."

"We moved about a lot after Malcolm was ordained. There was a restlessness in him. Nothing ever quite satisfied. We wanted to have children, of course. It was the Fifties and everybody was having children. Even though I had my career, I ached to be a mother. But it never happened. I never got pregnant. We saw specialists, of course. One of them finally diagnosed me with premature ovarian failure, rare and not treatable. I was in my mid-thirties when we got that news. We considered adoption, but the agencies we talked to judged us too old. And we prayed, as you might imagine, often together at night before retiring. Kneeling at the bed, side-by-side."

She was speaking more loudly now, in a normal voice rather than a whisper. Both Ludington and van der Berg still leaned forward toward her nevertheless, to signal attentiveness, perhaps sympathy.

"Then it seemed our prayers were answered, though answered in a most unexpected way. We had been at the Old Stone Church for about six months. Just after Christmas, the Christmas of 1969, a young girl appeared on our doorstep late one afternoon. It had snowed and was very cold. Malcolm and I both went to the door, the upper door of the manse, not the one to the kitchen. We were standing beside each other when Malcolm opened the door. She was standing there, shivering and blotchy faced, so young. She looked at me, then at Malcolm, and said, 'My name is Karen, and you're my father, I think. I don't have any place to go.' Then she began to weep."

Dolores McCrae seemed as though she might weep herself, but did not.

Van der Berg said, "May I presume to fix tea or coffee? Or would you like a glass of water, Mrs. McCrae?"

At first Dolores McCrae said nothing in answer to the offer, then, "Tea would be nice. The kettle is on the stove, cups are in the cabinet to the left, tea is to the right."

"Milk or sugar?"

"Just milk."

As van der Berg prepared tea for the three of them, McCrae fell silent again, tightly winding and then unwinding her handkerchief from her index and middle fingers.

"I have never told anyone before, you know. Not in these almost fifty years." She glanced at the wall clock she could see in the kitchen where van der Berg was searching for tea bags. "I have guests coming at 11:30, for lunch."

Silence rested in the little living room until van der Berg returned with tea. She handed the first mug to Dolores McCrae, returned to the kitchen and came back with one for Ludington and one for herself. Somehow, thought Ludington, tea was the more fit beverage than coffee for occasions like this.

Settled back in their places, McCrae resumed her tale unbidden. Ludington guessed that she was perhaps relieved to be telling it at last.

"Karen was pregnant, of course. And she was indeed Malcolm's daughter. He confessed it quite readily. He kept secrets; we all do. But he was a truthful man. He told me later that day that he'd had a relationship with a local girl from Bellefonte his sophomore year at Penn State. It lasted only weeks, but she became pregnant. They had already broken off their relationship when she told Malcolm about the pregnancy. He said that he never learned what became of her or the pregnancy. He told me her name was Cynthia. He said he could not recall her last name. He was nineteen, he thought she was seventeen. I asked him if she was beautiful. He said he couldn't remember."

McCrae took a gulp of tea, and shook her head. "I can't believe I am telling you this. I really don't know you."

But she understood that she had crossed a narrative Rubicon and continued.

"Cynthia had the child, of course, a girl. She named her 'Karen.' We learned this only because Karen told us. Her mother did not give her up for adoption, but she did not raise her either. Karen was raised by her grandparents, Cynthia's mother and father. Karen said she did not think they loved her. From what the girl would tell us, they were resentful at having a child foisted on them in their middle years. It seems they were neglectful in the extreme. Karen said they often told her that her mother had 'just run off to California' when Karen was two and left her with them. They didn't know where Cynthia was. When Karen asked about her father, they said he was 'some holier-than-thou Presbyterian preacher named Malcolm McCrae.' Cynthia may have kept track of Malcolm in the years after they broke it off. She knew that he'd gone to seminary. Perhaps he had shared his plans with her earlier, I mean during their relationship. At any rate, that's how Karen found us. She said all she had to do was call the Presbyterian Church in Bellefonte and ask after a Presbyterian minister named Malcolm McCrae. She's actually a very clever woman."

Her use of the present tense jolted Ludington. She had said "is" rather than "was." But he said only, "You took her in that day?"

"Of course. Her life had unfolded much like her mother's. A brutal home, if a home it was, then she found herself young, unmarried and pregnant, just like her mother. The father denied his paternity. Her grandparents booted her out of the house as soon as they learned of the pregnancy. She said they told her she was 'a whore like her mother.' Yes, we took her in. What else could we do? Karen guessed that she was about three months along. She was emphatic about not wanting the child. An abortion was not an option then, not a legal one at least. And Malcolm would have objected on moral grounds. He was quite conservative in many ways. The solution was obvious, Mr. Ludington. At the time it seemed providential."

She paused and took a sip of her tea. Ludington was confident that he knew what that solution was, but decided to let her reveal it on her own. He merely asked, "She lived with you in the manse?"

"No, of course not. That would have raised far too many questions, both in the church and in the neighborhood. We found Karen an efficiency apartment in a building on Second Avenue, a few blocks from the manse. Our plan was simple enough. We would care for Karen through her pregnancy. We would have a home birth. I am a nurse and would review the training I'd received in midwifery. Home birth was increasingly popular at the time. Karen would stay in New York for a while after the birth and then return to Pennsylvania to finish high school. We would continue to support her financially. She would leave the child with us. Malcolm and I knew we'd be leaving Old Stone in May, shortly before her due date. We planned to arrive at our next church with our adopted child, no mention of the fact that he or she was Malcolm's grandchild, of course. We had even created a fictitious adoption agency that we would say we'd used, should anyone ask."

She took a gulp of her cooling tea. "If the child were a boy, he would be 'Malcolm,' if a girl, 'Christine.' I have always disliked my name. It means 'suffering,' you know."

Van der Berg found herself wrapped in McCrae's story and could not help but blurt out the obvious question when McCrae paused, "What happened, Dolores?" She asked the question kindly. Somehow van der Berg's use of McCrae's Christian name seemed suddenly appropriate.

"The child came early, very early. Karen went into labor at her apartment the night of April 12th. She came directly to us. We had just finished preparing one of the bedrooms as a birthing room. I had brought items home from the hospital, things that might be needful for a delivery—cord clamps, sterile gloves, pads, analgesics. I had assisted at any number of hospital births in my career. I was working at New York Hospital at the time—not in obstetrics, though. In the ER. The delivery was quick, a very easy one, but the child was so tiny, and so early—maybe only 26 or 27 weeks. He was born the morning of April 13th. Malcolm baptized him in his mother's arms. He died the next day, on April 14th. I assume his lungs were simply too underdeveloped. That's often the case with boys that come way too early."

Ludington felt called to respond to this, not as an investigator, but as a pastor. "I am so very sorry. It must have been excruciating for you."

"It was for all three of us, even Karen, though she had no desire to be a mother then. Difficult as she was, Malcolm and I were coming to care for her. We were devastated. And, frankly, we didn't know what to do. We could hardly go to a funeral home. There was no death certificate, obviously. We didn't own a car, and even if we had, we couldn't imagine where we might inter the little body. Malcolm suggested cremation. It was not as popular then as it has become recently. But again, we simply could not go to a crematory with the body of a tiny infant. We were trapped. We had trapped ourselves. Malcolm found a shoebox. I fashioned a liner—a little bed—out of my old silk nightgown. It had been my mother's. Malcolm went to Wankel's for paraffin. He removed the log grate from the fireplace and opened the door to the ash pit. He built a pyre from kindling he gathered in Carl Schurz Park. Then the paraffin. We said our goodbyes, Karen and I, up in the room where she had given birth. Then Malcolm brought our son, his grandson, down to the living room. He said he would sweep it all into the ash pit afterwards. He said it was bottomless, simply bottomless, and no one ever cleans it out. He couldn't stay and watch. He came back to be with Karen and me. We held each other and wept, even Malcolm."

The weight of the horror and pathos of Dolores McCrae's tale pressed down upon both Ludington and van der Berg. Van der Berg was near tears, a rare event for her, Ludington knew. He was speechless. Even Dolores had finally found her tears.

To the heft of that horror and pathos, McCrae then added the burden of the guilt, the guilt that had weighed on her for fifty years. "For half a century, I've wondered. What if the birth had occurred in a hospital, a hospital with a neonatal intensive care unit? Would the child perhaps have lived? We had avoided a hospital birth because a grandfather adopting his illegitimate grandchild would have been ruinous for Malcolm's career in the ministry. At least, that's what we feared. But we might have been wrong. The question would haunt Malcolm for the rest of his life as well. He died with it. I'd like more tea, please."

She looked again at the wall clock in the kitchen as Ludington went to prepare her a second cup.

"I have someone coming soon. They'll stop, and the desk will call to let me know they've arrived."

She said this loudly enough for Ludington to hear in the kitchen. She accented the "they," a barb doubtless aimed at these guests who had not announced themselves.

Ludington returned with her tea and sat down next to van der Berg.

"Malcolm and I were coming to love Karen, not that she was especially lovable. She went back to Bellefonte and took a room in a friend's house. We paid her room and board. She never finished high school. She phoned once and again. A few years later, she called to say she'd gotten married. It didn't last but a year. Then she joined the Navy. She wrote and said that she wanted to see the world. I think she saw San Diego. We wrote regularly; she called occasionally and sent Christmas cards. Then, ten years after the baby, she called and said she was getting married again and would Malcolm officiate. He did. We flew to San Diego for the wedding. It was our first experience with air travel. The Navy had done Karen a world of good. Her new husband was in the Navy as well, an electronic technician. It was a good marriage this time. Karen had three children, now she has a grandson. Barry retired from the Navy some years ago. You retire early in the Navy.

He was from Nyack, and they moved back there. I don't suppose it was because they wanted to be near me. Barry inherited his parents' house. Up on the bluff. You can see the river."

Dolores McCrae carefully set her mug on the coffee table in front of her, rose, and went into her bedroom. She returned with the framed photograph Ludington had glimpsed on her bedside table twenty days before and sat in her chair. She passed the photograph to Ludington. It was of a woman in her sixties, a bit plump, with a head of magenta hair. On her knee was perched a boy of perhaps six, a handsome child with a mop of brown hair and intelligent dark-brown eyes.

"That's Karen and her grandson. He's named Christopher. What a pip he is. How I wish Malcolm might have known him."

The first real smile Ludington had seen crossed her lips.

"They drive over from Nyack every few weeks for a visit. They'll be here soon. I think you should leave before they arrive."

"Yes," said Ludington, "we should go. But a few things, Dolores. First, two promises, then a question. We will guard what you have told us. Consider it told to me as a pastor. I promise the story will rest. I also promise to find a fit and final place for the Little One to rest. And then there is a question: the comb?"

McCrae twisted the handkerchief she had pulled from the pocket of her blouse and wound it around the fingers again. "I took it from my friend's bathroom when I was in her apartment for Sunday afternoon bridge. I assume it belongs to her husband."

Perhaps she was about to offer an apology for this act of misdirection, but was stayed from doing so by the sharp ring of her landline. Dolores McCrae rose, took the few steps to the kitchen, and picked up the receiver of the wall phone.

"Tell them to wait a moment. I'm not quite ready."

She hung up the phone and walked back to the living area. She did not sit. "You should leave."

Ludington and van der Berg stood. He thought to embrace Dolores McCrae but did not. He said only, "Thank you, Dolores."

As they walked down the hallway, they saw a woman with magenta hair approaching. A little boy had dashed ahead of her. When he reached Dolores's door, he opened it without knocking, peered in, and called out loudly, "Gramma Doloooores, we're here."

The woman with magenta hair shook her head and smiled as they passed her.

# Chapter Forty-Four

*April 20—Holy Saturday*

Ludington opened the Volvo's passenger door for van der Berg. For the first time in ages, it did not resist. He drove carefully, aware that he was distracted, lost in thoughts that were far from the Cross County Parkway. Van der Berg said nothing until they exited south onto the Henry Hudson.

"You were right to promise Dolores that we'd keep this to ourselves, Dominie, though I assume you'll tell your wife and Harry. It seems to me that something like justice has been accomplished. Perhaps it has been effected by time, or maybe providence and grace."

"Agreed. But I must say that Dolores's question haunts me as it obviously does her, as it did Malcolm, as it surely does the woman we just passed in the hallway. What if they hadn't been so intimidated by their fear of judgment about adopting the child of Malcolm's out-of-wedlock child? What if they had toughed it out and planned a hospital birth and formally adopted? What if they had dared to be transparent about the whole thing? What if they'd not been so anxious about its effect on Malcolm's career? Maybe, maybe—born in a hospital with a NICU—that child might have made it."

"Dominie, that's a list of 'what if's' to rival mine. Do you think Dolores has forgiven herself?"

"I'm not sure she has. Time does not heal all wounds, no matter what they say. But time often dulls the edge of the anger and guilt. Not always, but often enough. Odd that it should. I mean, why is it easier to let something go—some wrong done by you or to you—after years have gone by than it is right after? The offense is the same. Nothing objective has changed. When it's new, the heat of it burns in you...burns till it finally cools. When it's fresh, you hold on to the precious little gem of your indignation, or you feast on your guilt in a way you half enjoy. But then, time does seem to work its way, sometimes anyway. Nothing reasonable about it. Grace has its own logic."

"Fifty years have passed," said van der Berg. "The woman ought to let it go. I pray that time may yet work its way with her. Maybe her telling the tale to us will make a difference. She said she had never told anyone before. It was rather like a confession, was it not, Dominie? Or maybe that little boy we saw will work his way with Dolores. This whole matter was always and precisely about children, Dominie. Wanting them or not wanting them."

Ludington did not respond to that last comment, though he knew it to be true. He feared that she was nudging the conversation toward him and Fiona and their unresolved issue of children.

Van der Berg said, "I have no regrets about my life... save one. I loved and was loved, not in the way I chose, but in the way I was made. Margaret and I were together for more than fifty years, and they were very happy years. We had only one regret, Seth, only one unhappiness. We never had children."

It was, Ludington realized, the first time in their relationship that van der Berg had addressed him by his Christian name. He knew that her doing so was intended to open a door to deeper intimacy. He was both honored and apprehensive.

"Adoption was not possible for two women in those days. Nor, of course, was artificial insemination. It was an emptiness for us, both of us. It still is for me. Not everyone in this world wants to have children. I think Harry and Georgia did. And Seth, I think you do as well. Why are you afraid?"

He launched into his accustomed answer, the one he used on both himself and Fiona—a vague and vogue discourse about the environment and over-population, lamenting a globe with a shadowed future. "How can you bring children into a world like this?" But as it tumbled again from his lips, he

251

realized that it wasn't true. The future of the world may be shadowed; an environmental apocalypse might be looming, but Seth Ludington suddenly had to own the truth that none of this had much to do with his anxiety about bringing children into the world.

He realized this as they were about to cross the Henry Hudson Bridge over the Harlem River. Perhaps it was changing its direction of flow as it did four times a day. Ludington judged the bridge, high above the river, to be one of the loveliest of the twenty-one on and off the island of Manhattan. But bridges, like life, cannot be seen in all their glory when you are actually on them. Glancing to the right, back over his shoulder, he could see the curious castle-like apartment buildings hanging over the Hudson from the sheer cliffs of Spuyten Duyvil. They looked like they had risen out of a German fairy tale. No one would ever guess that this, too, was New York City.

Ludington may have edged toward the truth about his fear of fatherhood, but all he said to van der Berg was, "I'll talk to Fiona. I promise I'll talk to her, Harriet."

She smirked at his use of her first name and said, "Talk doesn't make babies, Seth."

He dropped her off at her apartment building, returned the Volvo to the parking garage, and walked down to the church. The day was luscious, clear, and clean, warming into the sixties. The shoulder seasons were the sweetest ones in New York. When out-of-town friends asked about visiting the City, he always commended April and May or September and October.

He was in his study and at his desk by one-thirty. A couple pages of notes for his sermon of the next day lay neatly on his desk, demanding attention. Easter sermon expectations were always high. And Easter was notoriously difficult to preach. It was, after all, the same story every year. It had been so for the last two-thousand years. And it was, of course, a wonderfully far-fetched tale. Like most Christians, Ludington didn't pretend to understand the forensic details of Resurrection. Yet he trusted that Easter was somehow the truest thing that was ever true.

He had decided to preach Easter this side of the grave. It was, he would note to the congregation, tempting to reduce the promise of the day to the hope for life after death. But Easter also promises life before death—life deep and wide, empowered by the presence of the Living God with us. Or so he would preach. As he worked through the sermon, he skewed it toward hope—hope for this life—hope for life in the here and now and hope for the earthly tomorrow. He hit upon a phrase he was pleased with -Hope is nothing but trust set in the future tense. Was it his, or had he heard it somewhere? Is anything ever really original? It didn't matter.

He pressed the phrase into the logic of the sermon, a sermon that was increasingly focused on two things—hope and the closely related possibility that human beings can change. He told an anecdote to that effect, not a personal one, but one from a newspaper story he had read about a neo-Nazi in Nebraska who made endless harassing calls to a local rabbi. The rabbi met the calls with a love and grace that finally changed the man. Ludington closed the sermon with something John Cardinal Newman had said: "To live is to change, and to become perfect is to change often." He explained to the congregation that Newman used the word "perfect" in the sense Jesus used it—"accomplished" or "complete" rather than "without flaw."

The sermon was born of the truth that had come to Ludington as he was crossing the Henry Hudson Bridge: that he doubted himself. He doubted his ability to love a child in a way other than the way his father had loved him and his sister. He had long accepted the fact that his father's love for his children was conditional. It pained Ludington to admit it, but it was true. Perhaps all human love was somewhat conditional. But Ludington had always sensed that his father loved his children in a way that ultimately turned that love toward himself. His father's children were, in great measure, about him. Seth Ludington knew himself well enough to fear that he was capable of slipping into a like pride and vanity. And that had frightened him. It had frightened him for years. But people can change, can't they?

As he printed out the revised version of the sermon, Ludington understood at least two things about it. He knew that he was himself neither without flaw nor even close to being complete, in Newman's—or Jesus—sense. He also realized that his Easter sermon about the possibility that human beings can change was addressed as much to himself as to the two hundred souls who would gather in the sanctuary of Old Stone Church at 11:00 the next morning.

\* \* \*

After he finished the sermon, he wrote a long email addressed to the entire congregation of the Old Stone Church, an email he had been composing in his head for the last several days. After he finished it, he set Outlook to send it the next day at 11:00 in the morning.

It was nearly five o'clock by the time he had finished writing his Easter sermon and the email to the congregation. He went home to his wife to tell her about Dolores McCrae's confession. He had already shared his decision to send the email with her. He had told her Good Friday night after he had told her about Sara. Now, as they sat across from each other in front of the cold fireplace, he told her Dolores's tale, slowly, again omitting no discomforting detail. After he finished, they both looked into the fireplace and said nothing. Fiona finally said, "It's too damn sad, all the pain that your two tales of death kept secret have carried across the years, too many years." She went down to the kitchen to fix tea. Seth emailed Harry with a basic, five-sentence version of Dolores's story. He was not ready to speak with the man.

Then he phoned Patrick Sean O'Hearn. He got his voicemail and left the message he had promised the kid. "Hey Patrick, news. Not only was your great-grandmother a Protestant. Even better, you have a great-granduncle by marriage who was a Congregational minister. Your mom's grandmother, Anne Moore, had an older sister named Genevieve who married one Rufus Putnam—not the famous one, sorry. Yours was a Congregationalist minister. They had six children, one of whom—he would be your third cousin—became a Presbyterian minister, guy named Malcolm McCrae, born in Radnor, PA, in 1930. More precisely, Malcolm is—or was—your third cousin twice removed. Hope this sweetens the paper for your class." Ludington made no mention of Malcolm's child and grandchild, of course. Van der Berg had patiently explained to him the labyrinth of cousin relationships—first, second, third, as well as the "removed" business. Ludington thought he understood by the time she'd gone through it a third time.

# Chapter Forty-Five

*April 21—Easter Sunday*

E aster Day dawned even more eventful than Easters usually do, at
least those after the first one. The church was not full, but there
were more people in attendance than the year before—a whisper
of hope in that. The sermon landed on its feet, or so it seemed to Ludington.
He routinely preached from a manuscript. He didn't read from it, nor did
he even look down at it much. He usually had what he had written nearly
committed to memory. But he did take the manuscript with him into the
pulpit, in some measure, because it would rescue him if he forgot something.
More importantly, it saved him from the temptation to ad-lib—to add some
thought that had not weathered consideration in his study.

But his manuscript failed to save him on this Easter Sunday. After
offering Newman's line about human change—"To live is to change, and to
become perfect is to change often," two unplanned sentences—both honest if
glib—escaped his mouth. He said—where it came from he did not know—"If
human beings can't change, we might as well close this church down, and
every church with it." Then he said, "If I didn't believe that people can
change, I'd take off this pulpit robe and go be a greeter at Walmart." He sat
down in the chair behind the pulpit, dreading what was to come next.

The little Old Stone choir—two voices more than the usual nine—managed an Easter anthem after the sermon. Then it was time for Old Stone's
lamentable custom of an open mic time prior to the prayers of the day. He

had seen Cara Lundberg, sitting not halfway back as she had the Sunday prior, but having now placed herself conspicuously in a pew near the front. Ludington left the pulpit as he normally did at this point in the service, taking the hand-held pulpit microphone with him. He usually began this part of Old Stone's liturgy, dislike it as he did, by saying, "Would anyone like to offer concerns, something you'd like to be prayed for." Then an usher would walk down a side aisle, take the mic from Seth, and hand it to anyone who might have stood, wanting to voice a prayer concern. Many Sundays, no one stood to speak. Other Sundays, someone hesitantly rose and named a cousin with cancer or spoke of an unnamed grandchild struggling with school.

On this Easter Sunday, Seth Ludington began differently. He paused, just long enough to provoke anxiety in his listeners, though that was not his reason for stalling. "Those of you who are members of Old Stone Church have received an email from me, sent about an hour ago. In that email, I have related an incident that I was involved in twenty years ago when I was a college student. You will learn that I was morally culpable in the death of a young woman and her unborn child, my child. I have kept this a secret for two decades, but can no longer do so. I believe it makes me unfit to be your pastor, so I will convene a meeting of the Session for this Tuesday. At that meeting, I will ask the Session to call a congregational meeting so that you can accept my resignation as your minister." He paused but briefly. "I am sorry, sorry for what I did then and sorry for keeping it a secret, sorry for what I must do now, and I am sorry that it falls on this day of all days. But it had to be."

In that email, he had told the twenty-year-old story of Sara's death in a straightforward manner, including all the details he had offered his wife, everything except the hush money his parents had paid, and Cara Lundberg's attempt at extortion. Those were not his sins to confess.

No one in the congregation stood to speak any concerns they might have brought to church with them that day. Cara Lundberg did stand. Without looking at Ludington, she walked quickly down a side aisle and out of the church. Seth saw a number of hands reaching for cell phones, doubtless to check their email inbox.

He prayed for the church in the sober silence that followed. He did not pray for himself, nor did he pray for Cara or for her parents. He had already done so, just as he had already prayed for Dolores McCrae. He pronounced the benediction, and walked down the center aisle to the rear of the church, looking only at the stone floor under his feet, not at the expressionless faces in the pews. He did not greet at the rear door. Nor did he attend coffee hour. He retreated to his study to get out of his preacher's robe, perhaps for the last time. Fiona found him there. She embraced him without a word. They both hid there until they could get home without encountering any of the stunned members of Old Stone Church.

As they waited, there came a knock on the door. Seth and Fiona looked at each other, silently agreeing not to answer. The knock came again, more insistent, then an imperious voice, "Dominie, I know you are in there." Seth guessed that the shock of the last hour had led her to regress to her former manner of addressing him. The door opened as van der Berg let herself in, unbidden.

She marched over to the circle of chairs where her minister and his wife were sitting and claimed an empty one. "I have read your correspondence to the congregation." The woman was in a voluble mood, one she often adopted when she was anxious. Words to cover the worry. She changed the subject, though not really.

"That was a fine Easter sermon. I sense it may have been—at least in some measure—occasioned by our encounter with Dolores McCrae yesterday and our subsequent reflections as we drove back into the City—our conversation about forgiving one's self. Though I am aware that you generally complete your sermon preparation on Fridays, these matters clearly weighed heavily upon you." Van der Berg's verbal torrent did not pause for response. "You doubtless recall that while traveling in your auto, we inquired of each other as to whether Mrs. McCrae has been able to forgive herself, even after fifty years. We were unsure. Well, I do have to say that I hope you are not going to wait fifty years. Twenty is quite long enough." She offered a forced smile, "And I shall not wait twenty years to forgive you, though I must judge the sins of your youth to be exceptionally lamentable."

Fiona rose to embrace her, whispering a thank you in her ear as she did so. Seth said nothing.

When the three of them felt confident that all of Old Stone Church had vacated Easter coffee hour, Seth and Fiona took Harriet to lunch at the Lex Restaurant. They had reserved their back table a week earlier, quiet and isolated enough to permit private conversation. Seth had protested, saying he was in no mood to go, but the two women insisted. As they sat in the u-shaped booth, the mood was anything but Easter celebratory, though it was in some measure shaped by relief, relief at having the tale of the little bones in the ash pit nearly resolved. But more than any relief, the table was shadowed by Seth's email and announcement.

Ludington was dreading not only the impending Session meeting, but also final matters related to the bones, a few things he had to do in spite of the fact that his world was spinning off its axis. One loose piece of the puzzle was nudged toward its place when his phone pinged, alerting him to a text.

It was from Harry Mulholland. It read, "I'll talk to you about your announcement later. Eleanor and I decided it's time to talk. Like a lot of things, this has been hanging there for far too long. She wants you to be there."

He read the text and excused himself. He went to the restroom and texted Harry back, "When?" Harry responded immediately. "Tomorrow at 10:45 at the clinic." Ludington texted him back, "Meet you there."

He returned to their booth just as lunch arrived. Van der Berg had ordered her predictable Caesar salad, this time with salmon. Fiona was having the same. Ludington, remembering that he hadn't eaten in a day and was suddenly hungry, indulged himself with a burger topped with blue cheese, fries on the side. He decided to say nothing about Harry's text for the moment.

He and Fiona did not get home until nearly three. They both went upstairs to change out of their church clothes. Though he had long shrank from the thought of it, the other unresolved matter could not wait, not even until tomorrow. Ludington put on blue jeans, an old Michigan sweatshirt, and his new pair of Clark's desert boots. He had bought them, identical to the ones that had finally worn out, just two weeks earlier. He pulled the box they had come in off the closet shelf where it had been waiting for this day. It was larger than the average shoebox. He then found a white satin pillowcase in the linen closet, folded it carefully into a rectangle, and lay it in the shoebox covering the bottom and sides, rather like a nest. He told Fiona what he was about to do and went downstairs, through the kitchen, and into the cellar.

The box of old commentaries was still pulled up in front of the ash pit door. He sat on it and opened its door for the fifth time. He looked at the little bones and offered a prayer, a prayer for Dolores and Karen, for Harry and Harriet, for Fiona and himself. He had determined to pray like this weeks earlier when he first knew that this day might come and this task might fall to him.

He had also decided to use his hands, his ungloved hands, to do what needed to be done. The little bones deserved to be touched by human flesh. He carefully picked up each one—so fragile and tiny—and lay them softly in the satin-lined Clark's shoebox. He did not count them. He had checked, and had discovered that there are some 270 bones in a body at birth. The number decreases to about 206 in adulthood as some bones fuse. He did his best to place the bones in the box in a pattern as closely resembling the body of little Malcolm McCrae as possible. He hoped he had not missed any, but feared he had. There did not seem to be anywhere near 270. He went to the kitchen, found a mesh strainer, and gently sifted through the ash on which the bones had rested. This yielded a few tiny white bits, but he could not tell if they were bones or mere bit of ash. He closed the ash pit door and pushed the box of worthless old books back in their place with the others. They would all have to go when the renovation began.

Also tomorrow, he would phone Tony Spinelli at the funeral home on Madison. That institution and Old Stone Church had a long-standing relationship. Churches and funeral homes need each other for obvious reasons. Ludington had composed a tale for Tony that was proximate to the truth. He would say that he had been given the bones of a fetus, implying an abortion or miscarriage that had happened decades, maybe even a century, ago. He would not mention the manse, of course. "It's a touchy pastoral situation, Tony, no malfeasance, but it needs closure. Would you arrange for their cremation? I'll pay." Funeral homes were always desperate for clergy to officiate at services for unchurched clients, and were thus eager to maintain happy relationships with the ministers, priests, and rabbis in the neighborhood. They were also aware that clergy were often asked by bereaved families to suggest a funeral home. Ludington was confident that Tony would be helpful. He carried the Clarks' shoebox into the kitchen, bound it with a length of twine, and tucked it in the far back of a lower cabinet where Fiona would not happen upon it before he brought it to Tony in the morning.

# Chapter Forty-Six

*April 22—Easter Monday*

A trio of no-nonsense inspectors from the New York Department of Buildings were at Ludington's upper door at 9:20 on Monday morning, more or less as promised. Ludington asked them if they had any questions. They had almost none, inquiring only about the dates the house had been built and when it had been previously renovated. Ludington explained that he had to leave, but hoped to return by noon. "No problem," one of them answered—not two words Ludington expected from a building inspector. Problems were their reason for existence.

He went down to the kitchen and retrieved the Clarks' shoebox. He had the time, so he walked the eight blocks to the funeral home, the box tucked under his arm. He had phoned at 9:00 and was assured that Tony Spinelli was in. When he arrived, Ludington was escorted into Tony's office. It was furnished, as was the entire establishment, with Chippendale reproductions, the walls hung with muted landscapes, also all reproductions. The intended impression was one of restrained dignity and studied tradition. To Ludington, however, it all felt a bit *faux*. He lay the shoebox on Tony's desk and launched into his rehearsed story and request. Tony cut him off with a wave of his hand and a smile. He then said exactly what the building inspector had said half an hour before, "No problem."

Ludington walked the six long blocks east to the Yorkville Women's Clinic. It was another fine day, cooler than Easter Day had been, but real spring, not merely its harbinger, and so welcome. It was even more welcome to have the little bones out of his ash pit, out of his house, and being properly dealt with at last. He arrived at the clinic five minutes early to find Harry Mulholland waiting, dressed in his earthy tweeds, sitting incongruously and anxiously in one of the black leather Wassily chairs.

Ludington sat in the one next to him, and he said, "Thanks for coming. Eleanor asked.

Ludington's anger at the man had cooled, in some measure because time had passed, but more because it was obvious that Harry had initiated this attempt to resolve some very uncomfortable personal history. He could not but respect the man for doing so.

"This can't be easy for you, Harry."

"No, of course not. But it needs done. People can change, you know. You do know that, don't you?"

Eleanor Johnson approached them, walking confidently down the narrow hallway from her office to the clinic lobby. She offered a hand to Mulholland, and then to Ludington.

"Thanks for coming, pastor. I wanted you here. I also want you to rethink this resignation business."

They followed her to her tiny office with its three chairs pressed necessarily and uncomfortably close.

They sat, all three of them. Harry began, "I'm here to say I am sorry. I'm sorry for fifty years ago, for whatever happened. You left that fall. I didn't know where you went, but the truth is that I didn't really try to find out. I treated you badly, Eleanor. I was insensitive, disrespectful, careless."

She nodded and said, "We have stayed away from Old Stone all these years because I was afraid of encountering you, Harry, and back then, anxious about bumping into Jorge, especially after Henry and I married and had a family. But it's time to leave that behind, the silence and the fear, I mean."

She leaned forward in her chair, looked Harry Mulholland directly in the eyes, and said, "I had to drop out of Spence that fall because I was pregnant. I imagine you might have guessed that. In early October, my parents sent me to my mother's sister up in Massachusetts to have the baby. This was before abortion was legal in New York. I miscarried soon after I got there, at about three months. Awful, but a blessing, perhaps. It was too late to come back to the City for school. As you might have also guessed, I'm not sure who the father was. It was either you or Jorge."

Mulholland did not respond immediately. He looked at Eleanor Johnson and said softly, "Thank you for telling me. I am truly sorry."

"Harry, it was another kind of time, and I was a willing participant. My life was disrupted by it, of course, but the truth is that the experience ultimately led me to my career, to my work here at the clinic, I mean."

If forgiveness was needed between the two of them—and Ludington was not sure that it was—it had been offered and received wordlessly, given and acknowledged with the quick embrace exchanged before they left her office. On the way down the hall back to the lobby, Mulholland placed his hand on Ludington's neck, rubbing it rhythmically. Harry was as near to tears as the man ever came. Perhaps, Ludington thought, Mulholland's near-tears were occasioned by a sliver of peace come after half a century. Or perhaps they were near tears for a child he never had.

Harry Mulholland stopped, took his hand away, and looked at his pastor. "I'll say it again, people can change—sometimes. And there is forgiveness. I mean, it's actually possible—usually after some truth-telling, of course. Take it from me."

As they entered the lobby, both were jolted to see Fiona Ludington seated in one of the Wassily chairs, poking at her phone.

Seth gaped and said, too loudly, "Fiona, what on earth are you doing here?"

She looked up, just as shocked to see her husband as he was to see her.

"I might ask you the same. I was about to call you. I came in for a lovely little test, my dear. That's what they do."

Ludington sank in the chair next to his wife. Mulholland surmised that this was an encounter he was not called to witness, said his farewells, and made for the door. He turned back to them and said to both, "I'll talk to you tomorrow, Seth."

"A lovely little test, Fiona? That's one, one lovely I mean."

She looked down at her tummy and said, "I hope it's only one."

At this announcement of a pregnancy, he did not laugh. He wept—something he rarely did.

# Epilogue

The front wall of Old Stone Church's columbarium was covered with square marble tiles, all a matching beige veined in umber. Each tile covered a niche that accommodated a metal container of ashes, ashes properly named cremains. That word was a portmanteau of "cremate " and "remains." Ludington disliked it. Some of the tiles had names and dates carved on them. Others were unmarked and waiting. One niche was open.

Ludington began the brief inurnment service with a reading of the 23rd Psalm, *"The Lord is my shepherd...."* He then read the story of Jesus welcoming little children to come close to him, even as his overly-protective disciples tried to shoo them away. He read the Psalm and the Gospel from the crusty old King James Version because he knew it would please both Harriet van der Berg and Harry Mulholland. The two of them, plus Fiona and himself, were the only ones present. He had called Dolores McCrae and told her about the little service and asked if she and Karen might want to attend. He guessed that she would demure, which she did.

> *"Then were there brought unto him little children, that he might put his hands on them and pray, and the disciples rebuked them. But Jesus said, 'Suffer little children, and forbid them not, to come unto me, for of such is the kingdom of heaven."*

"Suffer," he thought as he read the word. Dolores means "suffer."

Ludington reached to the small table below the open niche. He took the brass box holding the ashes of the bones from his ash pit and slid them gently into the niche. He then lifted the marble tile from the table and snapped it in place over the opening of the niche. The engraving on its face read, "Malcolm, April 13, 1970—April 14, 1970."

Finally, he took up a prayer book from the table and offered the old Prayer of Committal—the one Dolores and Malcolm, and perhaps even Karen, would have known—reading it very slowly.

> "Unto the mercy of Almighty God, we commend the soul of our bother departed and we commit his ashes to their resting place, earth to earth, ashes to ashes, dust to dust, in the sure and certain hope of the resurrection to eternal life; through Jesus Christ our Lord. Amen."

# A Note from the Author

Please note that there is no Old Stone Church in Manhattan, and that its resemblance to any real congregation is quite unintentional. Should they go searching for it, New Yorkers and fortunate visitors to the City will discover a school parking lot and playground at its putative location. Likewise, no brownstone exists at the address of the manse on East 84th Street, and there is no Philadelphia Theological Seminary. However, the various restaurants that find their way into the narrative are all quite real and in our experience all worthy of a visit. Apologies to my friend Neil Gardner, the actual minister of the remarkable Canongate Kirk in Edinburgh, for replacing him with Fiona's father.

# Acknowledgements

We offer profuse thanks to our patient spouses and children who endured our inattentiveness as this book was being written. We express appreciation to all our persnickety beta readers—Steve Tracey, Fred Hasecke, Mark Smith, Terri Lindvall and Susan Whitlock, as well as our sister and daughter-in-law Claudia Gabel Lindvall for suggesting a brilliant valance to the plot. And of course, thanks flow to our tireless agent at Gersch, Joe Veltre, and to the fabulous editors a Level Best Books for their confidence in our work and their improvements to it.

# About the Author

M. M. Lindvall is a father-daughter writing duo. Madeline Lindvall Radman is a Television Writer and Producer specializing in true crime. Her work can be seen on A&E, Investigation Discovery and the Discovery Channel. Michael Lindvall is a published author of three volumes of accessible theology (Westminster/John Knox and Sterling) and two novels – *The Good News from North Haven* (Doubleday, Pocket, Crossroad) and *Leaving North Haven* (Crossroad). The former was on a *New York Times* bestseller list. He is the Senior Minister Emeritus of the Brick Presbyterian Church in Manhattan. Michael and his wife, Terri, make their home on the shores of Lake Michigan near Pentwater in the summer months, and "down south" in Fort Wayne in the winter. Madeline, her husband Tom, and their two children, Shea and Shepard, live in Takoma Park, Maryland.

SOCIAL MEDIA HANDLES:
Michael Lindvall is very active on both Facebook and Instagram, under his name.

AUTHOR WEBSITE:
https://www.mmlindvall.com/

# Also by M. M. Lindvall

By Michael Lindvall:

Michael had published two previous novels, both very different in tone from this series. *The Good News from North Haven*, (Doubleday and Pocket) and *Leaving North Haven*, (Crossroads).

He has also published a work of accessible theology entitled *A Geography of God*, (WJK).

CPSIA information can be obtained
at www.ICGtesting.com
Printed in the USA
JSHW020327230123
36575JS00004B/17